YEAR THREE
SUPERNATURAL ACADEMY

WSJ AND USAT BESTSELLING AUTHOR

JAYMIN EVE

Jaymin Eve
Supernatural Academy: Year Three
Copyright © Jaymin Eve 2020

All rights reserved.
First published in 2020.

Eve, Jaymin
Supernatural Academy: Year Two
No part of this book may be reproduced, stored in a retrieval system or transmitted in any form or by any means, without the prior permission in writing of the publisher, nor be otherwise circulated in any form of binding or cover other than that in which it is published and without a similar condition, including this condition, being imposed on the subsequent purchaser. All characters in this publication other than those clearly in the public domain are fictitious, and any resemblance to real persons, living or dead, is purely coincidental.

Text set in Adobe Jenson.
Cover design by Tamara Kokic
Book design by Inkstain Design Studio
Edited/Proofread by Lee from Ocean's Edge Edits and Amanda Steele

SUPERNATURAL ACADEMY

YEAR THREE

When you feel like you've been stripped to nothing but bone.
When you are tired and hurt and can't go on.
You have strength. You have worth. You are enough.
Also … your bones are sexy.
This will all make sense after you read Year Three.

Demi-fey Academy

Atlantea

Vampire dorm

Shifter dorm

Herbalism

SUPERNATURAL ACADEMY

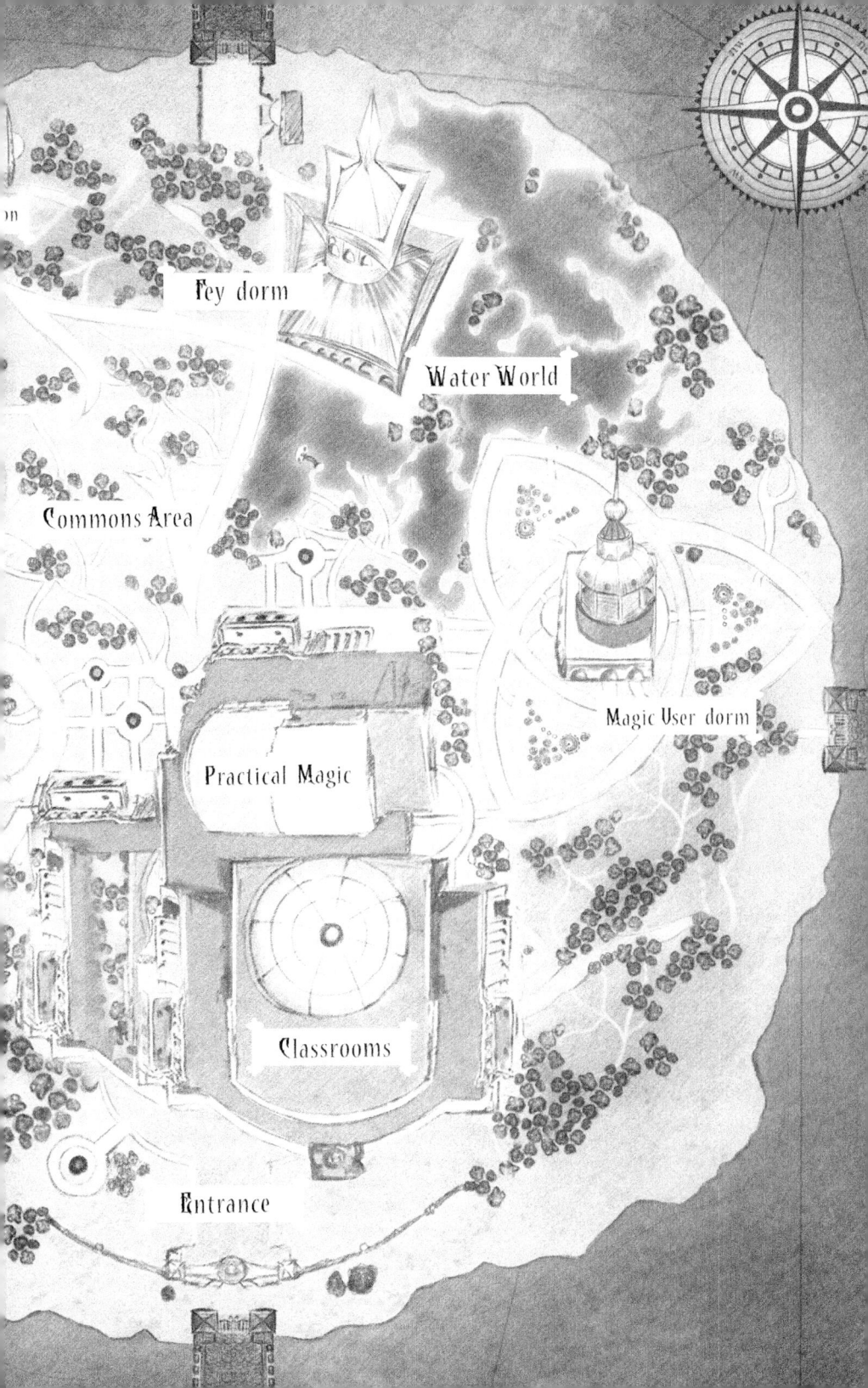

CHAPTER 1

For the first time in many years, I contemplated allowing another person to join me in the bathroom while I changed my hair color.

The yearly ritual was usually an act I committed alone, my time to erase the past and push for a new future. A new year to get it right.

Lately I'd been feeling a little off about the whole thing.

If the last two years at the Academy had taught me anything, it was that a new hair color didn't change my fate. I couldn't circumvent the truth of who I was, couldn't change my role in this world.

No matter how hard I worked, I couldn't seem to change a damn thing.

Still, the entire point of the different hair color—outside of the clean slate thing—was that it was the one thing I could control, the one part of my life that no one could take from me.

So the ritual continued.

This year I had chosen a color that meant a great deal to me, the color of the ocean when the sun's rays hit it just right, turning translucent water into a hue of greens and blues—when it was so clear that one could see down for miles. The color of Atlantis, its jeweled tones casting calm across the city. The color of my third year at the Supernatural Academy.

Aquamarine.

I once again had the fleeting hope that this color would be kinder to me than pink and purple … wishful thinking at its finest. There was no way I'd ever say it out loud though, tempting the Fates when those bitches hated me.

Swirling the mixture one last time, I was impressed with the perfect shade of aqua staring up at me from the dish. I'd already done the base prep-work to strip the purple away. If only I could strip away the scars from the year of purple as easily.

"You okay in there, Mads?"

"Yep, I'm all good," I called back to Ilia, not sure if that was the truth or not. Maybe if the nightmares would just leave me alone … if I got a decent night's sleep … if there wasn't a fucking god popping up whenever he felt like it to torture me. At least I'd ditched my phone so no more random texts, but he was still out there.

Biding his time.

Ugh. I needed to stop being such a maudlin bitch and accept that there was bad in every life, and I had a shit-ton of good as well. I needed to be happy about that. If I had one resolution this year, it was to find the happiness in whatever moment I could, because last year had been dark. Really fucking dark. I wouldn't go there again. I could never go back to that place.

Determination filling me, I lifted the bowl of color and got to work. I had this down to a fine art, and due to whatever special nature in my hair, new color took hold and stayed with bright perfect pigments for as long as I wanted it.

An hour later, I shut off the hairdryer and went back to my room to find Ilia and Larissa both fast asleep on my bed. A chuckle burst from me, before I managed to choke it down. Ilia looked uncomfortable, her long body scrunched up against the headboard, red hair smushed on one side and springy curls on the other. Larissa's head was in her lap, the new shorter blond strands tangled everywhere. Both of their mouths were open as they breathed deeply.

Guess I'd taken too long on my hair.

I ruffled the light aqua strands again, loving the feel of the silky lengths falling across my face. This new tone shifted the color of my irises from a deep blue to something closer to green. It was almost magical the way my skin and eyes adapted to the new hair, shading themselves to suit it. Some Atlantean/god power probably … one of the more awesome ones.

Stepping silently, I gently rearranged my friends so they were more comfortable, draping a blanket over them. Neither of them stirred at all, beyond exhausted, and I was glad we'd decided to forgo attending any of the New Year's Eve parties tonight.

That didn't mean the Academy wasn't filled with celebrating students. Many had returned to kick off the New Year's festivities before we started our new school year on the second of January. How the hell I'd been here for two years already… There was no denying my life had changed in almost every way from the first moment I was kidnapped by Ilia.

For the better. So much better. I'd take the pain just to feel all of the love.

With my bed fully occupied, I left the room, wandering pretty aimlessly through the halls of the magic users' tower. It was quiet, none of the usual witches and wizards dashing about. Even the common area only had three people in it, all of them watching a Christmas movie. It was still the season apparently.

Eventually I found myself heading to my favorite place here. The one building that drew me more than anywhere else. Or at least the people inside of it did.

The Atlantean mansion.

The Atlantean-five wanted to be with me tonight, not just because they got a kick out of my hair transformation, but also because it was my birthday. I'd told them I'd be by later after I hung out with my girls and drank some fey wine. The birthday thing really wasn't a big deal. I was pretty much the only one in my group of friends who even bothered to acknowledge the day of birth. Atlanteans were just not into it, and since we were almost certain most of us would live for hundreds if not thousands of years, it felt silly to keep caring about a number.

Some habits ... rituals ... they were hard to break though. Like my hair. Even if I was having the strangest feeling that maybe this would be the last year I changed the color.

Why it would be the last was still to be determined.

Taking the final set of stairs down to the common area of the dorm, I felt my spirit pick up at the thought of settling in for an all-nighter watching movies with my boys. I loved when we hung out together, family style. I couldn't wait to see Asher, my love, the sexy fucking god of an

Atlantean, who did things to my body that were probably illegal. Not to mention the things he did to my heart.

I had a dream, one that I didn't linger over during these trying times, but deep down I knew: I wanted to spend my life experiencing the world with Asher Locke.

With our family. Our brothers.

Axl, spouting off whatever cool random fact he was studying that week; Calen, flirting and asking me a million questions about Ilia, who he was lowkey obsessed with; Rone, strong and silent, but always with these moments that were so damn sweet my teeth would ache; and Jesse, my current pain in the ass problem. He would be brooding, doing his angry-at-the-fucking-world thing he had going on. Jesse and I were close, probably closer than any of the others outside of Asher, but lately he'd been withdrawn and absent.

I hadn't said anything, because I had an idea what was upsetting him, and he was entitled to feel all of the feelings. I deserved some of his anger. I'd leaned hard on Jesse when I thought Asher was dead. We'd gotten super close, and while I loved him, it was the love of a family member, not the love of a soulmate.

I just wasn't sure he felt the same way.

Only one brooding Atlantean owned my heart and soul, and that was Asher. I just needed to find Jesse his own perfect match and he'd understand.

Icy winds brushed across my bare arms as I stepped out of the magic users' dorm. The weather had been more unpredictable lately—Axl believed it was the newly "unlocked" powers of Asher, Connor, and me.

He was working on a spell to end the erratic weather inside the Academy, but he was only in the initial testing phase.

My feet moved faster as I dashed through the commons, noting that it was much busier here. Partying had a lot of hungry supes around, and I marveled at the magical appearance of food on the tables.

I could definitely destroy a burger—

"Maddison!"

I jumped as a tiny fairy appeared before me, brow furrowed and hands on her hips as she examined me closely.

"Mabs," I said, recovering quickly, smiling at her. "Where have you been? The library has felt empty without you."

Mabs was the literal queen of the fairies, an ancient, immortal, and frankly scary supernatural creature who had been the keeper of the Atlantean library for many years. It had taken us a long time to find it, but since the true Atlanteans were back inside the library walls, she was free to leave. It had been a few weeks since I saw her last.

"I went to visit some old friends," she told me, a look of confusion still on her face, "but your … energy, it drew me back."

She waved her tiny hands across me, gossamer wings flapping rapidly. She was dressed just in a thin, almost transparent white gown, and I wondered if her magic kept her warm in the frigid air or if she was immune to the cold.

"Your soul is dark," she murmured, and I made a coughing gasp sound.

"What?" I blinked at her, trying not to panic. Did she just say *dark*? Uh, that was definitely not a flattering color for a soul. I mean … how freaking dark was it? Like light gray? Or … brown, maybe? I mean, as long as it wasn't black, I had a chance, right?

Her tiny, perfect face scrunched up, like she was thinking hard.

Fuck.

My panicked thoughts were cut off as she shook away that pained expression, flying a little higher so we were eye level. "No, no, no. Calm down, Maddison. Your heart is going to pump out of your chest. It's not dark in an evil way. There's a heavy pressure inside your essence … it's dragging you down. Your spark and joy is fading."

"Fucking hell, Mab," I breathed, hand on my chest. "Way to scare the life out of a chick."

My soul was metaphorically dark, not physically. I could work with that.

And I didn't disagree. I'd felt it for days. Drowning in my fears … and the fucking dreams would not leave me alone. I'd almost lost everything last year, more than once, and I think I had some sort of PTSD, because the fear that this year would be even worse was terrifying me. Funny part was, I couldn't even remember what I dreamt. Just that it was red and fiery, and I woke up terrified and exhausted.

Fun times.

"I'm trying to capture the happiness," I told her. " I promise. It's just … hard, you know?"

"Don't let them win," Mab said fiercely. "If you let them get inside your head, you'll have lost the battle before it even begins. You can do this, Maddison. You would never have been blessed with your path if you did not have the skill, courage, and power to walk it."

I wanted so desperately to believe her, but she hadn't been there. She hadn't seen the way the gods handed our asses to us last year. It was pure luck that we'd made it out alive. Luck and Sonaris, who I now owed a favor to. A favor he could call on at any time.

Hence the nightmares.

"He could ask me for anything," I murmured, realizing that a large part of what was pressing on me was that. "I should never have given him that sort of power over me. I might have risked everything, and I feel like I didn't even try and fight as hard as I should have. I could have pushed through my fear, stepped further into the underworld and found the Hellbringers. I should have fought the gods then and there!"

I was just short of shouting at this stage, but she didn't seem bothered by it. If anything, there was a different look on her face … almost like *excitement*.

"Don't wait for him to come to you, then," she said, lowering her voice. "There's a way to destroy the gods, you just said it out loud. Now you need to figure out how to bring that plan to fruition."

Hellbringers.

The mythical creatures who could supposedly kill a god were never far from my mind. The one weapon that I might wield.

"It's too late now," I murmured. "I can't get back into the underworld. Well, even if I could, it's literally littered with gods who are probably not very happy with me. They're not going to let me stroll in there and find the very beings who can destroy them."

Mab smiled, a little intriguing smile. "There is another road into the underworld, accessible by the living. It will be difficult and dangerous. You'll have to take a journey that no supernatural being has survived before, and you won't be able to do it alone. But you can survive this."

"Will you help me?" I pushed.

Her lips pressed into a thin line. "I wish I could say yes. I want to help you more than I can tell you. But I'm sorry. I can't. I can't be trusted with original magic, and it's littered throughout that place. Just ... trust me, it's better I'm not there."

I wanted to ask more questions about that, because there was *a lot* she wasn't saying. But this wasn't the time.

"So who do I need?" I asked. "Asher?"

She paused. "Yes and no. He will be vital to this journey. But he is not all you need."

Fuck's sake, Mab. This shit was like trying to pry secrets from the dead.

Thankfully, before I could lose my shit at the ancient, powerful, possibly crazy fairy, she started to talk again. "Right now you're not ready, but you will be soon. The path will open to you when the time is right, so for now train your powers and bond with the other two born of both worlds."

Useful. Thank you. "How long do I have to train?"

Her eyes glazed over. "I don't see everything. It looks like there's one time only that the doorway will open for you. I sense that you'll be nudged in the right direction. When the timing is perfect."

I sighed. "You can't give me more information?"

She shook her head, focusing on me again. "No, I can't. As I said, I don't see everything, and I also don't want these words to reach ears they shouldn't. Evil lurks in the darkness. I have faith, though, that you'll learn everything when it's time for you to know."

Ah, yes, that old caper. Pretty sure it was time for me to know now. Or even five years ago.

Before I could say another word, Mab vanished, doing her too-powerful-for-her-own-good thing. To be perfectly honest though, I was glad she'd found me. Her visit had lifted a weight from me, only a minute amount but the sliver of hope that she'd given me cracked some of the darkness in my psyche. If Mab said there was a shot at defeating the gods, then I would trust her.

A shot was more than I'd had ten minutes ago.

CHAPTER 2

"Holy gods," I gasped, head thrown back, hands clenched around two pillows as my legs moved against my will. "Ash, seriously. Fucking hell."

He laughed, lifting me with both hands and pulling me onto his lap. "You're just so responsive."

I shoved him. "You know I hate being tickled."

More of his laughter rumbled across the room and I felt my heart swell. Just having him close like this was the best way I could think to spend my birthday. After Mab's shock appearance last night, I'd continued on to the Atlantean mansion, and the six of us had watched movies for hours. *Lord of the Rings*—my usual birthday movie marathon.

When Asher finally got me into bed, he'd loved me until I couldn't breathe or remember my name. He knew exactly how to touch me to drive me crazy, destroy my control, and my soul.

Fuck. I didn't care. It belonged to him anyway.

"What time is it?" I asked, straightening my top. I'd started the tickle wars, but he'd finished and won in spectacular fashion. Definitely my fault for insisting no powers be used. I was disadvantaged against his long-ass arms, and without my abilities…

"Just past 1 P.M.," he said, pulling me back to the bed, his body covering me, as a low moan escaped my mouth.

His lips pressed firmly against mine. I wrapped my arms and legs around him, pulling him closer, our tongues tangling together as we kissed like it was the first time we'd ever touched. It didn't matter that I'd kissed Asher so many times now I couldn't count them. The butterflies in my stomach never faded.

The need I had for him only grew stronger.

A heavy knock on his door barely even startled us. "Come on, you two, stop screwing." Jesse's voice got lower as he muttered, "…and making the rest of us nauseous." His voice grew louder again. "Get your asses out to the pool for lunch and a swim. The birthday girl needs to eat her cake."

"You want this or cake?" Asher murmured against my mouth, tracing a hand down my body, caressing the edge of the tiny panties I wore.

One finger slipped under and I moaned as he glided across my skin and down through the wetness pooling there. As one finger slid inside, my eyes closed and I decided that next time this was the game I'd play. Tickling was dead to me.

"Asher! Maddison! I will break this door down."

"Fuck off, Jess," Asher said, his eyes locked on me, a wicked smile on his lips as he pushed a second finger slowly inside.

"We'll be out in a minute," I gasped, sounding breathless, but fuck, Asher was driving me insane.

I heard grumbling, and the earthy lion shifter energy faded as Jesse walked away.

"You love teasing me," I gasped, my body moving as I swiveled my hips, needing the release that was hovering close by.

"I love *you*," he replied, before he shifted his thumb, and stroked across my clit. Pleasure exploded, the swirling sensations in my gut spiraling out of control as the world flashed black and white at me. I managed not to scream, but I was far from quiet as I rode out the orgasm.

"Gods," I groaned, falling back, limbs jelly. "One day my heart is going to give out when you touch me like that, and I'm not even going to be mad about it."

Asher's eyes darkened even as he laughed, fingertips brushing across my bare skin. "You're fucking adorable, but no more talk of dying. I'm not entertaining that thought. Not ever again."

It probably was too soon. Asher and I had both died, sorta, last year. Our mortal bodies had been destroyed to allow for our rebirth as god-ish entities, with a ton of new powers that were still developing and changing daily.

One in particular had been on my mind. "Have you noticed anything odd when we're close to each other?" I asked him, not sure if I was crazy or not. "Especially when we're touching."

Asher propped himself up on one arm, his broad chest very distracting, so I forced myself to focus on his face—not that it was any less distracting. "Like what?" he asked, his gaze like a caress as he ran it across me.

"Uh…" I cleared my throat, "I have occasionally been picking up on your thoughts. And I'm almost certain you've also heard mine."

It started late last year, Asher answering me when I was positive I hadn't said anything. At first I'd dismissed it, thinking maybe I had spoken out loud, but when it happened five or six times, I knew it was something more. I was sure I'd heard a couple of his thoughts too. Just random snippets, almost like a whisper across my mind, but it was there.

He was watching me closely, expression unreadable. "Does that mean something to you?" I asked softly. I'd caught up a lot on knowledge of the supernatural world, but I was still miles behind everyone raised in this world. That's what twenty-two years of thinking you were a human would do for you.

"It's not completely unheard of," he finally said, "especially for dragon shifters with true mates. Possibly Atlantean mates have the same gift. We are somewhat closely related to dragons. Our energy."

He leaned over and cupped my cheek. "We already know we're true mates, we just have to figure out how to trigger the bond."

I nodded, my head hazy as it always was when he was close. "And maybe we should ask Jessa and Braxton about the mind reading thing…?" I paused. "Or Rayge?"

Rayge was a dragon shifter—not confirmed, but I knew it—that I'd met in Germany. Asher refused to tell me what their history was, just saying that it was in the past and it was something he'd rather not revisit. I couldn't let it rest though. I'd only spent a few hours with Rayge, but I already knew he had too much going on to waste his life drinking in some tiny supernatural dive. Right now it wasn't a priority to find out his story, but I would be dealing with it once the god situation was over. For now, I'd continue to casually slip Rayge into conversations in the hopes that Asher would accidentally reveal some new information.

He grinned, perfect white teeth flashing. "Nice try, baby, but we're not talking about that scaly beast today."

Yes! A dragon was a scaly beast, right? He'd at least confirmed that much for me.

"Jessa and Braxton, on the other hand, are definitely viable sources on this mind reading thing. Be nice to know if we could communicate when separated."

Part of me—the human part I was sure—freaked at the thought that Asher might have free and unfettered access to my mind. Sometimes a chick just needed a little privacy. Like those times he pissed me off and I started planning ways to torture him. I'd lose my surprise attack, and that was essential to success.

On the other hand, I totally got the positives to us communicating from a distance. That would be a priceless gift. If we had that sort of bond, I might have felt his mind when he'd been "destroyed" and known he was alive. I definitely would have known later that he was only pretending to hate me to keep me safe. Saved myself a hell of a lot of heartache.

Hindsight was a beautiful thing.

"Come back to me," Asher murmured, and I shook my head, focusing on him again.

"Sorry," I said with a sigh, "I was just thinking that the mind reading thing, and even more important the communicating over a distance thing, might help in our battle against the gods."

He let out a low breath against my skin. "You haven't been sleeping well." He tried to hide his worry, but I felt it.

Pressing my face to his chest, I breathed him in. "I keep having dreams. I can't remember what they're about, but I always wake tired and ... scared. It has to be about losing to the gods—a manifestation of my own worries."

He wrapped me up so tightly that, for a moment, all my broken and jagged edges were smooth. "We will deal with the gods. Together. You don't have to carry this burden alone. In fact, just let me take all of it. I can't stand seeing your spark dull like this."

Mab had said the same thing, and I took a second to acknowledge how fucking lucky I was to have so many who cared. Especially Asher, who loved me more than I deserved.

"I love you," I said, voice thick with the emotions filling my chest and pushing into my throat.

He cupped my face in both hands, and I met those sea-green eyes, now traced with both silver and gold. "Live with me, Maddi, please. I don't want to be apart from you any longer."

My heart lurched, eyes burning.

I'd refused that request a lot. I didn't want to give up my dorm, the one thing that was mine ... a last piece of independence. At this stage though, it was pretty stupid to keep denying him. I struggled to sleep at all without Asher, the dreams so much worse, and on the rare occasions I stayed in my dorm, I usually ended up back at his place at 2 A.M. anyway. It was time to let go of the past and recognize that I could still be strong and independent with my mate by my side. If anything, we were stronger together. A fact that would no doubt come into play a lot in the next year.

"Okay," I whispered.

He stilled beneath me. "You'll live with me?" he asked, quirking an eyebrow.

I nodded, a husky chuckle escaping. "Yes. You're my future, Asher, and I'm done being stubborn about it. I don't want to waste any more time."

His lips crashed into mine and I welcomed him. Unfortunately for Jesse, I doubted we were going to make lunch today.

Maybe afternoon tea.

Asher pulled me up, shifting our bodies so that he held me back against his headboard.

Yeah, maybe not afternoon tea either.

CHAPTER 3

The assembly this year was a little different to previous years. Firstly, Princeps Jones was not here. I hated that he wasn't; it felt like a broken tradition, one I'd only just become a part of.

"He's so annoyed that the meetings ran over," Larissa whispered to me as we stared up at the teacher stumbling through his information. It was a professor I didn't know, one who taught advanced demon studies, and he looked like he'd rather be anywhere but here. "All the leaders are still there, arguing about what to do. Romania is the place to be apparently."

The princeps had been going back and forth to these meetings for months.

"Please tell me they at least found some sort of resolution?" I murmured back, trying not to make it look obvious.

We were still in the front row, because Larissa liked to be there.

She snorted softly. "All they decided is that until something is decided, no one will step foot in Atlantis. They're worried a surge of power could weaken the prison locking up the gods. In a complete contradiction though, once this meeting is over, a bunch of powerful magic users, Louis included, will head there to reinforce the door. Oh, and apparently Jessa and Braxton are seeking more advice from the queen of the dragons."

Clearly most of the supernatural community had no fucking idea how to deal with this situation. Gods. That was beyond their pay grade and they were scrambling for solutions that would result in the least number of deaths. The largest problem of all … killing gods was not easily done. Minor deities, maybe, because they weren't powerful enough to destroy the world with their free energy. But the full gods were a very different story.

Even if you did manage to kill one—an almost impossible task—you still had to figure out what to do with their power so it didn't explode the world. That was apparently where the Hellbringers came into it. All theory of course.

"We need to figure out their weaknesses," I murmured to Larissa. "Everyone has a weakness. The gods also have rules. Supernaturals have forgotten, especially about these gods that have been sleeping for thousands of years, but that doesn't mean they have none."

"We've scoured the library," Larissa said, dropping her head, her shoulders slumping. "There's nothing new."

Yeah, we kept coming back to the same thing. Hellbringers were the only weapon. It was the only fucking way. Hence why Asher, Connor, and I were even created. Even other gods had to follow the rules about their kind, and the Hellbringers were the best way to ensure they could kill and contain power.

We focused on the teacher again, or at least Larissa did. She felt it was her duty, with her father not here right now, to keep an eye on everything. I instead watched my friends. Calen's head was back, lightly snoring—Ilia, sitting beside him, kept turning a soft smile on him, all this emotion in her face. My fingers itched to capture that image, so she could finally see how she was so fucking gone over him, but a photo would probably just send her running. She wasn't great at dealing with strong emotions. A side effect from abandonment issues due to her upbringing.

She was giving it a decent try to make Calen and her work though, and I was totally digging their vibe.

Axl faced the stage, paying attention just like Larissa. I loved his new shorter hair, artfully spiked with just a few soft strands falling forward. The red was slightly stronger in the auburn lengths. Our genius. He'd definitely be able to tell us, word for word, what was said in this assembly.

I was distracted from Axl by a huge hand reaching over from the other side of Larissa, resting behind her seat. Rone. I wondered if they were going to step forward from the will-they-won't-they thing they'd been rocking for the last two years. I hoped they would, because the spark between them was strong. Gods knew neither of them had been able to extinguish it, no matter how hard they tried.

Asher, was on my other side, lazily playing with my hand, brushing his fingertips over it. His eyes were unfocused, gazed off into the distance, and I wondered if I could push into his thoughts and tune in on what had him so distracted. We'd experimented with it yesterday, but the moment I tried to actively hear his thoughts, I got nothing but a solid wall.

We were missing something, and I made another mental note to try and get in touch with one of the supes who might help. Jessa and Braxton might be out though if they were in Faerie, visiting the dragons.

As students started to move around us, I realized the assembly was over and I'd missed ninety percent of what was said. Hopefully Larissa wouldn't quiz me on how many students were here this year. Ilia shot a smirk in my direction, like she'd had the same thought.

"What's your first subject today?" she asked, pushing past a few students to reach my side. We followed the crowds out the door.

Reaching into my satchel, I pulled out the ever-changing magical schedule. We looked it over together.

MONDAY
10am – Sword and Sorcery Year Three
11am – Advanced Herbalism
12pm – Lunch
2pm – Advanced Attack and Defense Year Three

TUESDAY
9am – Herbalism
10am – Healing Magic
12pm – Lunch
1.30pm – History of Supernatural Races
7pm – Water Magic – Advanced

WEDNESDAY
9am – Sports Bonding
10am – Healing Magic
11am – Sword and Sorcery
12pm – Lunch
1pm – Advanced Attack and Defense

THURSDAY
8am – Herbalism
9.30am – Healing Magic
12pm – Lunch
1pm – History of Supernatural Races
2 pm – Race Morphology Advanced
3pm – Race Morphology – Demi-fey
7pm – Water Magic

FRIDAY
8.30am – History of Supernatural Races
10am – Race Morphology – Demi-fey
12pm – Lunch
1pm – Herbalism
2pm – Healing Magic
5pm – Advanced Attack and Defense

It was Friday today and I had a full day.

"History of Supernatural Races is up first," I said. "I legit can't even remember what we learned last year."

Ilia shot me a sympathetic look. "Well, at least you aced that class. So whatever you learned, you learned it well."

A sad chuckle escaped. She wasn't wrong, I'd done well in my classes last year. So well that they were talking of testing me out of my fourth year, allowing me to possibly graduate early, at the same time as my friends. It would no doubt depend on whether I was attacked by gods before or after this year's graduation.

"At least using your powers is pretty easy for you now," Axl said, lingering nearby. I swore he always knew when people were talking about school and grades, needing to be part of the conversation.

"Yep," I agreed. "Powers are easy, the book work not as much." Who the hell had time to read textbooks these days? I was too busy trying to keep my friends and family alive.

He wrapped an arm around me. "You know I'll help you with that. Don't stress for one second about it."

I hugged him back just as tightly, letting my head rest on his chest, absorbing the familiar energy and scent. Axl was the least volatile of the five, but his power was strong. And his extra special superpower was his brain.

"Thanks for all the help over the last two years," I murmured into his shirt. "I wouldn't be topping classes without you."

His chest shook as he laughed. "Yeah you would. Pretty sure there's literally not one thing you can't achieve if you set your mind to it."

If only. "Meet you in the library after school?" I asked, pulling away. "Let me know if you figure out how to stop the random weather."

He kissed my cheek. "You'll be the first to know."

I shook my head, noticing that somehow he already had a book in his hands, reading as he walked. He never tripped either. Another superpower of his.

"I'll see you at lunch," I said to Ilia and Larissa, hugging them both. Larissa was a year ahead of me, and we only shared one class, but had the same lunch break. That was a schedule requirement she forced her father to uphold, no matter what. Ilia was generally working for the Academy, but when she was here, we always made an effort to eat lunch together.

Calen dropped a kiss on my cheek, and then Rone and Jesse did the same. The lion shifter of our group turned away fast, still acting weird and cagey. He wouldn't meet my eyes, brushing a hand over my hair before he was off.

Narrowing my eyes on him, he glanced back once, shooting me a half-smile. Then he turned and strode away, long legged and graceful as all shifters were.

"He's hiding something," I murmured to Asher.

"Don't worry about Jesse. He'll work through it soon enough."

I stuck my tongue out at him. Typical dude answer.

He replied by wrapping huge hands around my biceps, pulling me closer as his full lips pressed into mine. As the scent of ocean and home filled my body, Jesse became a distant memory, and I lost myself for a bit.

"Fuck, I love you," Asher growled against my lips. "I still can't believe I have you back in my arms. It's why I need you to move in with me, because when you're not close the panic kicks in. That feeling when I thought I'd lost you … I don't want to experience that ever again, Maddison. Fuck." His chest rumbled, but he got himself under control quickly.

It was a feeling I knew all too well.

I'd been broken last year, into a million raggedy pieces. I never thought I'd find my way back to being even remotely whole. But apparently love was an amazing healer, and when you were bathed in enough of it, some of the cracks healed. I wasn't—and would never be—the person I was before losing Asher, but I thought of myself now as the Japanese people did with broken things. When they broke a bowl, they repaired it using gold. Highlighting the crack. Because your flaws make you who you are, and they should never be hidden.

I was littered with gold-infused cracks, and maybe that made me even stronger.

The chimes of the musical bells sounded and I sighed. "What class do you have now?" I asked, not willing to step away, enjoying this moment to be wrapped around him.

He pressed a lingering kiss to the top of my head and my eyes briefly fluttered closed. "I'm teaching water magic this morning, then I have some fight classes in the afternoon."

Pulling back to see him, I smiled. "Same schedule as last year, I see."

He nodded, brushing hair back from my face, tucking it behind my ear. "Yeah, there's really no point in me specializing in anything. I have Locke Industries, and water magic is my strength, so I'm honing my fighting and attack spells. I graduate this year anyway."

My heart hurt, and I tried not to let that show on my face. Asher leaned closer. "If you leave of course. Wherever you are, Maddi, is where I am. I don't even care if I have to take a permanent water magic teaching position to stay here."

I chuckled, and the vise across my chest eased. "Since you own half the school, and have your own house on Academy grounds, I don't think you need to worry about being kicked out." A darker laugh emerged. "And the gods might have wiped us all out by next year anyway, so let's not get ahead of ourselves."

Asher made a low, rumbling sound that started deep in his chest. "You can't think like that, baby. I know it looks bad, and at times we've been in way over our heads during this battle, but if there is one thing I know about you, it's that you're a survivor. And so am I. No one is going to tear us apart again, not your parents, or mine, or whatever gods they recruit. A path will show itself, and we will not falter."

Path. Exactly what Mab had said. I found that interesting. Maybe something was in the works, something bigger than any of us, because I was getting the "signs" … they were coming in loud and clear. "I'll try not to be such a downer," I said, forcing a smile across my face. "I have everything right now, and I'm going to enjoy it."

"That's my girl," Asher said, and then with one last kiss on the forehead, he laced our fingers together and led me to an archway covered in vines. He walked me all the way to my class, and we reluctantly separated at the door.

"See you at lunch," I told him, on my tiptoes for one last kiss.

He deepened the kiss, possessing and claiming my mouth, and then he was gone. Stumbling into the room, flustered and red faced, I sank down in a desk near the center. If I hadn't already died once, I would be certain Asher was going to be the death of me. In the best possible way.

CHAPTER 4

"Good morning, year three students."

Quark stood front and center, and I leaned forward on my desk, enjoying once again seeing his familiar face. The troll was someone I'd grown to like and respect. He was brash, unamused by idiots, and super smart. It was unusual for the demi-fey to teach outside of their academy, but Quark definitely walked to his own beat.

"In this course we've been moving through the history of our people, focusing on the wars for the most part. We might take a step away from that somewhat this year, but before we do, I'd like to pose a question to you all. Why do you think we focus so heavily on war when we explore the history of supernaturals?"

He generally started every class with a question, wanting to see lots of involvement and discussion. Hands went into the air, and the troll pointed to a vampire to the right of me: Brenda.

"We focus on war because it's the easiest way to showcase the very worst…" she paused for a beat "…and the very best of our people. And nothing else truly shows the division between our races and how far we've come to exist in the supernatural communities the way we do."

"War is a great way to see the repeated mistakes we keep making," I added. I meant to mutter under my breath, but the words came out louder than intended.

Quark met my gaze, his eyes super dark today. "I would agree with both points. If you study the history of supernatural wars, generally they all start in the same place. Usually because of our race differences. Usually because of misunderstandings. And often because of the minute—some would say insignificant—things that divide us." He leaned back against his desk, face somber. "At times I think we're learning from our mistakes, but then the next war comes along and I realize that we are forever going to repeat them."

It was so true. One of the shifter wars started because a vampire wanted their territory. Another war between fey and bear shifters because of a love affair gone wrong. All started by powerful, egotistical supes, usually filled with too much race pride and too little respect for all the lives that would be lost.

It was the same sort of bullshit that allowed the gods to think that what they wanted was more important than every other living being in the worlds. Those fucking gods, led by my parents, wanted to kill the Mother of All, absorb her power, and have the ability to completely remake the worlds. They were already super powerful, true gods, and yet that was not enough.

Time and time again, it had been proven that absolute power created absolute corruption. The gods were no exception, and even if they did manage to pull off their plan, eventually they'd fight amongst themselves. Pride and pettiness, we all had it.

A fury that was soul deep stirred in my gut, the sort of anger so strong it was self-sustaining with no help from me. The fact that these gods were willing to sacrifice everyone for their own selfish gains, that they would have killed all of my friends just to prove they could, just to hurt me, to make me do what they wanted … what the fuck was wrong with them? I mean, I was as guilty of being selfish as the next person, but I hoped I never reached the point where I could kill without thought or remorse for something as fucking stupid as more power.

That was abhorrent.

"What else can we learn from war?" Quark asked, walking through the desks. "Not even just the wars we've studied in this class, but on a larger scale. A generalization."

I put my hand up, already fired up. Quark nodded at me and words spewed from my mouth in a rush, most of it almost unintelligible because I was so pissed off.

"We've learned that most of the time, when people do terrible things, they justify it in their minds. In reality, those who feel justified are the most dangerous, and arrogant beings hear no reason. They will sacrifice lives for their crusade. They will sacrifice everyone, and in the end, believe that those lost should be grateful to have been part of their vision." I sucked in a ragged breath, the silence in the classroom heavy. "I appreciate and admire what Princeps Jones tries to do in this school, but most of the time, overcoming our differences is like plugging a leak in the ocean with your fingertip. We'll never stop the rushing tide, and everything ebbs and flows without interference. We are at peace now, but war will follow. It always does."

I realized I'd unintentionally sent power out in my speech. I dialed it back so that the heaviness would fade. Only it didn't. Because it wasn't just coming from me; everyone felt it too.

Quark arched one barky eyebrow. "Do you think good people ever win?"

I shrugged. "Good is a matter of perspective. It all depends what side of the war you fall on. For example … in the last great war between shifters and vampires, the shifters completely felt justified in defending their land, even though it was stolen from the vampires originally. And the vampires were justified in killing thousands of shifters just to prove the point of 'no one steals from us.' In both instances, the losers were the innocents sacrificed by their leaders. And those leaders … neither of them felt evil. They felt justified. As I said before, that's the scariest place to have anyone in power."

He smiled, an odd look on his foreign features. "Yes, it's quite scary," he said softly. "The way leaders will sacrifice everything for their cause, never considering the ripple effect of that."

"They never sacrifice themselves," someone muttered from the back of the room. A bear shifter. "My grandfather died in one of the wars, and his pack leader never even left the safe room."

Quark made a disparaging noise. "That's not the norm for shifters. The alphas are usually front and center of battle."

The bear laughed darkly. "Yeah, the silver lining to that story is that he was dragged out and sacrificed by his own people. The bears won that day, but in many ways they lost."

Quark threw his hands up. "Another great point about war. There is very rarely a true winner. So many losses on both sides. It's always a bittersweet victory."

All of these words were hitting me hard. Like he'd deliberately started this just to speak to my deepest fears. I knew a war was coming, I knew that's what the leaders were discussing right now in Romania, a war that could kill thousands—if we didn't figure out a way to cut the gods off before they started.

"And with that, it's time for us to move on from war," Quark said. If only it was that easy. "Year three for History of Supernatural Races will focus on the land of Faerie, and what we know about our origins."

I sat a little straighter, hoping he'd start with the Atlanteans. But outside of a brief mention, he moved on to the structure of the power system on Faerie.

Forty minutes later, the bell rang and I glanced at my eight pages of notes. I loved learning about our history and immersing myself in the supernatural races. The more I learned, the more part of it I felt. It was like the side of me raised human was fading with each year, with each new piece of information that entered my brain.

"For next class," Quark shouted as we packed up, "I need you all to prepare a speech on why the magic users are the most closely tied to humans. Remember to search through the timeline all the way back to the first crossing. To the Atlanteans. You'll have a more compelling argument. A good place to start would be with the question of how we all became so divided when most supernaturals that left Faerie, originally, were the same."

I jotted down the homework and lifted my satchel. It was the leather bag's third year with me and it was still going strong. I marveled at the quality of the bag Ilia had gifted me in my first year.

"What class do you have next?" a familiar voice asked, and I spun around.

"Simon!" I shrieked, throwing my arms around him. He was taller than me now, and more filled out, having lost all of that lanky youth he'd had in our first year. "I didn't see you in class."

He laughed. "You looked distracted and I was in the back row."

I shook my head. "I should have known you'd be in that class. Sorry I missed you."

History was Simon's thing … it was in his DNA.

"Next class is Race Morphology," I said quickly, smiling happily at him. "How was your time at home?"

He shrugged. "I hate to say it, but it was actually … okay. My parents didn't treat me like complete garbage. They even took me on one of their expeditions."

I snorted. "Let me guess, you topped our grade and they had to acknowledge that you're both smart and talented as fuck? They probably need you more than you need them at this point."

He shrugged, a half smile on his face. We were kind of blocking the path, so he linked his arm through mine and dragged me out of the classroom. Back in the hallway, we walked arm in arm toward the morphology room.

"I'm glad to see you looking happier than the last time I saw you,"

Simon said softly. "I've been worried about you."

Emotions swelled inside me, and I wondered how I could keep feeling all of these feels without exploding. "To be bluntly honest ... I've been worried about me too." I shrugged. "But, I'm working on celebrating the happiness I have now, so, in general, I'm feeling a little less maudlin about the whole thing."

Simon stopped in front of my next classroom, releasing my arm, and turning to face me. "The gods don't know who they're up against. I have never, for a second, worried that they would win. I know you, Maddi, and I know that you'll figure out a way to take them down…" His eyes jerked up to something over my head. "And with that, I'll leave you here. See you later, friend."

As he took off, power and heat washed along my spine, locking me in place. A firm hand pressed against my lower back, slowly tracing higher, heat burning across my skin and sinking into my blood. A shudder of longing ran through me as my eyes closed against my will.

It just felt so good.

"You can do anything, Maddi," Asher murmured, close to my ear, his body heat seeping into me.

Tilting my head back, I rested it against his chest, staring up at him. "Together we can," I murmured. "I tried it on my own and I was a fucking mess."

I'd been proud of how I survived without Asher, but something told me that time would have eaten away at my strength, until eventually I succumbed to the grief in a way that was not recoverable. Even now … I couldn't think about it. That time was so dark that it was banished into a box that I locked up tight, never to be touched again.

"Why aren't you in water magic?" I asked, not complaining, but surprised to see him.

Asher grinned. "Finished teaching that class already." I quirked an eyebrow at him, waiting for the rest. His smile just about melted my underwear right the fuck off. Sexy asshole. "And I might have forgotten to mention another class this morning, in the hope of surprising you. See, this year's Race Morphology class is so small they're combining third and fourth years."

I didn't even have to wonder what that meant. Happiness ripped through me. "We have a class together?"

His laughter was warm and husky. Spinning, I hugged him tightly and let out another cry at the sight of Axl, Jesse, Calen, and Rone over his shoulder. "All of you?" I choked out.

Fuck. I was a right old emotional mess these days. Damn hormones.

Jesse nodded, and for the first time in ages he met my watery gaze. "All of us, sweetheart."

CHAPTER 5

My old Race Morphology teacher had been replaced with someone new. A demi-fey.

I was sitting in the center row, Asher on one side, Jesse on the other. Calen and Rone were behind me, and Axl was in front. All of us watched as the centaur made his way into the room, ducking down to fit through the classroom door.

"Good morning, class," he said, his voice a rumble—I had to focus hard to understand him. "I'm Lennie, your new Race Morphology teacher. I generally step in for third and fourth year classes, because we focus a lot more on the demi-fey. As you can probably tell, I have some experience with demi-fey in general."

He threw his head back to laugh at his own joke, strong, bare chest shining in the lights that were above, and I couldn't help but laugh too. It was almost infectious. The centaur was a mix between a horse and human, the bottom half of him—the horse half—was huge and light brown in color. I knew nothing about horses and couldn't compare to a breed, but he looked strong and powerful, his dark tail swishing almost to the ground behind him.

In truth, the tail was the part that was weirding me out the most, but he was quite spectacular.

The top half of him was handsome—in a horsey-human way. His skin was a similar shade of brown to his body, just lighter.

The rest of the class was still laughing with the centaur, except for my guys, but they all wore smiles. It was weird though, because he hadn't really said anything that funny. And yet it was like it was comedy hour, and the teacher was the funniest creature alive.

"Centaurs can induce emotions in others," Asher murmured to me, his eyes warm. He didn't look upset, so clearly the teacher wasn't doing anything on purpose.

He brushed a thumb across my cheek, still broadly grinning. "This is a good look on you," he added as he twirled a long strand of aqua hair around his finger. "Pure joy. I'd like to see more of that."

"Why haven't we had classes together before?" I murmured.

"Because you would have failed," Axl piped up, shaking his head. "Books before boys, Maddison. Books before boys."

It was solid advice.

The centaur resumed his position in front of the white board. "Sorry about that. I promise that I don't deliberately push my power; it's an innate part of being a centaur. Something you will learn this year."

For the rest of the lesson, Asher played with strands of my hair, paying no attention to the teacher. Calen dozed in his chair and he wasn't even subtle about it—at one point, his head was back, mouth open. His favorite way to sleep, apparently. Rone stared out the window, and Jesse was drawing something in his notebook. I tried to catch a glimpse, but in his usual style lately, he hid it from me.

Axl and I were the only ones to take notes. When we finished class—the teacher had gone into details about gargoyles—everyone packed up. I shook my head at the guys. "You all took his class solely to be with me, didn't you?"

I should have guessed it. There was a reason there had been so few students they could combine a class—most supernaturals grew up in this world and already knew about the races. Sure, they could probably learn more specific details, but for the most part, this was all old information. Axl took notes because he was Axl, but the rest of them were here for me.

"I love you guys," I said, my expression sober. "I don't say it enough, and I know we've had our issues lately, but that doesn't change the way I feel."

Asher's right arm slid around me as he hauled me into his side. "Me the most though, right?"

When I didn't answer straight away, he jiggled me, and I burst out laughing. His chest rumbled and I took pity on him. "Yes, you slightly more. But that could change so easily if you don't stop using your caveman skills on me."

His laughter was low, stripping away my ability to resist him. "Technically, supernaturals never had cavemen, but I understand what you're saying." He leaned in closer. "And I personally think you love the side of me that wants to completely possess you."

Fuck. Where was the lie?

He gently placed me on my feet, pressing a kiss to the top of my head. As Asher pulled away I caught a dark look on Jesse's face. Our eyes locked and I raised my eyebrows in the universal silent question of "What the fuck is up with you?" but he just shrugged and turned away.

Heat and energy swirled around Asher. This was going to become an issue very soon if we didn't deal with it.

"Stop," I said loudly, using my power to slam the door closed so Jesse couldn't leave. Droplets of water crashed around us as I pulled moisture from the air, using it to do my bidding. It was almost second nature now to control the element in this way. It might have been an unfair advantage to use it against a shifter, who didn't have his own active magic, but I was desperate.

Jesse remained facing the door, his shoulders heaving as he struggled with himself. "I've gotta get to class," he muttered, sounding pissed off.

I moved closer, and even though I felt Asher's resignation, he didn't try and stop me. He'd learned that I could fight my own battles, and that I didn't particularly like being "saved" all the time.

"You're not going anywhere until we talk," I said to Jesse's broad shoulders, because the asshole still wouldn't turn. "What the hell is going on with you lately? You've been grumpier than the bear shifters at hibernation time."

The bears didn't actually hibernate, but I'd noticed they were crankier in the winter months. Had to be something to do with their animal counterparts. Or maybe they were just dicks.

"Do we have to do this here?" Jesse asked, his head cracking against the wood as he dropped it forward. "It's not even a thing. I just need some time."

My throat was burning and so were my eyes. Jesse was hurting and it was hurting me. Especially since I had no idea how to fix it. I turned to Asher. His eyes were traced with gold as his powers fought to surface. He was only a few feet away, but I knew he was about to move closer. Whatever it was that bonded us, the thing that drew me to Asher, and had from the first moment I saw him, it was getting stronger. Along with those errant thoughts, I could feel his emotions now.

I held a finger up asking for one more shot. He crossed his arms, a blank expression descending over his face as he nodded.

Turning back to Jesse, I reached out and touched him; his entire body seemed to rumble as a lion roar filled the room. No one moved, even though that roar would have scared most supes away. But it was Jesse. He wouldn't hurt us.

He wouldn't hurt me.

"Talk to me," I said softly, stepping even closer, my hand firmly on his back.

In one smooth movement, he spun and I was up in his arms. He slammed me into the door, his entire body pressed to mine as he held me, chest heaving, eyes wide. His pupils were like cat slits, the green in his eyes bright and glowing.

"For fuck's sake," I heard Calen say from behind Jesse, and I felt Asher's rage—it was crashing into the room and shaking the foundation. I felt all of that, but I couldn't see any of them around the raging lion shifter.

Jesse's eyes bore down into mine, his jaw changing shape as the beast took him over. "You can't fucking see it, Maddison," he rumbled, leaning in to run his nose along my neck. Inhaling my scent. "It's always Asher. Even though I'm the one who picked up the pieces over and over again."

Ah, fuck. I had really been hoping this wasn't the shit he was dealing with. I mean, I'd known deep down that this was all probably to do with errant feelings, but a tiny sliver of me had prayed to be wrong.

"Jesse," I said, trying to be gentle, but an undercurrent of "fuck you for manhandling me" still slipped into my voice. "I'm going to give you exactly five seconds to let me go, and if you don't, you won't have to worry about the pissed off Atlantean dude that's shaking this room apart." My voice got lower as my hair started to swirl around my head like it had a will of its own. "You'll have to deal with me."

Jesse's chest was heaving, and for a moment I thought he was going to fight my desire to be free, but at the four second mark he roared again and stepped back, letting me fall to the floor.

Fuck. *Ouch.* That kinda hurt.

Before I could stop him, he ripped the door open, barely missing my head, and stormed out.

I was an Atlantean demi-god so Jesse really couldn't hurt me. He knew that. Everyone knew that. But that didn't stop Asher from smashing his fist through the door that his best friend had just stormed out of. In the same instant, he reached down and gently lifted me into his arms.

We were all silent; no one moved until Axl stepped forward to magically repair the door.

"I'm going to kill him," Asher raged, the heat pouring off him in waves, the water in the air around us crackling and turning into steam as he got angrier.

Part of me ached at the way Jesse had just treated me, but I also got it.

He'd let whatever this was bottle up inside of him for too long. He hadn't spoken to anyone about it and he clearly was not dealing with it. I hadn't been the only one to go through shit last year. Everyone had. Jesse had to deal with Asher and me both "dying."

It was all too much.

"He's hurting," I said softly, tears in my eyes because my heart ached. Axl and Calen pushed closer, both of them reaching out to touch me ... offer comfort. Rone remained back, perched against a desk, his face a mask, even though his eyes were blazing. "We need to figure out how to help him," I choked out, sobs muffling my words.

"Jesse has timing," the vampire grumbled, his head shaking. "The entire world is falling the fuck down around us, and he wants to sulk because Maddi loves Asher." He tilted his head toward me. "Not that you're not worth crying over, Mads, because you are. But it's not like this is a secret dropped on him—it's been Asher and Maddison pretty much from day one. So why the hell is he taking it so hard now?"

I knew why.

"Because I was gone," Asher said, pain and anger bleeding into his words. "I was gone, and Jesse was there for Maddison. I've felt their emotions, and I know they love each other."

"Not the way I love you," I said without a moment's hesitation. "Not even close." I didn't have to think about it. Jesse was my best friend. My family. But Asher ... he eclipsed every other possible mate, and no matter what Jesse ... or *Sonaris* thought about it, there would never be another.

It was exactly as Rone had said, Maddison and Asher from day one.

"I know, baby," he said, resting his head against mine. The heat pouring off him had eased; his eyes were mostly green again. "I'm not worried about your feelings. But Jesse is going to be a problem until he gets this shit out of his system."

Musical notes rang out through the air, and since this room was no doubt supposed to have another class in it now, we hurried out—only to find a teacher and an entire class on the other side, waiting patiently for us to fuck off.

"Oh, I am so sorry," I said. "Minor power issue."

I had no idea how long they'd been there, but I was too upset to be embarrassed.

The teacher met Asher's eyes, and he must have read the lingering anger there. "No worries." His voice had a forced upbeat sound to it. "We're only a few minutes late…" He ushered his class inside.

It would have been amusing, but Jesse was occupying most of my emotions. And none of that was remotely funny.

Since the rest of us had lunch now, we wandered toward the commons. I wondered if Jesse would be at our table, and I quickened my steps, wanting to see him. Only the table was empty, mocking me with that fact. Mocking us all.

Asher's face darkened. He'd gotten himself mostly under control, but I could feel what was happening deep inside. The tumult of anger and pain still raged there.

We couldn't stay at odds like this. It wasn't good for anyone.

If *stronger together* was our motto, this current state was leaving us extremely vulnerable to the gods.

We had to fix it. Right the fuck now.

CHAPTER 6

Unfortunately, none of the Atlanteans equipped with testicles made my job of "family togetherness" easy over the next few days. I was literally the only one trying, and it was starting to creep under my skin like an itch I just couldn't scratch.

We fell into a normal routine for school life, and even though I saw Jesse in class a few times, he was acting the part of the most dedicated student ever, not even looking our way.

By the time Wednesday rolled around it was the first official sports morning, an initiative that had been started last year by Princeps Jones. It hadn't gotten any further than day one last year because I'd accidentally used my power that day to bring half the ocean to the Academy.

Whoops. My bad.

This was a take two, and Larissa told me her dad had high hopes it would unite the supernatural races in ways that were probably impossible to achieve. I loved him for trying though. Especially since I was going to use this mandatory event to force Jesse to deal with me. We were going to find our family dynamics again.

If it was the last godsdamned thing we did.

It was killing me to have this tension in the group, and not just me … Axl was not handling it well. Poor dude was basically living in the library now. Not that he hadn't always spent a lot of time there, but it was pretty obvious at this stage that he was avoiding home. I'd wanted to force us closer together and all I'd done was tear it further apart.

Today all of us were on the field. The weather was mild, and outside of a swift breeze, nothing at all to concern anyone. It was almost warm, and considering it was technically winter in this part of the world…

Bottom line: there was nothing that would result in me causing a huge scene by dragging half the ocean to the Academy and getting this bonding event canceled for another year.

"You wouldn't do that again," Asher said, doing our new fun mind reading thing. "You have control now. Frankly, I'm afraid of what you might be able to do once you've reached your full potential as an Atlantean demi-god."

I laughed, shaking my head.

The smallest of smirks tilted his lips. "You didn't say anything about canceling the event, did you?"

"Nope. That was you picking up on my thoughts."

Most of the time I got emotions from him, and some vague images, whereas he seemed to be getting actual detailed thoughts from me.

"Royal Atlanteans could hear the thoughts of their true mates," Axl said.

Asher and I both turned to him. "Are you serious?" I hadn't had a chance to properly research it yet.

Axl nodded. "Yep, I've just finished reading the second-to-last section in the library, and I found a book about the royals. It appears that those bonded in true mate relationships could communicate mentally."

"Holy shit," I murmured.

Asher pulled me closer, holding me tightly, and I relished the sensation of our bodies pressed together like that. "True mate," he whispered. "I like the sound of that."

When I pulled back, I found Axl smiling. It was the first genuine smile from him in ages. "Could this be a natural transition for us? The path to sealing our mate bond?"

He pursed his lips, thinking it through before answering. That meant he didn't know for sure and was trying to give us the most likely scenario. He hated guessing, but he would surmise based on the facts he had. "I think there's something in your power, Mads, something that's partially blocking the true mate bond. I've been wondering if maybe the tie you have to Sonaris is disturbing the natural energy of the mate bond. If that's the case, until it's resolved, you and Ash will always be straddling the line between what you have now and the full realization of a true bond."

Whatever smile I'd been sporting faded and I choked back some harsh words of denial. It wasn't Axl's fault, I had to remember that, but I really wanted to be growling the same way Asher was.

"Sonaris is not her fucking mate," he snapped, his power winding around us. Asher was a demi-god as well, maybe even stronger than me considering who his mother was. A mother that we thought was powerful enough to birth Asher with no father, just her energy, placed in a mortal queen of Atlantis.

I was born of two gods and a mortal queen too, as was my "brother" Connor. But neither of our parents were the daughter of the Mother of All, a literally original goddess with the power of creation.

Connor.

I hadn't talked to him for days, but I knew he was around the campus, being an arrogant prick. It was what he did best. Why he was still here when he didn't seem to attend classes was beyond me. Frankly, I could barely stand to even see his face. So much of my heartache was his fault. I fucking knew it was.

"Sonaris is an issue we'll have to deal with sooner or later," I finally said. "I owe him, and it bothers me, so I'm hoping we can get that finished. Then I can move forward with Asher, because he's my soulmate and Sonaris is just a leech that attached himself to me without permission."

Asher held me close. I didn't blame him. If someone was threatening our relationship, even in the tiny miniscule way Sonaris was attempting, I would be one pissed-off Atlantean.

It wasn't that I didn't trust Asher. I did. Completely. And if the last year hadn't torn us apart, nothing would. But I was possessive. I loved Asher and I would defend that to anyone who threatened it.

End of story.

"I would do the same. You're mine, Maddison James."

And there he went, reading my thoughts again.

A derisive snort echoed across to us. Jesse had edged into our inner circle, eyeing the three of us closely, as if trying to figure out exactly what we were talking about. His eyes brushed over me and our gazes caught. I choked on my words, the pain I saw in those green depths palpable, literally rendering me speechless. Jesse eventually shook his head, breaking the connection, before turning back to face the teachers. They had started to gather in the center of us all, ready to get this sports event started.

I rubbed at my chest, the ache deep and seated. I fucking hated when we were on the outs like this. Like I needed one more thing to stress about. Rone was right, Jesse had the worst freaking timing, but I could tell that he'd just reached the end of what he could handle.

So I was mad, but not too mad at him. And I was still determined to sort it out.

Today.

"Time to team up!" a gruff voice shouted, and I focused on the huge field again, surprised by the changes that had occurred in the short time since we arrived. The teachers had taken no chances with more magical mayhem, setting up the SSW area themselves. Supernatural Strategy Wars was a team sport played only by supes.

The huge field where the games would take place had been clear and open before; now it was filled with two mountains standing a hundred feet in the air. Legitimately. I'd seen the start as they slowly rose, but somehow, in my distraction, I'd missed the massive heights they'd reached. Not to mention there was a forest, a large, darkly enticing river, and some other rocky landscapes. The only cleared space now was right in the center—a flat grassy section that offered no hiding spots at all.

I still wasn't really sure about how this game worked, but thankfully we got a quick rundown before it started.

"You'll all form teams of four," said a male teacher I hadn't met before. I was thinking he might be some sort of physical sports instructor, judging by the tank style shirt and endless amount of muscles.

It was no surprise that I didn't know him yet; I'd avoided all the sports subjects, and not because I disliked physical activity. In my first year I'd been so far behind on learning about this world, I needed academics the most.

"One from each of the races," he continued. "You'll be allowed three attack and two defense spells today. The attack spells will disable any player they hit for twenty seconds, and the supernatural who shoots the spell will also be disabled from performing any more spells for twenty seconds. So make these offensive moves count."

He continued on with lots of other rules, mostly about using race gifts. They had limitations on what was and wasn't allowed. Vampires could not bite, but they could use their speed. The fey were allowed to use some elemental attacks, but only within the limitations of the five spells of the game. Shifters could shift into their animals, but they could not bite or maim the other team, and magic users were limited to the five spells as well, just like the fey.

"You said last year that the vampires and shifters are usually the runners, right?" I whispered when the teacher paused his explanation. I didn't remember much else, but that stuck with me.

"Usually the fey shields with one of the defensive spells and the vamp runs," Axl corrects. "The magic user is the one on the attack, more often than not, and the shifter herds them into place so that the attacks are not wasted."

Wasted. "So if I use one of the attack spells and don't hit anyone, I'm still unable to shoot again for twenty seconds?"

"Correct, and you will be vulnerable to an attack in that moment because you cannot defend yourself. The prime time to take out the other side is when they have their twenty second hold on magic."

Okay. Got it.

Maybe.

I was starting to get the vibe that it was very much like paintball and capture the flag, where you protected your flag while trying to steal the other teams. All I had to know now was what we were protecting, what the spells were, and who was on my team.

"Asher and I can't go together," I said, looking between our group. I'd been trying not to show my disappointment at that, but clearly I failed.

Asher chuckled. "Technically we can—we're born of the mixed fey-magic users race and I think we can represent either one of those."

Axl nodded. "Yep, mixed race players are allowed, they just have to declare who they're representing and then stick to strengths only from that race. It's a gray area, but they won't discriminate against those not pure. So you can go together. Team up with Jesse and Rone and you'll be a pretty unstoppable force."

Yeah, if Jesse, Asher, and I didn't come to blows on the field.

"What about you?" I asked Axl. He was a wizard, and in that case couldn't be on the team with us.

"I'll find a team," he said, "Calen and I will both have to see who needs a magic user."

Like we'd summoned her, Larissa appeared. I hugged her hard. "Girl, I love your braid," I said, admiring her thick strands threaded through with glittering ribbons and gems. They stood out against her blond hair and she looked gorgeous. She'd really been rocking new funky hairstyles ever since she went shorter.

She shrugged. "Trying something new."

"It's working for you," I replied. The teachers called for teams to come forward, and I moved into action. "Larissa and Calen or Axl can be on a team," I said, pushing them together. "Now you'll just have to find a shifter and fey."

It didn't take long. The Atlanteans had always been treated like gods in this school. Long before anyone knew Asher was literally a god. Other supes wanted their approval … their attention. They definitely wanted to be close to them. Calen and Larissa found their third and fourth in seconds, and Axl was dragged into a team of people he seemed to know already.

Calen coughed close to my ear. "Nerd squad," he said softly, his teeth shining brilliant white in the early morning light. "They keep vigil in the library with Axl when he's not in our exclusive section."

I snorted, shaking my head at him.

"Stay in your foursome and wait for further instructions," a teacher shouted.

Rone and Jesse stepped up shoulder to shoulder with Asher, and I faced off against the three of them, sighing at the sheer volume of devastatingly handsome dude staring at me. *How was this my life?* Seeing them like this, all together … it was almost too much for my poor female hormones.

Come on, I was only human. Or whatever.

"So, what's our plan, boys?" I asked, waggling my eyebrows, determined to pretend everything was normal, and maybe, just maybe we could have a little fun. "Are we going with brute strength, underhanded-borderline-illegal combat, or stealth attack?"

Rone's lips tilted up, and there he was, doing his avenging fallen angel thing. He'd looked the same the very first time I met him, only scarier. His somewhat permanent scowl had eased over the past two years, but he still had a reputation, a rep that might come in handy during our first SSW match. If I knew supes at all, a lot of this game would be won mentally … long before we had to get our hands dirty.

"I think Asher and Jesse on defense, Maddi and me on offense," Rone said quickly. "Maddi is fast and small. She'll be able to slip through areas we can't fit, depending where they hide their artefact. I'll be quick enough to intercept any of the spells so she can keep going."

I waited for Jesse to argue, because lately he seemed to just want to fight, but he didn't say a word. He must have felt the glare I was leveling at the side of his face, because his lips twitched, and he flashed me the smallest smile. For a moment, he reminded me of the old Jesse, my best friend, and not this moody stranger who had taken his place.

It was gone just as quickly though, and he was back to pretending none of us existed.

"You're team twelve," the teacher said when he stopped by our group. He reached out and handed Asher a small gold statue. "Keep your artefact safe. If the other team gets their hands on it, you lose."

It looked like it weighed nothing as Asher held it, but I sensed that it was damn heavy. "We'll call your number when you're up."

He left and a misty magic washed over us. I looked down to find the number "12" emblazoned across my shirt.

I loved magic.

We followed the groups across the soft grass to stand closer to the main field. Once we reached the sidelines, I noticed that it was actually divided into multiple smaller fields. "They'll play more than one team at a time," Asher said, watching me while I tried to take it all in. "During a game, you might be rotated into a new territory. You'll have to adapt, hide your artefact, and keep the other team off your back."

I snorted. "So basically the only real rule is that there are no rules, and the umpire or ref or whatever you call it can make a split-second decision that screws everyone."

"Right," the three of them said together, and I didn't let on how much I loved hearing them all in sync again. Just for a second.

Hopefully it wouldn't be the last time.

CHAPTER 7

Eight teams went out into the four territories, crossing a magical barrier that encased them in their field. Two of the territories were mountains, one a forest, and the last the dark waterway, with snow along one bank and what looked like a steam field on the other. Depending on the race rules around the water, Asher and I would do very well in that area. But we didn't get to choose.

It was all set out for us.

Team twelve wasn't called in the first set of eight and that meant I was going to have a chance to watch them all in action. Learn the way I did best: observation.

At first the teams stood in the cleared zone in the center of their territories, one member from each team holding their artefacts. A magic user stood between them, dressed in bright yellow, making it very clear he was the officiate of this match.

"Your spells are as follows," he said loudly, shooting some sparks into the air. In seconds, words started to form in the blue, cloudless sky.

Attack:
1. *Stun (scrama)*
2. *Fire (firenze)*
3. *Confuse (amentra)*
Defense:
1. *Shield (shisense)*
2. Camouflage (leta mina cora)

"Remember, you can use any of the spells, at any time, but with each spell you'll be powerless for twenty seconds after. If you're hit with a spell, it will stun or confuse you for twenty seconds. Fire will not burn your opponents, but it will send a ring of fire around them, stopping them in their tracks. It can also be used to burn through obstacles and the like."

I sidled a little closer to Asher. "If we stick together, I could use the first spell, then you, then Jesse, and then Rone, right? And by that time I'd be free to do it again?"

Asher flashed some perfect teeth at me. "Technically yes, because in this game the rules allow vamps and shifters to utilize magic as well. But to be honest, most of the time they don't bother with spells. It's weird for them and feels unnatural, so they stick to using their race strengths."

Rone muttered something about not being a fucking wizard and everyone laughed.

"Scowl and look scary," Larissa said, patting him on the chest. She was in team sixteen, and was nearby, waiting for her chance to go out. "That's your true strength."

He tried to glare at her, but she was too adorable to stay mad at. "Is that all I'm good for?" he asked, in mock horror, his eyes softening as he stared down at her. Those icy blue eyes didn't soften for many people, but they were practically melted pools of azure around Larissa.

Her return smile was so sweet, and that usually meant something asshole-ish was going to come out of her mouth. "You also give a wicked backrub and are super handy at reaching those high-up shelves."

I loved my best friend. Larissa had come so far from the shy, broken vamp I'd met in my first year, the one shunned for mourning her mother. This Larissa was fearless, and I couldn't be prouder of her.

Before Rone could retaliate, the matches got underway. The yellow-shirted officiate lifted his hands, sending words and numbers into the sky that indicated the draw system of what team played what. Lines connected those numbers and teams, and I assumed that whenever someone won, the eliminated team would disappear from the magical scoreboard in the sky.

"I wonder if we'll play you?" I asked Larissa.

She shrugged. "Eventually we might. It's a round robin style competition. The losing team gets knocked out, and the winners go on to face other winners until there's only two teams left."

Ah, that sounded like fun.

When the matches started, I paid attention. The teams directly in front of us—team two and team six—were in the mountain area. The vampire on team two dashed up as high as he could, no doubt planning on stashing their artefact in one of the rocky crevices. Vampires moved with superspeed and he was flashing about, confusing everyone about where exactly he was heading. On the other team, their vampire tucked the artefact into his shirt, heading in the opposite direction.

"How can anyone catch a vampire?" I asked, my eyes trying to track both of them.

Jesse made a disparaging sound and I lifted my eyebrows at him. Not that he noticed, since he was making a superhuman attempt to not look directly at me. He'd only slipped up once in days, and he clearly didn't want it to happen again.

He did speak though. "Shifters can keep up with them."

Sure enough, in the next five minutes, the bear shifter on team two, managed to pounce on the vampire from team six, and rip his shirt open. Only to find there was no artefact hidden inside. The bear roared, and it was so animalistic that actual chills raced across my arms. In seconds he was no longer a person but an actual freaking bear. No matter how many times I felt like I was finally getting used to this world, something new would then happen to surprise me.

Like, a two-hundred-pound person, turning into a six-hundred-pound bear.

"He offloaded it somewhere. Not bad," Asher said, looking impressed. "I never saw it leave his possession, but we don't have the best view from here."

The witch on the opposing team managed to shoot a stunning spell at the newly turned shifter, freeing her vampire counterpart. A clock appeared about the shifter's head; the twenty second countdown was on.

The vampire was on his feet in a heartbeat, and with the witch they took off. She had a clock above her head too, unable to produce another spell until her time was up.

"I feel like this could go on for hours," I said, watching as the teams went back and forth, searching for the artefact. Both vampires had hidden it effectively.

"The artefacts have a scent," Rone murmured, leaning forward, a gleam of competitiveness in that gaze. "Vamps and shifters can smell it, but they have to get quite close. One of them usually leaves defense to hunt it down if it's well hidden."

The other team's vampire was zooming up the mountain now, the witch right beside him, as well as their shifter. They must have been pretty confident in the hiding place, because all that was left on the ground was the fey chick currently zigzagging across the land, trying to confuse and evade the other team.

On the mountain, team two had spread out, with at least three of their members up there. I couldn't see the fourth, but I assumed they were trying to find the artefact.

Team two made a big mistake though—they stayed too close to their artefact, making it obvious where the general location was. The moment team six knew, the witch sent out a ring of fire, trapping two of the other team. The shifter took out the third. The vampire only needed about fifteen more seconds to find the artefact then, slamming his fist into the rock and disturbing its hiding place.

His fist rose in the air, gold glinting in the sun. A buzzer sounded and noise exploded around the area. We'd all been watching intently, and I hadn't even noticed that two of the other fields had finished their first round as well. Only one was left in an endless cycle of pass the parcel with their artefact, while the other team kept trying to stun and confuse to get it back.

"There's always one team," Axl said, shaking his head. "Their plan is redundant. No one can win this way, because one team isn't even trying to find the other artefact. They have all four players working on keeping theirs safe."

"What happens if no one wins?" I asked.

"After thirty minutes, there'll be a change up, and the limitations on spells will end for one minute. In that minute you can cast any spell and use any race gift to try and win. Generally, that sorts it out." Asher's eyes lit up and I could tell he was hoping that would happen, bringing with it all the chaos.

We didn't get a chance to see though. Our number was called up. We were against team thirty, so I gave Larissa a hug as we parted. Asher, Jesse, and Rone stayed close to me, all of us stopping on the side of our field. We were not in the water territory—we ended up in the forest zone, and my thighs were thankful that I wouldn't be climbing any mountains this round. I didn't recognize our officiate, but he was in their yellow uniform, so there was no way to miss him.

The eight of us gathered around and he ran through the rules quickly again. I almost laughed at the slightly green tinge to the faces of the other team. They looked like first years. Most of them probably didn't even know how to cast proper spells yet.

I almost felt bad for them. Almost.

When the officiate was done, we went back to our half of the field, and

I finally noticed—not sure how I even missed it before—that there was no sound inside here. I could see hundreds of students crowding around outside, but no sound reached us.

"No distractions," I murmured, forcing myself to focus on the game.

"I'm going to camouflage the artefact," Asher said as soon as we were huddled together, "and then hide it before anyone even knows I have it."

I nodded. "You'll be knocked out magically for twenty seconds, so I'll go with you in case I need to defend you with a spell."

"All four of us should stick together to plant the artefact," Rone said, "only scattering right before we hide it. That way, they'll have no clue which direction it went in, especially when it's camouflaged."

"We'll have twenty seconds of it remaining hidden," I reminded them. "Any idea where you want to drop it?"

Our half had forest, their half had forest, and then there was a grassy section that joined the two. "Up one of the trees," Asher said looking between them. "I'll search for a hollow to make it a little harder."

"I'll find the smelliest plants to stuff around it," Jesse said, looking focused and determined. He wasn't even scowling and that was a fucking nice change. "That will limit their ability to scent it easily."

"Everyone grab a stone," Asher murmured as the officiate announced the countdown. In three seconds, the buzzer sounded and we were off. "*Leta mina cora*," Asher said softly, and then the artefact swirled for a beat, turning into a stone. We'd all picked up stones at the same time, and then we took off. Asher passed me the artefact in perfect view of the other team—all who'd taken off after us. But I slipped it back to him as soon as we were out of sight.

The timer above Asher's head was counting down slowly. When it got to five seconds we split. I took off into a particularly dense part of the forest. I wasn't sure how much of this was real or illusion, but everything felt just as it would in an actual rainforest. Lots of associated scents and noises, even some insects and arachnids scattered around.

I couldn't hear anyone pursuing me, so I planted my stone first, hiding it in the hollow of a giant tree. Its base was so large it was at least six feet across. I wasn't sure anyone was watching me, but I played the part like they were.

When I was done, I exited the forest, ending up in the clearing between both sides. I was there alone, not another member of either team in sight—until a vampire dashed past me, and before I even registered what I was doing, I shouted *scrama*, sending the spell into him. He tumbled down, his body motionless.

I dashed toward him, thankful there was no telltale black shirt and broad shoulders that would mean I'd spelled my own team. I'd reacted so quickly there hadn't even been time to really see who was running past me.

When I reached the vamp, the countdown clock was at ten seconds, so I quickly flipped him over, ready to frisk him. I wasn't expecting much, because I figured they'd dumped their artefact straight away, like we had. But as soon as he hit the ground, the golden artefact tumbled out of his hands, and with a laugh I scooped it up and held it high.

They'd clearly thought we were all busy in the forest, and I'd not only ducked out at the right time but had somehow been fast enough with my reflex shot spell to hit a vampire at full sprint. Probably that was an extra skill that most supes didn't have, but it wasn't like I tapped into any of my powers. Pure instinct.

Thank you, Supernatural Academy, for developing those reflexes.

Or maybe it was all the practice I'd been doing lately. I was determined to up my game since the gods made me look like I was all but human. I refused to be taken down so easily again.

Either way, we got the artefact in about two minutes. Another burst of laughter left me. This game was fun.

The buzzer sounded, alerting the rest of the players that we were done, and my guys emerged from the forest, shaking their heads at me standing there with the golden statue in my hands.

"Go, Maddi," Rone whooped, scooping me up and swinging me around. "That had to be some kind of record."

I shook my head and smacked him on the arm to let me down. "Dude, it was a lucky fluke, nothing more."

Jesse actually smiled at me, directly at my face, and for a moment we all pretended he didn't hate my guts. "Nothing you do is a lucky fluke, Mads. You're just naturally good at competitive sports."

I'd never had much chance in my life to know if that was true or not. Sports back in America were expensive, and the schools I went to didn't have a whole lot to offer in their curriculum. But it was a nice thought.

We all left the field and the other team's artefact was handed to our officiate, before we rejoined the sideline of supes shouting and cheering. The morning bell rang soon after that and all the games ceased.

"Since this isn't anything official," one of the teachers shouted, his voice magically amplified, "we'll stop there. But next Wednesday we'll pick up from the same round robin draw. Thanks for today!"

I was already looking forward to it.

CHAPTER 8

When I was finishing up my classes on Friday, I found myself in the Atlantean library. I had an hour to kill before everyone was meeting for dinner. Axl was already in there, and so was Mab. She'd been coming and going, visiting friends, so it was nice to see her again.

"Maddison!" she exclaimed, fluttering over to send a burst of magic around me as she got closer. "I've missed you."

"I missed you too," I said, smiling broadly. Mab had a way about her; she made me feel both intensely safe and happy, even if part of me never forgot that she was one of the scariest creatures I'd ever met. "Where did you go this time?"

She flapped her wings hard enough to create a small breeze, elevating to my eyeline. "I was in Faerie," she said simply.

I blinked at her, waiting for her to expand on that, only she just continued flapping her wings and smiling.

I pushed when I couldn't take it any longer. "What were you in Faerie for?"

"I was talking to some old friends," she said, without hesitation. It was always her answer though.

I sighed. "Are you going to tell me or will I have to pry every bit of information out of you?"

Her smile never faltered. "You've got to learn to ask the right questions, Maddison James."

A snort escaped from Axl, but otherwise he remained silently reading in the corner.

"Okay," I said softly. "Did you learn anything in Faerie that is pertinent to me, or to Atlantis, or the gods who we are currently trying to stop from destroying the worlds?"

Her smile grew wider. "Why yes, my lovely friend, I did."

Energy swirled in my center and I tried to calm the racing of my heart.

"The cage keeping the gods inside the underworld will last only one more moon cycle. A reliable source from the inside said that the gods are teaming up and sharing their powers. Looks like Lotus is taking more than her fair share and will be the head runner for this final battle. Oh, and Galindra's allies turned on her, and joined forces with your parents. Galindra has not been seen since she was locked inside, despite the other gods searching to find her."

"Why are they searching?" I interrupted. "They can't kill her without the Hellbringers, right?"

Otherwise locking her in with them was a really bad idea.

Mab lifted her head, face no longer wreathed in happiness. "Technically they could, but they know that her energy might destroy them all. So they won't risk it. Not without the Hellbringers. And they can't control those little devils without you, so they're at a bit of an impasse. I'm guessing they just wanted to detain her, maybe a bit of torture to weaken her. The usual."

I blinked.

Scary. Ass. Creature.

"She no doubt still has some allies in there," Mab continued. "All powerful beings collect allies. It's essential. They'll be hiding her."

Rubbing my hand on my chest, I hoped the soothing motion would keep some of the panic contained. "One moon cycle. So ... one more month. That's all the time we have? What about the path? Is it here? Because we're legitimately running out of time."

I mean, I had a countdown clock over my head now, similar to the one we'd just seen during SSW. Mine might not be actually visible, but it was there.

"Your path is not set in motion yet, but ... it will be soon. This countdown is a catalyst that will pave the way. Don't worry."

Yeah, telling me not to worry was like telling me not to breathe. It was almost part of my nature now.

"Anything else I need to know?"

She nodded, fluttering even closer, her voice lowering. "You need to train with Asher and Connor. The three of you ... there's a bond between you. Beings born of multiple energies: god, Atlantean, Faerie. The three of you together have a power that needs to be explored. It's very important."

This wasn't the first time she'd told me this, but it was the first time I truly took heed of her warning. "I haven't seen Connor in days. Is he even in this school still?"

"He's in the library most nights," Axl spoke up. "Usually gets in late though, around midnight."

I could work with that. Since he wasn't responding to my texts, he was going to get an in-person visit. Mab wouldn't give us advice or warnings lightly, so it was time to pay attention.

The fairy queen flew away, clearly satisfied with the information she'd shared, and I sat next to Axl. He handed me a book, without even lifting his head from the one he was reading.

I didn't question him; I'd learned not to do that. Axl was a billion times smarter than me without even trying, and if he handed me a book, it was one I had to read.

Flipping it open, I found myself staring at an image of two people having sex. The sensual sort of sex where they were so intertwined that I almost couldn't tell which limb belonged to who. What the fuck was this, the supernatural Kamasutra?

I raised an eyebrow at my friend, but he just nudged me with his shoulder.

"Chapter twelve," he said.

Flipping past many more scenes of love making, some with multiple partners, I found myself at chapter twelve. There was no title on this chapter, so I had no idea what to expect, but if this was just advice on how to achieve some sort of ten-hour orgasm … I was totally going to high five the fuck out of Axl.

The chapter was set out like a diary, as were so many of the ancient texts from the original Atlanteans. Third line down the words *true mate bond* caught my eye, and I settled back, reading it closely. There was a bunch of text in ancient Atlantean, and then below was the translated version.

He'd been my best friend for many years. Someone I both loved and admired, but it wasn't until we took the final steps in our relationships, with both words and actions, that the bond was triggered.

It's the strangest thing ever. I can feel Jaffin. Feel his emotions. And I can hear his thoughts when he stops shielding them from me. Communicating mentally ... it has changed the dynamics of our relationship. We've grown so much closer. He tells me that it's because of his father, who is brother to the king. The royal line has the power to communicate with their true mates.

We are unique. There is no one else I've spoken with who has experienced this.

Jaffin believes we will ascend to godhood when the new babies are born. It's said that the gods can not only read each other's minds, but they can share their power. Especially between true mates.

An organic power share that would make that couple near unstoppable.

I feel this is to be for us. Limitless power.

The next few sentences were about the god babies who were due any day. I still couldn't quite wrap my mind around the fact they were referring to me. Especially since this text was some ten thousand years old.

It was very clear though, from everything we'd read, that at the time the Atlanteans had been excited about our births. An excitement that would soon turn to horror.

Instead of the riches they'd been expecting, we were their downfall.

My parents were such fucking assholes. Their selfish actions had triggered a response from some powerful being, possibly the Mother of

All, destroying everything.

"You think Asher and I might not only be able to read minds, but also share our power?" I asked Axl. "Once we get this bond worked out?"

"We need to address the issue of Sonaris," he said bluntly, finally looking up. "It's impossible to truly know until that happens. I've been reading everything I can find on these subjects, but the royals didn't seem to keep the same level of diary commentary as the commoners. I haven't found anything solid. And the gods certainly didn't journal their lives into Atlantean libraries."

Big shock there. Sucking in deeply, I closed the book. "Sonaris is a real pain in my ass. But you're right. It has to end now. I'm going to force him to settle this debt between us the next time he shows up. Then we need to figure out how to break whatever metaphysical ties he forced on me before I was even born. There has to be a way. There's always a way."

The concern on Axl's face was enough that I wanted to scream, but he didn't tell me it couldn't be done, and I took that as a small positive sign that there was still a chance. I needed there to be a chance.

Asher's energy hit me moments before he entered the room. Whatever tension had been building inside relaxed. When he reached my side, his power and scent covered me, sinking in deep, and I was home.

"Your emotions are all over the place," his voice rumbled in my ear. "What's wrong?"

Axl and I quickly detailed everything we'd discovered, and I added extra information from Mab. "So we have one month," I finished. "And there's no path. And I have no clue. And it's driving me fucking crazy."

He was quiet for a second, and somehow more tension left me, like he was leeching it from me, slowly. Absorbing it … or at least sharing the burden of my worries with me.

"The path will show itself," he murmured. "I'm not sure how I know, but my power is giving me a sense of what is to come. It won't be long."

And just like that, I felt even better.

Axl was back to his books, and since I was exhausted from school and study and stress, I yawned and grabbed my bag.

"You ready to go home now, water baby?" Asher asked, his hand tracing teasing circles on my back.

Home. The concept had been so foreign, but that was no longer the case. I had family who felt like home, and I had a home that felt like everything. Tonight was the official move-in night, but we were supposed to wait until after dinner.

"Food?" I reminded him.

He spun me so I was facing him and I drank in every sexy inch of him. Hair was tousled, shorter on the side, longer on top. Green eyes shimmering at me. Bronze skin with the uniform shirt partly unbuttoned to reveal long slices of tanned muscles.

I realized I was hungry, but not for anything I could get in the commons.

"Fuck food," I said, grabbing his hand and dragging him out.

Axl's laughter sounded from behind us. "Maybe you should have read more of that book," he called after us, and I flipped him off over my shoulder.

It was dark outside when we emerged from the main entrance of the library, and there was a massive storm building. It looked like one of those crazy ones that only hit inside the Academy. The timing was brilliant as usual, with me about to carry my stuff across campus.

At least we had magic.

"Some days it feels like it's getting worse," I said, staring up.

"It is," Axl said from behind us, and I jumped because I hadn't heard him follow.

"You figured out how to reverse the spell yet?" Asher asked. I could tell that no one had a doubt that Axl would figure it out; it was just a matter of when.

Axl shifted his heavy stack of books in his hands, nodding as he did. "Yes. But it requires magic from the four races, some Atlantean energy—I can provide that—and for the moon to be in a specific position, usually associated with the middle of its cycle."

Asher stared up, eyeing the moon, barely visible behind the tumult of the weather. "So about two weeks?"

Axl nodded. "Yes. I've started preparing, and when Princeps Jones returns I'll make sure it's all squared away with him. Unless of course he enjoys the random weather, and in that case I'll just write my case study up for future reference."

It took some effort, but I managed not to laugh at him. Axl was the best value, and the most loyal, loving friend, but at times when he acted more robot than supernatural, it really amused me. "Good luck with it all," I said, managing to keep a straight face.

A figure dashed around the building, skidding to a halt before us. "When you weren't waiting at the table in the commons," Calen said, not sounding even a little winded, "I figured we were jumping the gun on getting our girl all moved into the house."

Ilia appeared at a much more sedate pace, shaking her head at Calen. "Dude, I could legit kick your balls up into your throat right now. You're a total pain in the ass. Everyfuckingthing is not a race."

In one move, so fast it was almost untrackable, he was in front of her, arms wrapped tightly around her. "Oh, why you so mad, babe?" he said. "Is it because you lost the race?"

She choked out a snarl laugh, sounding like she didn't want to be amused but was. "It was not a race, you overgrown child," she huffed.

Calen laughed, and her eyes went very dark and I swallowed a laugh. Calen was in so much trouble. In two rapid movements, she clocked him both in the throat and in the gut, landing gracefully on her feet when he dropped her. "Don't be mad, *babe*," she mocked. "Not everyone can win in a fight. Because I like making up competitive events and not telling anyone about them."

Calen wheezed through his next breaths, humor gone from his face. He wasn't mad though. Nope. Dude was legit eye-fucking her. And Ilia liked it.

"We're totally moving me in alone," I joked, turning to Asher, who was watching our friends with a resigned look on his face.

When he focused on me, though, that look morphed into something darker, possessive. "I've waited a long time for this day. I got you, Maddi. We don't need any help."

He stepped closer and I couldn't breathe. I forgot that anyone else was even near us as I tried desperately to suck in air and moisten my dry lips. "Let's go," I finally choked out. "I'm ready."

I'd been ready for a long time. Fear held me back, but no longer.

CHAPTER 9

Ilia and Calen did manage to help, as did Axl, Rone, and Larissa. Jesse didn't show up at all. I tried not to let it hurt me—I tried really fucking hard to put myself into his position—to understand that he was hurting and this was how he was dealing with it.

But I just wasn't that big of a person. Jesse was family to me, but family or not, I wasn't letting something toxic like this current dynamic stay in my life. I might have hurt him, but I was trying to fix it. If he'd talked to me at all, explained how he was feeling—if he even said once "you're important to me but I need to step back for a bit"—I would still be upset, but not on this level. He was treating me like he couldn't stand being near me.

He wasn't doing it to anyone else either. I'd seen him laughing and joking with his brothers, including Asher, but the moment I was there, he shut off and disappeared.

Maybe it was selfish of me, but it hurt to have him act so cold. I missed my friend.

"That was easier than I expected," Asher said, pulling me back into his—*our*—soft bed. We snuggled into the clean sheets that already smelled like ocean and life. "You really don't have much stuff. A bunch of clothes that Ilia definitely picked out for you, and about three things from your life before the Academy."

I chuckled, turning to bury my head in his chest. All of my shit was already packed away—thank you, magic. Even my clothes were neatly stacked or hung up in the large walk-in closet. The only thing I still had out was my old knife.

"This blade has seen me through a lot of life," I said, staring at it, shifting the rust-marked silver-colored handle through my fingers. A snort escaped. "Did Ilia ever tell you I pulled this on her the first night we met?"

Asher shook his head, five o'clock shadow scraping across my skin deliciously. Reaching out, he wrapped a hand around mine, enclosing me and the knife in his huge grip. "How long have you had it for?"

I thought for a moment. "You know, I'm not sure. Years, definitely. I got it from one of my mom's boyfriends, and it definitely came in handy a few times. Sometimes a chick just needs a blade to remind people that her body is hers; they have no right to it. It's almost symbolic at this stage, a tribute to everything I've been through. Everything I've overcome."

He was silent, that scary silence where he was contemplating bad things. But since no one was here for him to kill right now, he eventually relaxed.

"The knife stays," he said gruffly. "It'll go in the cabinet."

He had a large, almost ceiling-high, white timber cabinet that sat against the wall near his door. Inside were photos of his family—well, the family he believed were his parents growing up—plus many other pieces from his childhood, including some artefacts he searched out with his dad, and a collage of weapons collected over the years. That cabinet held some of his most prized possessions.

He got off the bed, lifting me with him. Together we crossed to the large piece of furniture, and I stared up at all the photos as I had done many times. Young Asher was one of my favorite things in the world. As a small child, his power and strength were obvious, even if they were covered by a sheen of innocence, baby-faced cutie that he was. For a brief moment, when I saw those photos I could picture my own child. Our child.

Gah. Not something I was ready to contemplate for many, many, many years. Maybe ever. Depending on how the god and danger situation in the world eventuated. I wouldn't risk having a child in a world that might destroy them.

But the errant thought still hit me every now and then.

"We would protect them," Asher said, voice soft but with a deadly undercurrent. "The world would have to cave in around us before I'd let anything harm our child."

"I know," I said, hopping up on tiptoes to reach a small space high on a glass shelf. My blade slid into that spot like it had been made for it, and Asher closed the front panel.

"This information on Atlantean couples," Asher said as we moved back to the bed, "was there anything else that might help?"

"I legit have no idea what we would do without Axl…" I shook my head. "He's saved my ass so many times with his unending knowledge of fucking everything."

Asher's full lips quirked at the corners. "Yep. Mine too. For most of my life. He's always had his head buried in books."

I'd pretty much told him everything already, so we just went over what had been in the diary entry again, including the information about the gods sharing power.

Asher was silent for a moment. His face contemplative as he considered what we'd learned.

"Maybe the next time Sonaris is around, we can try and get information from him," I suggested.

We both knew that he would be around, although, thankfully, I hadn't seen him in over a week. Maybe he was bored with me already. That would be really great news. Asher's expression shifted from contemplative to murderous at that suggestion, but thankfully my stomach chose that point to growl loudly.

With a shake of his head, he laughed. "Better feed my mate before she kills me."

I smacked him hard on the shoulder. "Jerk. I've never even tried to kill you."

I mean, not really.

Asher laughed as he dragged me out into the living area, and I was excited to find that someone had already ordered dinner. The delicious smell of tacos wafted around the room, and I guessed it was Calen we had to thank for the food. Tacos were one of his favorites.

Rone stopped in front of us. "I was just coming to let you know dinner was here. Are you all unpacked?"

"Yep." I nodded for extra measure. "There was hardly anything left to do after using Axl's nifty little unpacking spell."

"When you code it specifically to a supe's energy," Axl said from where he was perched on a kitchen stool. "It unpacks much more accurately."

I shrugged. "Couldn't fault it. Everything is placed just as I would have."

Larissa patted him on the shoulder as she walked past, a tray of glasses filled with water and other drinks, in her hands. How she held the tray and managed to pat him at the same time was beyond me—super strength probably helped. "If you five weren't already filthy rich, you could make a fortune with these inventions."

Axl's cheeks went a little pink. "Thanks."

Aw, my humble genius.

Looking around at my family, all of them setting the table so we could eat together, I felt a surge of happiness. More than happiness, it was contentment. The thought that someone could come along and destroy that … I had to figure out this path. I had to figure out how to stop it.

Asher made a sound next to me, a rumble of annoyance. "Where is Jesse?"

Jesse might not have been acting too differently with Asher, but my mate still knew it was hurting me, and I could sense how much it was pissing him off.

Feeling his emotions was a daily occurrence now.

"He's on his way," Calen said, taking a seat beside Ilia. "He texted before that he was in a meeting."

Yeah, right. A meeting at 10 P.M.

I needed a subject change. "Is your dad back yet, Larissa?"

"He should be back tomorrow or the next day," she said, sounding relieved. "I spoke briefly with him earlier and the meetings have wrapped. He said that he's coming back with everyone and that they have a lot to tell us."

The meeting in Romania had been going on for too long, and I was desperate to know what they'd decided. Not that I thought there was anything those supes could do. But if even one helpful thing came out of the meeting, it would have been worth it.

So many powerful and important supes were there.

I should have been there, but had decided to stay here, just in case. I didn't want to bring trouble to their secret meeting place. What if Sonaris followed me? What if other gods were out there tracking this situation? The risk was too great.

I would just have to wait for their updates.

We all sat at the huge whitewashed table, extending out the sides so that we had more space to fit. My favorite part of this table was the curved legs, carved all the way to the ground, thick and solid.

"Should we wait for Jesse?" Larissa asked as she handed out drinks. She knew everyone's favorite. Mine was water with a hint of lemon and mint. Asher preferred sweet iced tea. As did his brothers. Everyone drank a ton of water though. We were born from it after all.

"No," Asher said shortly.

"He knew what time we were eating," Rone added, a bite in his tone.

Both of them were the most pissed with him and neither bothered to hide it. Calen and Axl were making a little more attempt to stay neutral.

At least there were tacos to distract me.

Asher dropped two on my plate first, and I was pretty sure that if anything in the world proved someone's love, it was their willingness to feed their mate before themselves.

"Thank you," I said, biting into it so fast that the filling went everywhere. The first touch of spiced beef and vegetables on my tongue had an almost inaudible groan leaving my mouth. "So damn good," I mumbled. "This is one of my favorite meals."

Asher wasn't eating, he was watching me. "My favorite too," he said, and the look on his face ... I was suddenly hungry for a lot more than dinner. "Later," he promised quietly.

"I live here now," I said, blinking at the realization. I mean, I knew that already, of course, but it really hit home in that moment.

I lived in the Atlantean mansion.

"For at least the next year," Rone added, already finished his eight tacos. He ate neatly and left almost no mess. He didn't even have sauce on his shirt, and I wasn't sure how that was possible.

Mental pressure slammed into me ... of my own making. "What if I don't graduate this year?"

"Then we'll all be here for another year," Calen said.

"You'll graduate early," Axl added. "You're already ahead in all your classes, and we've got the teachers pushing fourth year work on you. You're handling it, no worries."

Not a hundred percent accurate, but I was somewhat keeping up.

Going back to my taco, I took my second bite just as the front door slammed open and in marched Jesse. Well, it was more like a wobbly lurch, if I was going for accuracy.

He ground to a halt when he saw all of us around the table, his brilliant eyes dimming as they ran across all of us. One by one. Until finally … he finished on me.

My taco was forgotten as the two of us remained locked in each other's gaze. Fuck. I had forgotten how green his eyes got when he was upset, almost unnaturally green. The contrast to his dark skin was startling, but in the best kind of way.

Everything about Jesse was striking, and he was also such a fun, nice guy. Usually.

The perfect package.

Just not for me.

A scowl crossed his lips. "You started without me. Huge fucking surprise." He slurred some of the words and I was getting the picture of just how wasted he was. It was hard for shifters to get drunk—he must have been working at it all day.

"Jess," Asher said softly. "Don't do this, brother."

The stark pain on Jesse's face in that second almost broke my heart; all of my righteous anger against him faded into nothing. All I wanted to do was hug him until everything was okay. But maybe a hug from me was the exact opposite of what would make it okay.

"I gotta swim," Jesse muttered, spinning and hurrying out of the room as fast as his drunk ass could move.

"I'll go after him," Calen said.

"No," I said, standing. "This is about me. I need to deal with it."

Pushing the chair back, I stepped away from the table, only stopping when Asher wrapped a hand around my forearm. "Maddi," he said, warning in his voice, "I don't think you should be alone with him. He's not … acting himself. He hurt you last time."

Leaning down, I slid my free hand around Asher's neck, pulling him closer to me. "It's going to be okay. He didn't hurt me, and I need to deal with it. I promise not to push him too hard, but if I don't confront him, we'll never move past this."

Asher didn't want to let me go. I could see the indecision on his face, the tumult in his darkening eyes. But he wasn't one to pretend women needed their white knight to save them. He let me be the savior sometimes too, and I appreciated that about him, because he was alpha as fuck and it was hard for him to let go.

But he still did it.

"It's just Jess," I reminded him. "He's not going to really hurt me."

"Ten minutes," Asher finally conceded. "Tell him to pull his head out of his ass or we're about to have more than words pass between us."

Pressing my lips to his, I kept the kiss short. "I'll be back soon," I promised.

He held my arm until the last second, not wanting to let me go, but he did. He loved Jesse too. No doubt he hoped I'd be able to bring our family dynamics back.

CHAPTER 10

J esse was already in the pool. As I stepped closer to the water, the briny scent invaded my nose and my heart grew a little lighter. This was water from our oceans, and despite the shitty reasons I was out here, I had a moment of happiness. It had been a while since I'd had a chance to swim, but I lived here now, and could venture out any time of the day or night. That was a huge win.

Jesse was adept at ignoring me, so I didn't even bother trying to catch his attention. I just stripped off my clothes, leaving on a plain black bra and underwear, before diving right in. Everything was crystal clear below, and within seconds my lungs adjusted and I was breathing as easily as I could above the water. Despite the dark stormy sky, it was not dark at all below. My eyes picked up every pigment of light and amplified it until it was almost as bright as day.

I could taste the faint scent of lavender from the cleaner the guys used on the tiles outside. There was also some new water in here—it had rained yesterday. The fresh water and salt didn't mix well at first, but eventually it found its symbiosis.

Jesse had flipped over, watching me as I swam toward him. "We need to talk," I said when I got close. "Please, Jess. We can't keep going like this. It has to end now."

He couldn't speak under here, but I could tell from his face that he wasn't happy. He didn't run away again though.

We rose and hit the surface at the same time.

He opened his mouth first and I didn't try to beat him to it. I wanted him to talk to me.

"I love you," he said.

Everything stopped. The water even stilled.

Jesse dropped his head, and I tried to gather up the pieces of my aching heart.

"I tried really hard not to care this much, Mads," he continued. "Fuck. I did everything. I've not been able to touch another girl in a year, and it's not for lack of trying. I've tried. With as many as I could. But they're not you."

Jesus. I wasn't sure I could get through this without losing my fucking mind. How could I fix this?

He met my gaze and my lips trembled as I fought the tears lingering right on the edge. *Not about you.* This was not my pain, but I hurt all the same, because I loved Jesse too. Just not this way.

"I had it together," he said, a dark laugh emerging with the words. "I'd slotted you firmly into the friend-sister zone, and I wasn't going to touch it again. But … Asher died." More laughter, derisive … cynical. "What sort of fucked up best friend moves in on his girl when he dies? I mean, I would never want to lose Ash. He's my fucking family, but when it looked like he was gone, when you were crumbling … holding on to me. It … broke the box I had you in."

I clenched my fists to stop them trembling. Jesse had stopped talking and I knew it was my turn, but I couldn't figure out what to say.

"I'm so sorry." The words spilled before my thoughts caught up. "Fuck. I wish there was something I could do or say to fix this. Trust me. I would literally do anything."

"Except the one thing I need," Jesse sighed. "I know I'm being a dick about it. I know it, Maddi. I see and hear it every single time I'm around you lately, but I just can't get myself together."

I squeezed my eyes closed, briefly, before finding some fucking backbone. "I'm not saying any of this to hurt you, but there will never be anyone for me other than Asher. Sonaris tried by tying our energy together, and still he's not even a blip on my radar. I love you too, Jess. I will never deny that, but it's not the way I love Ash. He's the part of me I didn't even know was missing."

"Can't fight fate," Jesse murmured, and it was so fucking sad I wanted to scream.

"You have a true mate out there as well," I reminded him. "Someone who is going to make these feelings you have for me seem like nothing."

Jesse growled; the lion was coming out to play. "Don't bet on it, *friend*. I've been fighting my feelings for you for two years. If they were small or insignificant, it wouldn't have taken me this long. It wouldn't be getting worse."

Well, fuck.

"What do you need from me?" I asked. This was about what Jesse needed, even though I was pretty sure I'd never done anything for him to think I wanted a romantic relationship.

I mean, I had leaned on him last year, when Asher died. But dudes had to start realizing that just because a chick is their friend, and cares about them, and loves them, doesn't mean they have any right to her heart or her body. I'd never given him one indication that my feelings were more than friendship. He'd made that leap on his own.

Still, I wanted to fix whatever part of our relationship I could. I just needed Jesse to tell me what he wanted me to do.

He didn't answer me and was not looking my way now.

Letting out a ragged breath, I nudged him. "You need me to back off? Leave the room when you enter? I can do whatever it takes to help you through this. Ash and I will tone our PDA down…"

He finally met my gaze. "I would appreciate that," he said. "Not the part where you stay away, but the part where I don't have to see you and Asher all over each other. It makes me want to punch … something."

"Fair enough," I said, forcing a smile. Not touching Asher every second of the day was going to be difficult, but if it made Jesse's life easier for a short time, we could do it.

"And there's another thing…"

He trailed off and the air turned chilly. I wasn't sure if it was reacting to Jesse's energy, or if it was just a random weather change, but it was eerie all the same.

"What?" I said. "If you need something from me, I'll do my best to give it."

"Kiss me," he said.

Whatthefuck?

"Jess…" I started and he held his hands up, huge palms, water dripping down them to the water below.

"One kiss. I just want you to know for sure, to experience this with both of us, and make the most informed decision. I mean, how can you truly know without ever kissing me?"

His lips twitched then and a gust of air left me as I lunged forward and punched him. "You fucker. You legit had me going for a second there."

Jesse threw his head back and laughed and I sent a plume of water into his face.

"I knew letting you watch *Twilight* was a bad idea," I grumbled.

His grin was large and genuine and something relaxed inside of me. "I'd never do that to you or Asher," Jesse said, scrunching his eyebrows. "I might have been team shifter for most of the movie, but that guy was a selfish fuck when he put that on Bella."

It amused me to no end that he was a secret Twihard.

"So … we're okay?"

Jesse nodded, some darkness filtering back in the green depths of his eyes. "I'm working on the okay thing, but I promise not to keep acting like a prepubescent kid that didn't get his favorite toy."

Stepping forward, I grabbed his hand. "And I promise to stop being so insensitive to your feelings. You're one of the best people in the world, and you're going to make some chick very happy one day."

He hugged me. Tight and hard, but only for a second, before he was diving under the water again, swimming like he could outrun his demons that way.

If only it was that easy.

Chapter 11

As reluctant as I was to leave the water, I decided not to intrude on Jesse's time any longer. If I wanted us to find our way back to a better place, I had to do my part as well. I had no idea what Asher would say about us toning down our affection in public, but he loved his brother, so hopefully he'd at least try.

Life was complicated.

Just as I was sliding back into my jeans, I felt a ripple of power, and since it wasn't the first time I'd felt it, I gritted my teeth and made my way around the side of the pool to where Sonaris waited.

"Thought I might have gotten rid of you," I said in greeting. "Haven't seen you for a while. It was nice."

He grinned, not even remotely deterred by my prickly comments. As he straightened from where he was leaning against the wall, I noted that he looked particularly put together tonight, wearing a black dress shirt and pants, hair perfectly styled.

"We're bound, my little princess," Sonaris said with a drawl. If I was anyone else, that power and tone in his voice might have sent a shiver down my spine, but I'd been around Atlanteans for two years now and I was somewhat immune. "You'll never get rid of me."

"Famous last words," I spat, because it had already been an emotionally fucked day and the last thing I wanted to be dealing with was this absolute tosspot of a cocksmoker.

"We should swim," he said suddenly, and it was completely my own fault that I wasn't prepared for him when he snapped his hand out and grabbed on to mine. In seconds, he zipped us away from the Academy, using that instant transmission way of travelling only the gods could do. And it was fucking annoying.

I had no idea where we were, but it was daylight here, and we were on a picturesque beach with palm trees and crystal-clear waters.

"I like your hair," Sonaris said. "It's almost fitting that this year you chose my favorite color."

"Take me back. Now," I bit out.

He shook his head and I reached for my magic, ready to both kick his ass and open a step-through to get me home. "You don't own me," I said, my voice deeper than usual as power swirled through me. "Tell me right this second what the favor is, or don't come near me until you're ready for it to be fulfilled."

Fucker was always smiling. I didn't like it. I didn't trust him. There was something about Sonaris that stirred my senses in the worst way. It reminded me of when I thought I was human, and I'd be walking somewhere late at night, somewhere dangerous, and every hair on my arms would be standing up. Because I knew I was in trouble. I knew evil lurked around me. Sonaris was the evil, I just hadn't figured out his plan yet.

But I would.

His smile vanished, and maybe, just maybe, that was even more terrifying.

"Okay, if that's your wish," he said softly. There was an undercurrent in this tone, but it was hard to discern the extent of his anger. "I know what I want for my favor, and I'm ready now for you to know it as well."

Riddle talking fucker.

"Well…"

He stepped closer and I wanted to back up, but that would give him the power. And I'd die before I did that. "I want you to spend one month with me, on my island, exploring my world and getting to know me. You think you have it all set with the young Atlantean, but how can you know when you've never given anything else a chance. You're very young yourself, and to commit fully to one without exploring other options … not something I can allow."

My head spun for a second. Was this some sort of cosmic joke? I mean, Jesse had just pulled the same move on me in the pool, only he'd at least been somewhat kidding. Sonaris wasn't.

"When does this month start?" I whispered, knowing that I'd bound myself to this deal and could not back out of it. In reality, of all the things he could have asked for, this wasn't the worst. Although, the timing could be better. According to Mab, one month was all the time I had until the gods released. Maybe Sonaris knew that and was doing this for that very reason. I was no doubt about to find out.

"Right now," he said. "This is my island. It's perpetually summer here, and no one comes into my waters without my permission. It's private and safe. It's the perfect—"

"Prison?" I interrupted.

His features tightened minutely before he smoothed his expression again. I was finally getting to him, destroying his perfect facade. "I could have asked you for anything," he reminded me. "Anything."

I swallowed roughly, and he took another step toward me so there were only inches between us. "Remember that when you act like this is the worst kind of punishment you could receive. I assure you, it's not."

"I have school," I said, shaking my head. "I want to graduate early this year. I can't skip an entire month."

He opened his mouth but I pushed on.

"Not to mention that I've heard from a reliable source that the gods will only remain in their cage for another month at the most. I have to figure out how to stop them before that happens. Otherwise we'll all be fucked."

Sonaris grimaced. "You curse a lot. It's irritating and a sign of limited intelligence. I know you're not of limited intelligence, so maybe tone it down."

Did he just seriously…?

"Fuck. You."

Now I was the one smiling. This piece of shit thought he could come in here and tell me how to…

My internal rant was cut off when he grabbed me, hands tight around my biceps, and it was in that moment I saw the true monster inside of him. A monster he'd been hiding … trying to woo me using fake charm. I hadn't fallen for that, though, and now he was done acting.

I was finally going to see the real Sonaris.

Power surged under his palms and I reacted with my own, shooting energy back at him. He flinched but didn't let me go. He was so strong, one of the strongest of the gods, and I'd been stupidly complacent, thinking of him as nothing more than an annoyance. A nuisance.

Now I was probably going to pay for that in some sort of horrific way.

His power wrapped around me, invisible to the eye, but it felt like thick coils of rope, binding every part of my body, including my own power, rendering me completely vulnerable.

That old fear of being held immobile still flickered inside of me. I'd mostly gotten over that since coming to the Academy, but I'd never lose it completely. At least if I focused on something else—aka destroying Sonaris—I should be able to handle it.

"If you'd ever figured out how to truly tap into your powers, we probably wouldn't be having this conversation right now," he said angrily, roughly shoving me away. I sprang back like I was connected via an invisible string to him. "You'd be able to kill us all without blinking an eye. But since you're still woefully ignorant, I'm going to take advantage."

Fuck. He was lucky I couldn't kill him with nothing more than an eye blink, because he would no longer be breathing.

"You'll never make me love you," I told him, my mouth the only part of me that could still move.

Sonaris laughed, throwing his head back, strong bronze neck corded with muscle and veins the only thing I could see.

"I don't want your love," he said when he stopped laughing. "Love is weakness. I want a powerful partner at my side. One who has energy that complements my own so I can utilize that source as well."

And there it was. Finally we had the truth.

A truth that made sense.

He'd told me that he wanted a mate. That he was lonely.

But that was all bullshit. He wanted a mate alright, one he could share power with. And by share, he meant to steal their power. This bastard had tried to manipulate a true mate bond so that he'd have access to my energy.

What the fuck was it with gods always wanting more power?

My energy surged in protest, crashing uselessly at the binds holding me. My skin grew clammy as I fought, trying any spell I could think of. But nothing worked. A long drawn out battle scream ripped from my throat, and I focused more than I ever had before, not hiding from the heat that swirled in my gut. I let it all loose. Sonaris cocked his head to the side, examining me, the warm inviting smile replaced by a smirk. It was actually less creepy, because this was the real god now, no pretending to be anything other than a psycho.

"You're absolutely spectacular," he said, brushing a finger across my cheek. I snarled and jerked my head in an attempt to bite him.

I was under no illusion that I was the most beautiful, or smartest, or even the most powerful supe around. I was none of those things. But there was something in my energy that drew these powerful men to me. Jesse, Sonaris, even Asher—though I did believe we were truly soulmates. The connection went both ways with Asher. It certainly didn't with the other two.

I tried a different tactic. "There's a true mate out there for you," I told him softly, quenching some of my sarcasm and anger in an attempt to connect on an emotional level. "It's probably someone you least expect. Shit! It could be a human."

He scoffed. "I need a power source to draw from, not a black hole to suck it out of me. If my mate was a human, I'd kill her before she could weaken me."

My eyes narrowed. "You're already one of the most powerful gods in the fucking world, and still it's not enough. What if you did have my power? It wouldn't be enough after a while either. You have to learn to be satisfied with what you have. Especially when you're already blessed."

His smirk wavered, just briefly, and for a second I wondered if I'd gotten through to him. His irises dilated as he remained unblinking, staring at me. Then that moment was gone. He shook his head like he could shake out my words in those two swift movements. He picked me up and threw me into the water off the side of the island.

As the cool liquid closed over my head, a sigh escaped. I was still bound, but being in here actually made me feel a tiny bit better. The water was surprisingly deep, and since I remained bound up like a mummy, I could do nothing but sink.

Shadows danced beside my face and I managed to flip over to see what was following me.

Sonaris.

"You need some time to think," he said, conversationally. "Since I have you for a month now, I'm going to leave you here for a while. I'll be back to check on your attitude soon."

He moved through the water the same way he'd stepped through the air, like neither was a barrier to his movement, both there to support and help him. So graceful.

I wondered if he'd die just as gracefully. Because I was going to fucking kill him. Even if it took me the rest of my life.

I would figure out how to destroy that god.

Chapter 12

When I hit the bottom of the ocean floor, I managed to flip myself over to lie on my back. The pressure down here was not uncomfortable and I had no problem breathing or seeing clearly, but I was still bound. With no Sonaris to focus on, I was having some trouble with that old fear again.

Breathe. Just breathe. In and out. In and out. *You're okay. You're alive.*

The water was my home. Not my enemy. There had to be something I could do to help myself. Closing my eyes, I focused on the currents, drifting around me. After some time, even with my eyes closed, I could sense everything around me. The billions of creatures. The life and death of the great circle happening down here.

My heart beat in rhythm with so many others, and when I finally opened my eyes, I wasn't surprised to see hundreds of creatures around me.

I'd done this before. Called the sea animals to me. Not on this scale though.

There were so many. More than I could see or count. They spanned way back to what looked like a whale. It should have been eerie—okay, it was a little freaky—to have them all just hovering there before me, like a captive audience waiting for me to say something highly inspirational.

Inspiration wasn't really my thing though.

"Can you get word to Asher?" I asked. "Tell him that I'm okay and I'll be back as soon as I can free myself from the binds."

Two dolphins, close to me, sent out their squeaks and whistles. I wouldn't swear on it, but it definitely felt like they could understand me. In any case, they zoomed off and I crossed my fingers they were going to figure out how to "speak" to Asher.

Asher. Dude probably flipped out when I disappeared. Ten to one he punched Jesse thinking he'd killed me and buried the body. Hopefully their fight didn't last long before they figured out there was another enemy in their midst, and that we had to stop fighting amongst ourselves.

"If only we had our mental link secured," I muttered. "Would make it a hell of a lot easier."

We hadn't figured it out yet though, so we'd just have to wing it and hope for the best. Maybe Asher had learned to speak dolphin in the last few months. Weirder things had happened.

A shark, its teeth alarmingly close to my face, brushed against me. I decided to think of it as solidarity and not him sizing me up to eat. Not that gods could really be eaten by a shark, especially not Atlantean gods. I was mostly god, so that had to count for something, right? Right!

"If you *can* eat gods, I have a few for you ready and waiting," I said, to cover my unease. I both loved and respected all the creatures under here, and that respect meant acknowledging the apex predator that was the shark. Emphasis on the predator part.

The shark brushed against me again, its sandpaper-like skin turning the bare flesh of my arm red, before it healed. It did it again, and I was starting to get the idea that it was trying to tell me something.

"Can you break my binds?"

It stopped rubbing against me and I sensed that meant no.

"Are you rubbing against me for a reason?"

This time it nudged me.

Okay, a nudge was a yes, and no movement was a no. I hoped.

"How do I get free?"

It bumped me for the fifth time and I was at a loss. It didn't move back as fast this time, lingering close, continually scraping my skin. Each time it did, there was a strong tingle when our skin touched, and after a few minutes of that my skin no longer turned red. If anything, the shark's sandpapery touch was almost … soft.

Sea creatures didn't have power like gods, but every living thing held energy, some stronger than others, and this shark had quite a lot actually. Energy it was sharing with me … strengthening my own…

Clarity hit me. And with it came horror. "Stop! No more. You're giving me your energy. Your life force."

Nudge.

I tried to shake my head, but my limited range of movement was not really conducive to that. "No. Please. It will kill you."

Nudge. Nudge.

"No!" I shouted, and the bindings holding me shifted just a little. Rage swelled again, swirling the water around me. Everything was tinted in shades of red and burnt orange, like fire had ripped across the ocean floor. Only it wasn't fire.

It was me.

In an instant I was upright, still bound but no longer prone. The creatures surrounded me in a large circle, moving with the water that churned from my energy. Sonaris appeared in my line of sight, and he tried to blast through my animals, but they didn't shift, held in place by me. Something dark and foreign broke through the normal heat of my power and words spilled out.

"You made a mistake, Sonaris."

My voice was amplified, blasting through the water.

The god didn't look upset. If anything, there was something akin to satisfaction on his face.

"You. Are. Magnificent." He uttered each word slowly, pausing between.

"If you say that to me one more time…" I seethed. I couldn't seem to control my emotions, and the sea animals around me reacted, turning as one and … attacking Sonaris.

"No! Stop!" I screamed, but they didn't listen. He was going to destroy them all. He was going to tear them into a million pieces of meat, turning the water red with death and destruction. Panic ripped through me. It almost overshadowed my fury. I couldn't let innocent animals die, especially ones trying to help me.

I lost sight of the god, buried beneath hundreds of fish. I pushed forward, aiming for the general direction he'd been last. I zipped from one place to the next, and as I approached the largest mass of animals, it finally hit me that I was actually moving. My arms and legs, and all body parts.

Had Sonaris released me? Or did I break free on my own?

No time to worry about it. I had animals to save.

Using my power, I scattered the ones in front of me, moving them—gently—out of the way. Unlike when Sonaris tried, they moved for me. When I finally reached the epicenter, I expected to see death and destruction. This was where the god had been ... but there was nothing. No carcasses or blood.

Not even Sonaris.

It was like he'd just vanished completely.

"Where did he go?" I asked, looking between a pair of sharks.

Both shifted in the direction of the surface and I shot up. Again, a smart person would have just opened a step-through and gotten out of there, but I was beyond controlling myself at this point. The fire in my vision grew larger. That bastard had tied me up. Bound me with power. He'd wanted to hurt my fishy friends.

I burst out of the water, droplets scattering all around, and for the first time gravity didn't yank me back down. My power surrounded me, and ... I was drifting in the air. No, it was more like manipulating water particles in the air to keep me afloat. I could use those same water particles to shoot me around, and it legit felt like I was flying.

Probably the coolest thing ever, and in different circumstances I would have been whooping and hollering at how awesome it was. But that was the last thing I felt like doing at this moment.

Sonaris was going down.

I'd seen only a small fraction of the island before, but from my current elevation, twenty feet above the ground, I had a very good view of the surrounding area. It was an island with gorgeous white sand and lots of palm trees. Patches of forest appeared further back, and I could make out a waterfall near the center.

Sonaris's private sanctuary wasn't large by any definition, but it was stunning. Too stunning to be claimed by someone like him.

The water followed my mental command, sending me zooming over the trees toward the center of this island. Once I got near that waterfall, a small treehouse came into sight. Cleverly camouflaged into the surrounding landscape, I might have missed it if I wasn't looking so hard.

"Sonaris!" My shout had power behind it and the foundation of the house shook. I tried to dial it back because I didn't want to destroy something so perfect. It didn't deserve my wrath, but maybe it was hiding the being who did.

"I'll give you to the count of three," I said, not even bothering to yell this time.

He would hear me.

Sure enough, in the next two seconds he appeared, and he was smiling again.

Fuck. I really wanted him to stop doing that.

"I knew it wouldn't be long before you began unlocking your true potential."

Deep inside, I felt what he was saying. The shark started it, sharing its power with me. That boost, and my fear of killing the creature, had unraveled the bonds I'd been mentally keeping on my power. All along it was me stopping the full release of my energy. Maybe because I'd always feared what might happen. Feared I wouldn't be able to control it.

But no more.

Sonaris had done exactly what he set out to do—forced my hand—but now he had to deal with me at full power.

"Are you going to let me go? Leave me alone?" I asked as he rose in the air, hovering across from me.

He shook his head. "I can't do that. You're too powerful. One day you'll usurp me as the god of the oceans. I won't relinquish my role."

He almost looked apologetic about this.

I could read between the lines with the best of them. "So … it's join you or die?"

"It is," he replied.

At least he was honest.

I should have been afraid, but all I had was understanding and acceptance of what was going down here. It was the inevitable conclusion.

"I will never join you," I told him. "My heart … my soul, my power … they're mine. And even if they weren't, there's no way I'd give someone like you more power. Someone who just wants it for their own gain." Storm clouds swirled over Sonaris's head, super obvious in the blue skies above. "If I ever choose to share my power, it would be with my family. With Asher, and the other Atlanteans. Not with you."

Thunder rumbled, and the ocean, visible far off in the distance, was no longer crystal-clear waters of blue and green. Now darkness lurked below, a tumultuous swirl of water, and a clear reminder of the power of nature. Especially nature controlled by this fucking megalomaniac.

"Last chance," I said, already knowing he wouldn't take it. "Just walk away. Be satisfied with the huge amount of energy you control now. Take my word that if you don't abuse your power or position, I will never come for your godhood. I promise."

He moved faster than a streak of lightning, and I knew this because literal lightning followed his movement a step behind. Our bodies slammed together and I gasped, expecting pain and blood. But my skin was all of a sudden as strong as diamonds. Then again, so was Sonaris's.

Diamond slamming into diamond sent out an almighty cracking sound. I felt the fizzle of the storm power as it attacked with him, hard and fast, but it didn't hurt like it should. My energy sucked it in like they were long lost friends. My mother was a goddess of storms, my father a god of the underworld, and Sonaris had added god of the sea to my power arsenal.

In hindsight, it was a very bad move on his part. His power called to mine, like recognizing like.

"You never should have shared power with me before I was born," I bit out, slamming energy back into Sonaris. "Nothing you have will work against me. Not like it should. Your power recognizes me."

His roar was music to my ears. Long gone was the confident god with that fucking smile, thinking he was top shit. Nope. He'd created his own worst enemy, and then prodded at me until I had the power to take him on.

I mean, no doubt I wasn't going to be able to beat him easily, but I'd at least have a shot now. I also had a few extra moves up my sleeve that I'd learned from Asher and Louis. Those two did not fight like gods.

My fist slammed into Sonaris's face, and I marveled at the strength coursing through me. I didn't stop at one punch either, swinging my other arm around, clocking him with my elbow and pushing him back across the island. It took me all of five seconds to figure out that while Sonaris had been trained to physically fight at one point in time, he hadn't kept up with that training. His movements were sluggish and shaky, like he was trying to remember how to even throw a punch.

This was my shot.

As we fought, I used the elements to my advantage, pushing water and storm energy behind each hit. Sonaris countered though, slowly getting himself into proper positions. He landed a couple of clean blows that actually really fucking hurt. I got him right back with a straight shot of my own.

It was amazing that I was somewhat holding my own against a god, but also frustrating that we were so evenly matched.

The gods had wanted control over the Hellbringers because they were the only beings who could kill a god without the energy destroying the world. They were a conduit for power, and could direct it in small increments around so that it didn't explode with the force of a billion nuclear bombs.

Or so my research indicated.

At this point it was all theoretical.

The truth was, the Hellbringers were the "safe" way to kill a god, but there were other ways. Axl had actually found a few suggestions. One was a spell. You had to get close enough to touch them, infect them from the inside out. Their power would turn on them, before they exploded into a million pieces. Complete self-destruction.

Infecting them wasn't an easy or simple thing, and for most beings they'd never have the power to do so. They'd never have the power to even get close.

But I was a god myself, with energy that recognized Sonaris's. I just wasn't sure how to handle the power fallout if by some small chance I succeeded in taking him down. There was no point in killing him only to blow up the rest of the world.

Sonaris slammed his hand on my chest, bringing me back into the fight, and I gasped at the invasive feel of that. Not even because of the hand, but because of his slimy power beneath it. "You thought to take me out?" He laughed. "Me? Little girl, you have a lot to learn. Don't you know that whenever a god shares power with another, they create a path between them. It was almost too easy."

Apparently, I did have a lot to learn. My power froze within me, everything shutting down. The second time Sonaris had done this to me today. His energy oozed under the surface of my skin in the most degrading insidious way, seeping into my very being. He was doing exactly what I'd been planning. He hadn't said the spell yet though, so I still had a shot.

"We could have been brilliant together," he murmured, leaning close. Our lips brushed and I tried to jerk back, but had no control over my limbs.

"You see," he continued, "I knew you were planning on locking on to my powers, but you clearly didn't know that whoever locks on first has all the control. You're still so new to this world. Now, if you were a lot stronger than me, there would be a possibility of you breaking free. It'd be hard, because I'm draining your power as we speak, but there'd be a shot."

He was draining my power. I could feel it slipping away, leaving me empty and aching inside.

This was not the same as Axl's spell. This was something completely different. Something I hadn't even known was possible. A whimper escaped as heat filled my chest, expanding into his palm. "I'll miss our beautiful children," the crazy fucker said. "I already pictured them, with white blond hair and big blue eyes."

My teeth clenched even tighter. I was fighting a losing battle trying to get away from him, but I didn't give up. The heat grew, hurting me now. My skin no longer a diamond, but some sort of crumbling paper burning in a flame.

I'm dying.

The thought hit me as my body arched, moving closer to Sonaris—against my will—as he drew more and more power from me. His head dropped back, a look of contentment filling those strong, broad features. His skin rippled with strength, the bronze pigment growing darker, his hair lengthening, as if every part of him was influenced by the new influx of power. When he returned his gaze to mine, his eyes were blue ice, very similar to my own, and I felt like I was about to burst into dust with a puff of air.

"Goodbye, love," he whispered, leaning in to kiss me.

The moment our lips touched, a flicker of fight filled my body, and I grappled with his hold, desperate to break away. No one got to kiss these lips but Asher.

Asher! The scream reverberated through my mind and expelled from me in a silent rush. I couldn't speak, but I could call for him. I would not die without fighting for us, and in this situation I was desperately scraping for anything that might give me a boost.

I'd already exploded apart in a ball of energy recently. I wasn't keen on doing it again. Something told me that this time there was no coming back.

Maddi…

It was a single word in my mind, dark and filled with rage that literally burned through me.

Asher?

I mentally followed the path of his rage. He wrapped me up, covering me with his power, and I found a little more energy to hold on. Energy that Asher shared with me.

The dolphins sent me images of where you are. I'm coming.

CHAPTER 13

My heart soared, swelling and beating rapidly. *The bond.* I'd felt it there. A real, tangible connection as our powers mingled together. It was so brief, but I knew we'd finally broken the last barrier. My godhood was free, and the bond was bursting to life.

But … as quickly as it had appeared, it was cut off. A lingering strain of his power remained within me though, giving me enough strength to jerk my knee up and slam it into Sonaris's balls.

The god had expected I was all but dead and hadn't even tried to block the shot.

Diamond skin or not, every man crumpled when cracked in the jewels.

Sonaris let out a curse, his bellow probably heard back at the Academy. He jerked away, face wreathed in pain and annoyance. He tried to come straight back for me, but I was already using what remained of my "borrowed" power to scoot me toward the ocean. This was pure instinct, and maybe a little insane, considering I was being chased by the god of the ocean, but I felt like it was my one shot at surviving.

Storms chased me across the sky, and I felt the touch of Sonaris's power right before I plunged into the blue-green water. A slight murkiness had invaded since I was last submerged, but not as bad as when the storms fully raged. I didn't sink this time. Immediately I was surrounded by animals; they pushed into my space, supporting me.

Sonaris crashed into the water behind us, his power almost visible it was so strong now—thieving bastard. The water churned murkily, growing as dark as the stormy skies above.

"What did you do to me?" Sonaris cursed, bellowing through the water. I used the water to move my body back, with a little help from a dolphin and stingray wedged under my arms, but I wasn't moving fast enough. Sonaris was only inches from me, hands out and ready to finish the job of killing me.

Heat washed over my face just as Asher burst into the sea in a blaze of power and golden energy. Literally. He was completely gold from his skin to his eyes to the tips of his hair. Our eyes locked as he danced in the waves, looking freaky as hell. And absolutely glorious.

He took me in, one full sweep, and if I could describe rage as having a taste, it filled the ocean, overwhelming my senses. In a motion so fast I couldn't track, he powered through the water to Sonaris, slamming into him.

Asher wasn't as stupid as me. He didn't give the other god a second to attack him.

I sensed that he'd seen—through our bond—how Sonaris had

attacked me on the island. He was now doing the exact same thing back.

As he locked on to the god of the ocean, his golden energy brightened to a point that was literally blinding.

I heard shouts, a choking, strangled sound, and in less time than it took to adjust my sight to the new golden glow, it was all over. As the light faded, my eyes were drawn to Asher's broad shoulders a dozen or so yards from me. He was half hunched over and very still. I frantically searched for Sonaris, but there was no sign of another being.

My power was still beyond drained, my body fragile and frail, but using the water I pushed myself forward.

"Ash," I said softly when I was close. "Asher, are you okay?"

He didn't turn or acknowledge me, and I was starting to get a very bad feeling about what I might find when I reached him. He was still covered in his golden power, even if it was no longer blinding. The energy pouring off him … it reminded me of the first moment I saw Asher after thinking he was dead. He'd been in the sky, trailing after his insane god of a mother. He felt like this. Foreign and cold.

I'd thought I lost Asher that day, that he'd been taken to the dark side, corrupted by power.

The fact that I was getting the same vibe right now chilled me to my fucking core.

The water around Asher heated, ripples streaming from his back. He was burning up the ocean…?

A hand grabbed me before I could move any closer. Jerking myself free, I spun to find Axl.

"*What?*" I gasped. "How?"

He reached for me again, and this time I went to him. "Are the others here?"

He nodded, jerking his head behind him. Shifting my head, I eyeballed Jesse, Rone, and Calen, who were all gliding through the water toward us. Despite my fatigue, I had enough energy to thank the fucking worlds for sending me my family.

When they reached me, each of them touched me briefly, a reassurance that I was alive. More energy flickered inside of me, desperately trying to rejuvenate from the massive power of the Atlanteans.

"Something is happening to Asher?" I said softly, and all of us turned toward him. He still hadn't moved, shoulders hunched. "I think he killed Sonaris."

Axl cupped his hands and blew out a water bubble-like substance. I blinked as it expanded, and then he popped his head right into it, waving me over like I should do the same. I didn't hesitate.

Inside there was no water and we could talk.

My fucking genius.

"Asher definitely killed Sonaris," Axl said without preamble.

I gasped. "It was the only thing that made sense, but at the same time … fuck."

Axl shook his head. "We were slower in following. but I can feel the energy trying to explode. Asher's not strong enough to keep it contained, and the power of a god like Sonaris could, theoretically, end the world."

Jesus. Fuck. Fuck! This was one of my greatest fears when going up against him.

"Sonaris took most of my power," I said softly. "I have nothing left…"

That sparked Axl's attention, and his face did that dreamy half stare that was common when he was contemplating something. "I think I have an idea," he finally murmured. "But I need you to open a bond with the five of us." He cleared his throat. "Well, four of us. You clearly have a true mate bond with Asher that has finally reached fruition. We are all bonded to Asher. I think between the six of us … there's a chance."

A chance was the best we could hope for. "Am I strong enough to do this? I'm completely tapped out and, fuck, it sounded complicated in class." I spoke as fast as I could; we were running out of time. If we weren't Atlantean, the heat of this water would have killed us already. Asher was at blowing point.

"You can do anything. And we will help you." Before I could protest, Axl broke the bubble, reaching out to take my hand. Jesse moved in to my other side, Calen next to him, and then Rone last. The five of us joined hands, forming a circle. Axl shot energy through my palm, but it didn't stop there. It ricocheted around through all of our hands, joining us together.

After being so drained, it was like sticking my hand into an electrical socket. My body lit up, sucking down the power, until Axl tugged on my hand and shook his head.

Right. Right. I wasn't here to drain them. I was here to form a permanent bond with my guys. It wasn't a completely unheard-of concept for me. We'd studied it in class before, the theoretics of it, and the consequences.

The largest worry was if one of us messed with dark energy. Struck out on a nefarious scheme to take over the world. That supe could utilize the bond for both power and control, and with that in mind, there were very few supes in the world I'd form a bond with.

But these five … they were as close to family as I'd ever had. I trusted them implicitly. We also had no other option if we wanted to save Asher.

Oh, and the entire world. Let's not forget about it.

Rone, on my other side, squeezed my hand, and I sucked in a deep breath. It might be a blessing that I really had no time to freak out, because I was just going to go for it.

I'd only had one lesson on these connections, but I remembered it clearly. Gathering as much of my energy as I could, basically everything left, I bundled it into the shape of a missile, and with one thought in mind, sent it zooming along the path already created between our hands.

Keeping my mind laser sharp, I didn't look at Asher, because if I did I'd probably fall apart. The key to success here was keeping control of this energy. I couldn't falter for a moment. It got harder with each of the guys … some of them were so much stronger than I anticipated—especially Jesse and Rone. My missile wanted to stay with them, basking in their strength.

Axl was the weakest, but that was only compared to the other three. In general, his power was a low, humming buzz that would pack quite a punch if used in the right way.

Team his energy with his brain power, he was super scary.

My spell touched each guy, gathering small parcels of energy as it moved along, forming a circle that contained power from all of us. By the end my limbs were shaking. My chest ached. My hands burned. I wasn't sure how you knew when it was complete, but instinct urged me to keep holding on.

None of us moved, not even when the water bubbled around us and Asher dropped to his knees, dust from the ocean floor bursting up around him, like he was made of lead and weighed a thousand tons. It was going to be a race against the clock…

CHAPTER 14

I didn't have to worry about knowing the right time to let go. The bond cemented in the same way I figured a volcano would erupt. Hot and destructive.

Our hands fused, making it impossible to separate, and then it clicked into place. I could feel them in my chest, in my energy, just slivers of each guy, but I also knew exactly how to tap into their energy if I wanted to.

Now use your bond to Asher and take the power.

I jerked, my eyes widening as I stared at Axl. He'd literally just spoken in my head.

His presence disappeared the moment our hands weren't joined, and I sighed in relief. It was one thing to be bonded—I mean I loved them— and it was no hardship to be part of their lives like this.

But to have five dudes in my head at all times…

Nope. I couldn't do that.

Asher.

This time it was at least just my own inner voice urging me forward.

My power had regenerated enough that I could zip with ease through the simmering water. My skin was strong, not burning, even though it was clearly beyond boiling point under here. There were so many dead animals around us and I wanted to cry and vomit at the sight and smell. But there was no time to fall apart.

If I didn't get to Asher, we'd all be dead.

When I was only a few feet away, I blanched at a blast of fiery air in my face. How the fuck there was fiery air under the water, I didn't know, but shit was weird these days and I didn't have time to question it.

That golden light was once again building around Asher, blinding me, but I didn't need to see. I could feel him through our bond.

Lurching forward, I slammed my hand onto his back. White exploded behind my eyes and I felt like half of me was being ripped apart as our bond kicked in. Before I could figure out what to do, my body jerked forward, power funneling into me. My empty well filled, overflowed, and then the surge of power shot to Rone. The vampire threw his head back, veins standing out starkly in his neck, hands clenched. He took a lot, but nowhere near enough.

There were still three to go though.

Calen was next, the magic user bracing himself, his stance strong and wide, water not moving around him. His jaw clenched as the power made itself at home in his center. But there was only so much Calen, and way too much power. It didn't linger once he was filled up, moving onto Jesse. The shifter showed the least reaction, except for a slight twitch of his jaw. He took the most power, and I gasped when it finally burst free, and into Axl.

The last one.

I saw his face settle into one of resignation, and in a blinding moment of clarity I knew that this much power was going to kill him. There was no one else for it to go to. We had completed the circle.

Axl was going to be destroyed.

"No!" I screamed, trying to jerk my hand from Asher, but it was fused. The circle was not finished, and I wasn't free until it was.

"Axl, let it go!" I was shouting, but just like the rest of us, he couldn't break the bond.

Our eyes met across the water, and I saw the apology there. Like he'd already calculated this and knew all along that one of us would die. That he would die.

My scream was so long and drawn out that my ears and throat ached when I was finished, water churning around me, gold filling my vision as Asher fought the hold too.

Axl's body arched, and then he jerked a few times, like he was having a seizure. He crumpled to the ground, face first. In the same moment, my hand was released from Asher, and … I felt my mate in my mind and through our bond. He was back, stronger than ever, but whole.

"What happened to Axl?" he asked, voice rumbling, eyes gold. He was back in control, energy filling every pore. All of us were rocking an overload of energy.

"The power," I sobbed, grabbing his hand and blasting us over to Axl. "He took too much power."

In my newly formed bond with the five, I searched for Axl's familiar energy, but it was barely a wisp, and considering how strong the others felt now, that could only mean one thing.

He was fading away.

When we reached Axl, Jesse had him cradled in his arms, the others around them, faces creased with devastation.

"What's happening?" I cried. "Shouldn't the power have exploded him? Why has he just gone ... limp like this?"

In truth, six of us shouldn't have been enough to take a god's energy. It was probably only that Asher and I were gods ourselves, and the other's were four strong Atlanteans. But still...

Had Axl done something else? Had he known this was coming?

Asher didn't answer, but there was a moment where our eyes met and I recognized that look. He was going to risk himself to try to save our brother.

Before I could voice my worries, Asher moved at god speed, yanking the lifeless Axl into his arms. Then he was swimming like a bullet through the water, up and out, heading toward the island. I followed right behind, the guys with me. I tried not to panic, praying for a miracle. Who I was praying to, I didn't know, but I was sending the vibes out into the universe.

When we caught up to them, they were on the beach. Asher had his hands pressed to the chest of his lifeless brother. The golden energy around him increased, pushing us back.

"My mother is the daughter of the goddess of creation," Asher snarled. "I will not let Axe die. I don't care what I have to sacrifice."

His eyes met mine. "Do it," I said. "Do whatever you have to." He was strong, strong enough to do this and save himself. I had to believe that.

"He took that energy and buried it like a bomb inside," Asher spat out, his hands shaking on Axl's chest. "Used his damn life force to keep it in place."

"Nothing stronger than a life sacrifice," Rone said, sounding robotic as water dripped down his face.

"Not on my fucking watch," Asher growled. "The power is still there. I'm going to make sure it gets used."

All of us watched him, none of us exactly sure what he was planning. I had faith that whatever it was, he was capable of making it happen.

Asher had spoken to me briefly about his time with Galindra. He'd never gone into detail, preferring to move forward from what was a truly horrific experience for both of us, but it was clear she had taught him things—things that might hopefully save Axl.

If it worked, every second of agonizing pain I felt during Asher's death would be worth it, because I couldn't lose any of my family.

I couldn't lose my Axl.

Jesse wrapped an arm around me and the strength of our new bond kicked in hard. I could feel his emotions: fear, worry, hurt, anger, all churning like a pot of crazy inside him. But he held it together … and he was trying to hold me together.

Asher's eyes closed, and I barely breathed as I waited to see if we were about to mourn another member of our family.

"Look," Rone whispered, and I managed to look away from Axl long enough to see the twinkling lights falling from the sky above us, drifting down in waves and swirls, covering us and the land.

"What is Asher doing?" Calen murmured, lifting his hands to catch what looked like stardust. *Gods, please let this work.*

Asher and I had both cheated death; our friend could do the same. There was a beat of complete silence, all of us coated in golden sparkle that very much reminded me of the glitter in Asher's eyes when he was all powered up.

Then Axl gasped.

The sound filled the clearing and a strangled sob escaped me.

He jerked, but not in the way he had in the water, this was a jerk of a body coming back to life. In a split second he was up off the ground, floating above us, eyes wide and blazing.

I took a tentative step forward. "Axe?" I said softly, not wanting to startle him. There was a blank expression on his face, but his eyes ... his eyes were now a bright startling aqua, almost the exact same color as my hair.

The bond I had with the five guys flared to life, and it was Axl fueling it. His power was so strong that it hurt my very bones with the intensity. Asher stood before me, protecting me as he always did. He'd killed a fucking god for me, and he'd risked everything to save Axl...

I had to ask. "What is he?"

That wasn't our Axl.

"The world needed a new god of the ocean," Asher said softly. "There was so much energy left, I had no choice but to reform Axl into a being of original power." He shifted his stance, covering more of me. "Give him a second ... he's adjusting to the change."

It was what I'd suspected, but part of me hoped it wouldn't be true, because we might still lose our friend in a different way. Gods, they weren't like us, and Axl being turned like this, in such a traumatic way…

I was scared of what Asher might have created.

On instinct, I rose up into the air, flying toward him. The Atlanteans blinked with slack jaws, and I remembered that they hadn't been here when I discovered my new ability. When I unlocked my powers.

Asher didn't look shocked; he wore a mask of determination, rising up with me, wanting to get to Axl first. It didn't matter which one of us got to him though, as long as one of us did. Axl needed a friend to remind him of who he was.

More power … god of the oceans … he was still our Axl. This was our one shot to pull him back before he was lost to the influx of power flooding his every cell. I'd been born a god, or mostly god, and it still had been a huge adjustment when my power first released. Then again when I "died" and was reborn to my god body. And finally, just before, when the shark had shown me how to release the final hold on my energy.

I understood what he was going through. We had to remind him of who he was.

Reaching him first, I wrapped my arms around his middle, gritting my teeth through the blast of power. "Axe," I said, squeezing him tightly. "Come back to us. It's just power. It's not you."

Our bond flared and I had the briefest thought that maybe this was fate's way of ensuring that Axl wouldn't face this alone. That he'd find his way back through the bond.

I held on tighter. No matter what he threw at me, I took it without letting go, all the while talking to him through our bond.

At first, I didn't think it was working, my soul weeping at the thought, but I didn't give up. And neither did Axl. Slowly, piece by piece, he found the strength to drag himself away from the power. When his arms lifted, wrapping tightly around me, I finally let the tears fall.

Our hug went on for a long while, and after some time I pulled back just enough to see his face.

His eyes were still brilliant blue-green gems, unfamiliar to me. But the face was all Axl. "Maddi," he rasped. Hearing my name from his lips, the familiar way he always said it, was every-fucking-thing.

His eyes shifted up over my head to Asher, who'd been right behind me the entire time. "Thank you, Ash."

I turned to see Asher shake his head. "I'm sorry, brother. I hoped the sacrifice would come from me, but it was you that lost something. Your mortality is gone. Your Atlantean side is now one with the gods. There's no going back from godhood."

Axl shrugged, and through the bond I saw that he wasn't upset by it. "A sacrifice I would have willingly made to save all of you, and the world. I was prepared to die. This is a much better option." His laughter sounded natural, albeit laced with a lot more power. "And now I have a lifetime to gather information. It's not all bad."

The ocean behind us surged. Axl shook his head as his power swirled, visible across his skin in arcs of electricity. Using my own energy, I pushed through the bite of his elemental power and sent soothing vibes into Axl. It occurred to me that now I shared an even stronger bond to this Atlantean … god. Sonaris's power was Axl's power now, merging into new DNA, different but the same.

Kin, I said to Axl in his mind, our mental connection present while we were touching. That one word was enough for him to calm his energy, the storms dying off.

Frustration creased his face. "I should be stronger than this," he bit out, uncharacteristically angry.

"It will take time," I reminded him. "You've been a god for exactly one minute, and in that time you've already had the control and self-discipline to pull back from the addictive power. I've been there, dude. It's not as easy as it looks."

"The gods will break free from their cage any day now," he reminded me. "This is not a great moment for me to have to figure out a new godhood and power."

I flashed him a smile. "Actually, you're pretty much our new secret weapon, Axe. We now have the god of the ocean in our corner…"

He snorted. "A shit one that has no idea how to use his powers."

I patted him on the shoulder, slowly releasing the water holding me aloft, sinking back to the sand. Axl and Asher followed.

"Didn't know you could fly too," I said with a smirk at my mate.

He returned that smirk with a scowl. "When you take off heading toward danger, I suddenly have a ton of new powers to access." His lips twitched. "Plus, I'm pretty juiced up, thanks to all the power we absorbed from Sonaris."

Yes, that was very true. In a way, we were all connected to Axl more than ever.

When we landed on the sand, Rone hugged Axl so hard I heard bones creak, but he didn't flinch. "There's nothing you can't do when you set your mind to something," the vampire said as he pulled away. "Nothing. This is just your most recent challenge, and all of us know you'll succeed."

Axl squared his shoulders, a glint of determination filling those new eyes. "You're right. My new mind is easy to get lost in, but once I figure out the system, I sense I will really enjoy the benefits of being a god."

He half turned to Asher. "Is there something the gods do, though? Something I should specifically know in regards to being the god of the seas? Surely it's not all just 'look cool, be powerful, and fly around?'"

Asher clapped him on the shoulder. I could feel through our bond how truly happy he was that Axl was still here with us. "I have no fucking idea, but I think I know the perfect book for you."

That was absolutely the right thing to say. Axl looked both happy and relieved in a way he hadn't since awakening. Books were his thing. And his excitement over a new one to read, was a huge clue that this was still our Axl. We would get through this.

Together.

CHAPTER 15

The next few weeks passed in a rush of school, research, and fuckups. Most of the fuckups were from Axl as he navigated his new godhood, but thankfully two very important people were finally back. I hoped they might be able to shed some light on our situation.

Louis and Princeps Jones had returned yesterday, many days after they were supposed to. Apparently something new had arisen in Romania, delaying them, but they were finally back. The moment we heard, all of us rushed to their office to hear the news. Larissa hugged her dad for the longest time, and I wasn't surprised to see tears in her eyes when she pulled away. They were close. For years he'd been both her dad and her only friend in a world that mocked her for what they perceived as race weakness.

She had struggled with him gone for so long.

Louis hugged me tightly, and shook hands with Asher, before he stopped on Axl. His eyes widened just a little, those purplish depths curious and wary. "Well, well, well…" he said softly, tilting his head as he examined Axl. "I know you told me what happened, but seeing it in person … feeling the power." He let out a low whistle. "Insane."

"I'd appreciate any advice," Axl replied, taking a deep breath. "I'm kind of blindly groping around in the dark, hoping not to kill anyone. You helped Maddi figure her powers out. Can you help me?"

Louis took a step closer to him and held up a hand, palm facing Axl. "May I?"

At Axl's nod, Louis dropped his hand right onto his chest and a blast of heat rocked through the room—my face felt a little raw.

"Interesting," Louis said, lips twitching like he wanted to laugh. "I have a few thoughts on how to help you. Let's talk after this meeting."

Relief flashed across Axl's face as he nodded. "Great, thank you."

The sorcerer examined him for a few minutes longer, before turning back to focus on the rest of us.

"We want to hear everything that's been happening here," he said quickly, "but first we'll tell you what was decided in Romania."

There weren't enough seats for us all, so we just moved in closer, letting Louis and Princeps Jones stand on the other side of his desk and face us.

"A task force has been formed from the strongest supes in the world," Louis started. "They're already converging on Atlantis, and will set up a home base there in anticipation of the gods releasing. The reason we took longer to get back, was I had to duck to Faerie and procure some ingredients to make spells and potions. They're not going to stop the gods, but they might give us an advantage.

"Jessa and Braxton are still in Faerie, with the queen of the dragons. She has a plan ... something she learned from the ancient ones. She got part of a message to Jessa, but then they lost contact."

Princeps Jones let out a sigh as he rubbed at his temples. "I stayed behind to get the group together," he said tiredly. "For what good it might do."

"Every little thing helps," Louis said. "Now we just have to hope Jess and Brax get back in time. This disturbance in the balance of gods is causing disturbance in Faerie again, and we only just got the last balance issue over there sorted out."

I completely understood his frustration and worry. Jessa, and all of the Compasses, were his family. He also had a new member of his family coming into the world soon. Knowing Louis as I did, he would have locked everyone he cared about away if he could, but he happened to care about a ton of supes who did not like to be overprotected.

"So, what do we do now?" I pushed, needing a game plan. This waiting around was frustrating, to say the very least.

There was a knock on the door, and when it opened on its own—magic, bitches—Connor was framed in the doorway.

"Sorry I'm late," he said, strolling in. "Overslept."

I glared at the supe I'd spent days looking for but who had been nowhere in sight.

He looked like absolute shit, hair disheveled, eyes puffy, and I was wondering how in the fuck a being born of gods could even look like that. When I woke now, it was difficult to tell I'd been asleep. No more puffy face or morning breath.

Gods rarely looked unkempt.

Connor had figured out a way.

"Are you still drunk?" Ilia asked, scowling as she crossed her arms.

Connor tripped, shaking his head. "No. I'm absolutely, totally, not even a little bit drunk. I've been sick, okay?"

She snorted. "You're a god. You don't get sick."

He flipped her off, half falling into the wall as he attempted to lean against it. "How do you know? None of us know jack fucking shit about being gods, and if they do, no one is sharing with me. What I do know is that if you mix fairy wine and demon's brew, and drop some pixie dust in the bitch, gods can get drunk. FYI for future parties."

He winked at me, and his head dropped back as he slid down the wall, snoring and drooling at the same time. I blinked, staring at him. "I haven't even seen him since school started. Has he literally been drunk for nearly a month now?"

Asher scowled at the idiot passed out on the floor. "Connor never could handle disappointment or change very well. I'm guessing the last year of his life has gone nothing like he anticipated."

I snorted, anger slapping me hard. "Are you fucking kidding me." Connor should be proud at how adept he was at pissing me off. "*He's* not handling it very well? *Him*? That poor fucking guy. Let's all feel sympathy for the asshole who set most of these events into motion because he was a brainwashed dumbfuck who couldn't think for himself. All of us are dealing with this shit. All of us. And some of us have suffered much worse than *Connor*, the poor little Atlantean god."

It took more control than I'd admit not to walk over and kick him in the ass. Drinking for a month so he didn't have to deal with reality. If only all of us could be so irresponsible.

Somewhere deep down, a blooming sliver of sympathy tried to rear its head, to remind me that Connor was clearly struggling and I should be kinder about it. There was some guilt too—I definitely should have tried harder to find him over the last few weeks to make sure he was okay.

The guilt and sympathy were not enough to overtake my anger though. I couldn't forget everything he'd done and hidden from us. It would take a long time for me to trust and forgive Connor. So, for now, he could sleep on the floor. After all, he made that bed.

"Before we were rudely interrupted," Ilia said, shooting Connor an even darker look than I was—that girl could hold onto grudges like nobody's business—"Mads asked what we should be doing to prepare...?"

Louis crossed his arms. "A few things that I was going to suggest have already been completed. Maddison has opened a proper connection with the other Atlanteans. The five of them have a new, strengthened power, and much more control. I can see it between them. We also have Axl now, and he may just be what we need to tip this battle in our favor." He turned to him. "What would you say to being stationed on the front line?"

Axl was nodding before he'd even finished. "Yes. I figure it's a good opportunity to learn from the strongest in how to control my power."

Louis looked excited by the prospect of playing with Axl's new power.

"Fantastic! I have some ideas of how to utilize the new god in our corner. It could be our one advantage."

Axl looked pleased by this. I was excited to see him embracing the changes with the same enthusiasm he embraced every experiment in his life.

Louis turned back to me. "I'm excited to see that you and Asher have completed your true mate bond."

Fuck yeah we have, Asher murmured in my head, and I swallowed hard, because I had an actual visceral reaction to him talking to me like this. A reaction that was not appropriate in a room full of supes.

I focused again when Louis continued: "But, Maddi, you need to do the same with your brother. Not exactly the same, of course…" I shuddered at the mere thought. "But the three of you are unique beings, and part of the message from Josephina, the dragon queen, had to do with the three of you and a combination of your powers. It's very important. We won't know how important until they get back with the entire message."

Mab had said the same thing, and I was not stupid enough to keep ignoring that advice. "Okay, I'm going to work on that straight away … as soon as I sober that moron up."

Connor let out a particularly loud snore to help prove my observation.

Looked like I was going to have my work cut out for me.

"Is there an updated timeframe on the gods releasing?" Asher asked. "Could our power be used to strengthen the prison?"

Princeps Jones spoke up again. "It could be any day," he said. It hurt my heart to see him looking so defeated. Even his voice held little inflection. "The supes there now, monitoring it, have mentioned that the energy-cage is cracking."

"At least Sonaris's death didn't explode them out," I added, because it had been a very real worry when he'd first died. After all, it was his magic that locked them in there in the first place.

"As long as Sonaris's power exists in the world," Louis said, "his spells will remain active."

"Could my favor still stand?" I wondered. "Owed to Axl now?"

Louis nodded. "Most likely. Did you agree to anything?"

"I agreed to spend time getting to know him. A month on his island."

Louis rubbed at his forehead, almost subconsciously, like he was thinking it through. "I can't tell you for sure, but I suspect you'll end up at that island again one day to fulfil that request."

Axl met my gaze and he smiled. "Vacay on the island," he joked.

A chuckle escaped before I could stop it. "Deal. Once we handle the gods."

His smile didn't fade, and I was so relieved that more and more of Axl's personality bled back into him every day. His eyes had not returned to his beautiful color, but I was growing used to the startling green-blue they were now.

Louis clapped his hands, shaking off some of his fatigue. "Great! Now that's settled, I have a mate to check in on, and a new god to train. I'll talk to you all soon. Inform Princeps Jones if there are any new developments, otherwise I'll be back when Jessa returns."

We waved him off, and I wasn't sure why, but Louis's return had made me feel worse, not better.

Maybe because this was it, the final countdown, and I wasn't sure we were going to win this time.

Chapter 16

A true mate bond between regular supes consisted of an ability to sense the other, feel their emotions, and know if they were in danger or hurt. A true mate bond between dragon shifting supernaturals had the added bonus of mental talk—communicating in each other's heads.

And a true mate bond between Atlantean-supernatural-gods … we had no fucking idea what that entailed, but it sure as shit was taking Asher and me through a bunch of new experiences, one being the mind-blowingly intense sex, where we shared more than just our bodies, but also our energy.

I was growing addicted, and now used any excuse to get Asher into bed. Or the pool. Or on any usable surface, really. I mean, it was my one chance to escape the mental load of daily worrying. Asher, and his magic as fuck hands might be the only thing keeping me sane.

In the week since Louis and Princeps Jones had returned, Axl had left for Atlantis, and the rest of the defenders were stationed on the island. According to their last report, the cage was eighty percent compromised, and we were talking days until the gods released.

I'd just hung up from video chatting Axl—I missed having him in the house. It just didn't feel right when one of us was away.

"I'm going to bed," I said, both exhausted and needing some alone time with Asher. The only downside to living in a full house of family ... not a lot of time alone.

"I'll be there soon," Asher said, his eyes dark as they traced down my body. The long slow leisurely stare was enough to burn my blood, but he didn't touch me. We were keeping our promise to Jesse. Barely.

Things were actually a lot better between all of us, so that was worth the small sacrifice.

I'll be waiting, I replied mentally.

His hands tensed on the couch, and I could tell he was fighting against just getting up and throwing me over his shoulder. Jesse said something and with an almost resigned sigh, Asher turned back to his friend. I'd let them have a few minutes before I started the mental torture. This new link between us was starting to grow on me, for more reasons than one—especially the fact that we could "touch" without being anywhere near each other.

Something I was about to take full advantage of.

Slipping into our room, I took a second, breathing it in. I'd been doing that a lot lately, that scent of Asher and me, mixed together, ocean and salty air, power and life. It was fast becoming my favorite scent, and with days until the final battle, I was more determined than ever to embrace the little things.

Crossing to our bathroom, I dropped my clothes on the floor, before cranking the shower, letting the water and steam fill the room. Ever since discovering my heritage, so much of my personality made sense. I loved the water, I always had, and since pools were not readily available in the neighborhoods I grew up in, and the ocean was not nearby, I had to make do with showers and baths. The moment I'd had any house to myself, I'd be in the water.

Asher had a really amazing shower. Huge. Great water pressure. Shower heads surrounded the stall, so spray hit me from all directions. The water was all recycled through a large system too, so we weren't even wasting water. We reused all of it.

Guilt free showers were the best.

Guilt free and maybe a little naughty.

It was much easier now to slip into Asher's mind. I couldn't see through his eyes or even hear all of his thoughts, but I was aware enough to know he was still chatting to Jesse. They weren't chatting about anything important. Just dude talk. A little about Axl's new powers and the class Asher had to teach tomorrow.

Reaching for my body wash, I squeezed a small amount into my hand, breathing in that botanical scent. Nothing fake around here, our senses were too strong, but I did enjoy products touched by nature. Lathering it up, I started to wash myself, slowly, moving my hands across my sensitive skin. It didn't take long for Asher to notice, and I realized that he'd had one "eye" on me since I walked away.

My breathing was a little heavier at that thought, knowing he was as turned on by me as I was by him ... it was a heady feeling. My hands moved lower, slicking across my stomach, and I started to forget what my entire point of this had been. Teasing Asher was one thing, but I was actually torturing myself, because I was seriously in need of a decent orgasm.

As my fingers slipped toward the ache between my legs, I tried to stifle the moan on the tip of my tongue. I shouldn't have bothered, because in the next second hands gripped my hips, jerking me back into his hardness. The moan spilled out as Asher's hands replaced mine, soaped up and rubbing across my clit, another slipping between my folds and entering me. One finger, then two, fast and hard.

"Is this what you wanted, baby?" he breathed in my ear, but I literally couldn't speak, because an orgasm crashed over me in the same second. I cried out as I rode his hand. Asher held me up through all of it, and before I could even finish experiencing the first wave of pleasure, he spun me so that we were facing each other.

His hands remained on my hips, just short of biting as they held me in place. We played this dominance game quite a lot, and Asher almost always won, but I got all the pleasure ... so who was the real winner?

His mouth crashed into mine and I returned that kiss with as much force. As I opened my lips further, his tongue dominated me, taking whatever it wanted, drowning me in his taste. He pushed me back so he could sink to his knees, needing more room to fit his giant body. He sucked my clit into his mouth, his tongue gliding over the sensitive nub that was still pulsing from my last orgasm. I cried out, fisting my hands into his hair and holding him tight to my body as he moved lower, licking me in one long line from bottom to top. He did this over and over until I couldn't feel my legs. How in the fuck did someone feel this much pleasure and not die? My brain might just explode from the overload.

Asher's mouth continued to destroy me, and right before my second orgasm, he connected our minds, sending every one of his desires through me.

I came, stars dancing across my vision as everything went black around the edges.

Fuck. Not even in my wildest dreams could I have ever imagined someone loving me as Asher did. He wanted to possess and devour every single part of me.

I came again.

"Jesus," I groaned. "You are literally going to kill me, Ash."

His dark chuckle trickled across my body and I basically died. My body crumpled and it was only Asher hauling me up into his arms that stopped me hitting the floor. "You can handle it, love," he murmured, before our lips met.

I could taste myself on his tongue, mixed with his intoxicating taste. It gave me extra energy to wrap my legs around his waist. I slid onto the long hard length pressed between us in one smooth move.

"Babe," Asher groaned, his head tipping back slightly, the water running over his face. Was there anything sexier than a man in the shower, hair slicked back, droplets of water tracing the hard planes of his face? The answer to that was no. Fuck no. There was not a single sexier thing.

He pressed me back to the wall, giving himself enough leverage to slam up into me over and over, my body jerking against the force.

I loved every second.

I'd already had multiple mindblowing orgasms, and I didn't expect another to be so close, but ... it was Asher. Pretty sure there was no limit to the number of orgasms he could wring from me.

"Hold on, Mads," he growled. "I can't go slow for you, love."

I shook my head. "I don't want slow," I gasped, before tightening my hold on his broad shoulders. My head rocked against the wall as he fucked me even harder, but I didn't care. Pain was not an issue. This felt like heaven.

The spirals of pleasure were not what I'd consider a slow build this time. They crashed into me with the same power that Asher was fucking me with, and I somehow managed to stifle my scream, even though I lost the ability to think as white light exploded behind my eyes.

Moments later, Asher slowed before he jerked inside of me, coming hard, his body firmly pressing mine into the tiles as we rode out our orgasms together. Our minds were still somewhat joined, and I could feel his pleasure and love for me. And the slightest concern he might have hurt me with his passion.

I kissed the only place I could reach ... his neck. "You didn't hurt me," I whispered against his skin, pressing more kisses to the smooth strong lines of his throat. "I loved it."

His tongue traced over my skin, licking the water droplets up as he tasted me. I was still feeling the aftershocks of sex, a delicious ache taking root in my body, reminding me of the pleasure. For a second, I wished we could stay like that. Forever. Just Asher and me, locked in our own world, without any of the drama and stress that was happening in real life.

I'll keep you safe. No one will take you from me again.

A shiver of foreboding traced through my body. *Don't tempt fate like that*, I told him, wrapping myself even tighter around him.

He shrugged, stupidly confident, as most powerful men were.

What if the thing you battle, I said slowly, *is me?*

He knew about the dreams, the nightmares that more often than not kept me awake, but what he didn't know was that I'd recently remembered one small detail. The fire and red I felt, they were from me. My face, awash in flames, was the last thing I saw. When I awoke with fear in my heart, I knew I was the demon that might end it all.

"I will fight for you against anything," he drawled, voice husky. "Even against yourself. If you're trying to destroy the world, Maddison, I'll either be destroying it with you, or I'll figure out how to bring you back to me. There's no other option."

I laughed, even though I felt no real humor. "You'd destroy it with me?"

His laughter was more genuine. "Yes. Where you are, that's where I am. We are two halves of the same soul. You'll never be alone again."

Using his powers, he switched the water off and stepped out of the shower. I was still wrapped around him, our bodies joined.

Actually…

Asher was definitely ready for round two, his rock-hard dick sliding against my sensitive core as he carried me to the bed. Bonus points for me … boy had stamina.

The second time, he made love to me like he wanted it to last for days. The pleasure was different. More intense. And when I finally fell asleep, the dreams stayed far away.

Not even they could take on Asher when he was determined to keep me safe.

Chapter 17

Two weeks later, the words I'd been dreading came down the line from Axl.

"They'll be out by tomorrow or the next day."

Louis was beside him in the video chat, and I could tell from the grim look on their faces, that this was the final, final countdown. The supernatural taskforce had managed to delay it as long as possible, and we were a few weeks over Mab's original estimate … they'd done everything they could.

"We'll head to the island straight away," I said, leaning closer like I could see through the screen to the prison. "Any word from Jessa and Braxton?"

Louis shook his head. "Nothing. I'm worried, but I can't leave to find them. The gods are powerful, maybe even more powerful than they were when they went in."

Asher, at my side, remained silent. All of us took a second to let it absorb.

"If they're even more powerful," Louis continued, "we have no hope of stopping them. We barely had the power to buy time. Now, I'm not sure if we'll do anything except die at their feet the moment they emerge."

Axl shrugged, his eyes downcast. "I just wish I could do more. Apparently, it's not easy to learn god powers in a month."

Louis dropped a comforting hand on his shoulder. "You've done remarkably well. Don't beat yourself up. The timing for all of this is terrible. We're doing the best we can."

A heavy sigh left me. "What if ... once they're free, I use my power to fly through the prison and see if I can track the Hellbringers? Might be too little too late, but it's something."

If Jessa got back in time, we might have had another plan, but this was the best I could come up with. My path hadn't shown up like Mab predicted. And I'd spent too long waiting around for it.

"Can't we just kill them all?" Jesse asked, stepping in behind us. He'd just gotten home from classes. "I mean, Asher killed Sonaris and he was super powerful..."

Louis shook his head. "I've considered it, but there are no beings strong enough to do what you all did. And you're already tapped out taking any extra power. It nearly killed one of you, and Asher shouldn't do that again. A lot can go wrong. You all got lucky this time." His eyes shifted to meet mine. "Maddison's idea is solid. The Hellbringers are still our best—our only, really—option. The three of you will need your bond to control them."

His eyes locked with mine. "Have you bonded with Connor?"

I groaned, running a hand through my hair, leaving the aqua strands in messy disarray. "No. He's an idiot who never listens. He doesn't want to bond. He's keeping us out of his mind and energy, and we spend most of our sessions together arguing."

Louis's expression, normally open and relaxed, was dark and hard. His aura was scary even through the phone. "Stop waiting for his cooperation. We don't have time to baby him through this bump in the road. Bottom line, you three are possibly the only chance to keep the world as it is now and not reformed by gods who care nothing for mortals. Connor needs to step up. Don't come to the island until that's complete. You're useless to us otherwise."

He ended the call and I fumed, my own guilt eating away at me. I hadn't tried hard enough. My brother was no doubt having a midlife crisis. Trying to keep him sober for longer than five minutes was a challenge ... but there was no more taking it slow. Connor was going to bond with us, whether he liked it or not.

"Give me five minutes," I said to Asher. Mostly because he looked like he was going to kill Connor if the idiot mouthed off one more time. "My brother and I need a little heart to heart."

Asher snarled again, shooting a dark look at the pathetic excuse for an Atlantean sprawled across the sand of the beach world. "Tell him this is the last chance I'm giving him. When I walk back in here, he better be on his feet, ready to figure this shit out."

He turned to leave, pausing briefly to drag me into his arms, pressing a rough kiss to my lips. "I desperately needed that," he told me, the slightest vibe of good humor creeping back in before his anger descended again and he left to walk it off.

Once I felt Asher's energy fade away, I focused on Connor. Using my power, I swirled water around him, jerking him up off the ground and to his feet.

His eyes went very wide as he blinked stupidly at me. "Wha—?"

He choked as more water crashed into his face, drenching him completely.

I'd been practicing the last few days with one of my professors, pressing harder into my ability to manipulate water and the elements within it. I could now, without too much effort, remove certain minerals and increase others. It was not the easiest of skills, because it required huge levels of concentration, but I was starting to see that I could manipulate any substance that contained even the slightest trace of water.

Like the alcohol he was so fond of. It contained water from Faerie—which was not an issue. Water was water, when it came to my power.

Holding him in the air, I reached for more energy, marveling at how much stronger I was since Sonaris. His death ... it had boosted more than just Axl. All of us had a new influx of strength, and I kept praying it would be enough to fight the gods. For now, it was more than enough to strip the alcohol from Connor's system. I needed him sober, and there was no time left for him to do it on his own. I should already be at Atlantis. Instead I was here, babysitting this fucking fool.

As soon as Connor realized what I was doing, he started to fight me, but it was a pathetic attempt.

"How are you so strong?" he snarled, trying to stop me from removing the toxic booze from his body. It was seeping out in bubbles that smelled horrific; it was a constant battle with my gag reflex to keep going.

"We killed Sonaris," I told him. This was not common knowledge, so I wasn't surprised when he choked and coughed.

"You did what? How? How has the world not ended?"

For the first time since we started these sessions, Connor was showing an interest in something other than getting drunk.

"We almost died," I told him, voice flat. "The power was too much for even the five of us to take, and Axl, who was last, absorbed the final energy. He was prepared to sacrifice himself, because the power of a soul's death would be enough to house the last blast of Sonaris's energy."

Connor couldn't even stop drinking long enough to remember his own name, so he probably didn't comprehend that level of sacrifice. But it deserved to be mentioned. Axl deserved to be known as the hero he was.

Connor's bloodshot eyes squinted at me. "I saw him though. At the meeting. I'm sure, now that I think about it, you all felt more powerful there."

"Axl is the god of the ocean now."

The silence was long and filled with tension, until he shook his head. "I don't believe you. Gods can't just be made from mortals like that." For the first time in a month, he sounded completely sober.

Yanking the last of the alcohol from his system, I sent it up into the air, exploding the droplets in a fiery blast. "I don't owe you any further explanation. You asked why I'm so much more powerful and I told you. End of story."

I released the water, letting him fall to the ground. He was on his feet in an instant, eyes clear, face confused. "How did you do that?" he asked. "Stripping the alcohol? My natural barrier should have stopped you from entering my body like that."

I shrugged. "Maybe you should have spent more time using your power and less time drinking. I'm not sure you have any barrier left at all."

He was steady on his feet, eyeballing me like I was a piece of shit he'd just stepped in. "I really don't like you," he said flatly. "This reality … I don't want it. Why the fuck do you think I drink?"

"So you don't have to deal with things like the rest of us!" I sniped back. "Newsflash, buddy, you don't just get to check out because shit is hard. The gods are almost loose again. We're talking days … or hours at this point. Who do you think they'll come after the second they get out and kill all of those on the front line?"

His gaze was steely; I preferred it to the glazed-over look he'd been rocking recently.

"Us," I reminded him. "We are what they want. Our power. Our abilities. And right now, you're a hot fucking mess that will be taken in by those dickhead-deities in seconds. I can already tell that you're so weak you'd roll on us in a heartbeat and damn the entire freaking world."

Again. I wanted to add but didn't.

Connor had been helping the gods behind the scenes for many years. Leading the Arterians, a now defunct secret group of Atlantean warriors. Even if he didn't fully understand what he was helping the gods do, he still did it. He was weak, and that was the worst character flaw to have in this fight against power hungry deities.

I stepped closer. "Here's a reality check … I'm not letting you roll on us again. I don't care what I have to do. Genetically, we're siblings. Genetically, I know you must have some strength of character in there." I growled at him. "Fucking find it."

His jaw was set, that look of disdain still boring into me, and it was clear that my current tactic was not reaching him. My patience was at its limit, but I decided to give it one more shot, and approach him in a different way.

"Talk to me, Connor," I said, letting whatever iota of concern I could muster filter into my voice. "It can't just be the god situation that has you drinking ... there has to be more to it?"

His jaw twitched and his mouth opened, but then he slammed it shut and shook his head. "I'm not doing this with you. You don't really care. You've never even acknowledged that I'm your brother outside of that lovely 'genetically we are siblings' statement from a second ago."

Guilt ripped through my gut again, leaving a slightly sick feeling behind. He hadn't said it with any emphasis, more like he was just stating a fact, but there was resignation in his voice. He knew my "concern" right now was just a front to get information from him.

"You did a lot of shitty things. You hurt me, you took from me," I reminded him. "But if it makes you feel any better, I've started thinking of you as my brother, even when I'm mad at you." This was the truth.

I took another step closer and he didn't back up, eyeing me warily. "You consider me to be your brother?" he asked, voice so low I almost missed the question. "Family?"

I nodded. "Yes. You're my family, whether I want you to be or not. Our parents, they're evil..." I sighed. "But I'm hoping that you're not the same.

I have this stupid hope that someday, if we can win this war, we might actually have a relationship. I want to believe there's good in you."

He swallowed so hard I could see his throat working. "I did it for family," he choked out. "To finally have a true family. A place to belong. Then we met our parents…" He shrugged. "And you know how that went. Not exactly the happy family reunion I envisioned."

Understatement of the century. I was finally starting to understand why he'd been acting the way he had. It all made sense now, especially his actions recently. He was grieving. For a lost dream.

"You wanted a family," I breathed, and my chest hurt, because that's all I'd ever wanted in my life too. And then I'd met Asher, and the Atlantean five, and Ilia and Larissa. Even Louis and Princeps Jones, who'd both been like father figures to me.

They'd become my family and I was never alone or lonely anymore. I hadn't needed our parents. But Connor didn't have any of that.

"You and Asher used to be friends," I reminded him. "You pulled away from everyone in this crazy pursuit of a family. A family that could have been part of your life all along…"

He was never one of the Atlantean-five, but piecing together what I'd learned about the guys and their relationships, he could have been part of it. He'd chosen to take a different path.

"Stand with me, Connor," I said, reaching out my hand to him. The first time I'd offered myself freely to him. "Help me save the world, and then we'll work on our family. We'll work on you and me."

He stared at my hand, hesitation on his face as he fought against self-preservation … and his need for someone to give a fuck about him. I'd clearly hurt him in the past when I dismissed him, probably not my finest moment, but he also wasn't completely blameless.

He placed his hand in mine, and the second my fingers closed around his, energy flared between us. Asher must have felt the jump in my power, because he was back in the ocean room in a heartbeat, racing toward us. He couldn't get any closer because there were visible arcs of power spreading around Connor and me.

You okay, Maddi?

His voice washing through my mind was a soothing balm to my frazzled nerves.

All good. I think this is the connection. Our energy is ... curious.

Connor didn't fight me. If anything, he was urging the connection forward, and I squelched the small part of me that wondered if he hadn't been playing me all along. We both had a long way to go in building any sort of trust. But we had to start somewhere.

We just needed time. The one commodity I was basically out of.

When our energy was satisfied, curiosity sated, we were released from the hold. "I can sense you," Connor said, almost in awe. "Nothing crazy, just a small sliver of your power. Like I'd know if you were in trouble or not."

I nodded. "Yes. I feel the same sliver from you."

Him and five other Atlanteans. I was amassing a veritable army of energy signals inside my own power, and I liked being able to tap into all of them to know they were safe and not in pain. Only with Asher could I go deeper.

Just as it should be.

Asher would always be part of my soul, but the others ... they were part of my heart, and my family.

Chapter 18

"You ready for sports bonding Wednesday?" Larissa asked, head back as she enjoyed some unexpected sun at breakfast.

I grimaced, spooning more yogurt into my mouth. "I wish. Louis wants us on the island today. He has no idea how the gods aren't out yet, but our time is up." I wasn't even wearing my uniform, since I knew his final call and step-through would be arriving any time. Instead I wore ass-kicking boots, jeans, and a long-sleeved Henley. This was my battle armor.

"Louis will send a step-through soon, so we don't create any sort of power imbalance by showing up any other way," I told her, scraping the last of the yogurt from the tub.

Larissa's face was wreathed in worry, but before she could voice any of them, Ilia dropped into the seat beside me.

We were both distracted by how disheveled she looked. "You're not going to Atlantis without me," she said, voice raspy. "If the gods are killing us all, I'm going down with you, bestie."

I didn't comment on that, because there was no way in hell she was on the front line. This was a war with the gods, and as badass as she was, Ilia was still just a regular supernatural. And I loved her too much to risk her life, even if I would have preferred she was at my side. It was bad enough that the Atlantean-five would all be there. Ilia and Larissa was not happening.

Deciding a distraction was the way to go, I leaned back so I could take her in. "Girl, what did you and Calen get up to last night?"

Her shirt was on backwards. Her hair was completely sticking up on one side of her head, red curls looking more like a tumbleweed.

"I mean … did you look in the mirror at all?" Larissa asked, sad humor tingeing each word. She'd argued to come with us as well, but unlike the headstrong Ilia, had finally conceded that she would not be much help, and would probably end up a liability in this fight.

Ilia grinned, never embarrassed by anything. I had a sense that we could walk in on Calen and her screwing, and she'd just grin and ride her man like the confident bitch she was.

"We kind of … fell off a cliff," she said, reaching out to snag some of the toast sitting on the table. It was just plain old buttered toast, but she inhaled it like it was the best thing she'd ever eaten.

I pushed a glass of water toward her—she looked like she needed it. "Uh, how did you fall off a cliff?" I asked, enjoying this moment of normalcy. It might be one of the last—

I cut that thought off quick fast.

Ilia shrugged. "Apparently when you have sex in a car, you should be careful not to hit the gear stick with your ass. It would be a good idea to have the handbrake engaged as well. You know, for extra safety."

My lips twitched. "Your car went over a cliff?"

She nodded. "Yeah, it happens. Took us a few hours to climb out, because I kind of knocked Calen out when I punched him, and then I had to half carry him up the cliff."

I caught Larissa's eyes. "We should stop asking questions now," I said dryly.

She snorted. "Probably for the best."

Ilia glared at us both, before going back to her toast. "You bitches should have more sympathy. We were naked when we climbed out, because our clothes went AWOL and I had to steal these from a house nearby."

"You know the shirt is on backwards, right?" I said with a burst of laughter, before I cut it off.

She looked down; eyes wide. "Well, fuck. I'm a hot mess."

I shook my head. "Girl, you're a total hot mess. But that's okay. We've got your back."

Larissa and I pushed the rest of our food away and all but hauled her up, dragging her back to her room. I got her into the shower, and Larissa dug out some clothes that were more the style of our usually very put-together, glamorous friend.

"Calen will probably be the death of her," Larissa said, laying the clothes out on the bed.

I leaned back on the wall, waiting for Ilia to finish showering. "Probably, but I don't think she'll complain. I've never seen her this happy."

I'd never seen either of them this happy. Fuck. We couldn't lose this life. I wasn't ready. I'd only just freaking found my place in the world.

"How's Rone?" I asked Larissa, desperately needing anything to focus on other than gods killing the entire world.

"We're in a good place," she said with a small smile and a shrug. "A really good place. We talk all the time, share our feelings, eat food together, and co-exist in every way a couple would." She paused with a harsh sigh. "Except for sex. We're basically friend zoned, and I have no idea how to get out of there. It's shit in this zone."

"Dude," I said. "I feel that. It's certainly not fun when your feelings go deeper, and you want more, but you're also scared to lose what you have now. I guess you just have to ask yourself, will you be happy if things stay the way they are forever?"

Larissa's white teeth worked across her lips, the slightly pointier vampire fangs visible against the pinkish brown. "I'm torn. Maybe one day I'll get over my attraction for him in this way, and then we can exist *happily* as best friends. We're very good at being friends. I wouldn't want to lose him in my life. But…"

She trailed off, and we both knew what she hadn't said. *What if she didn't get over her attraction?*

Could she live a half-life like this forever?

I hugged her quickly. "You don't have to make any decisions today," I reminded her, when I pulled back. "Hell, you don't have to make a decision in the next hundred years. We live for a long time. And right now, in these tense, high stress situations, it's like being in a constant state of intense emotions. It's hard to know your true feelings. I say give it some time and see where it naturally leads."

Look at me being optimistic about having hundreds of years. If the gods got their way, we might not even have two days, but no one should go into these battles without a little hope.

And here was mine.

"Should I go on dates?"

She didn't particularly look thrilled by the prospect of dating again.

"You deserve to be happy," I reminded her. "If Rone's not giving you what you need, if he's not stepping up, then it's up to you to grab at whatever means to happiness you can. If I've learned anything over the past few months, it's that life is unpredictable, and sometimes you just have to take a risk." Probably a contradiction to my last piece of advice, but I wanted her to be in control of her own happiness. "If there's someone you want to date, then I say … yes. You should go on a date."

The shower shut off and we straightened, waiting for Ilia. "I don't want him to think I'm doing it to make him jealous," she said softly, "but I also won't wait forever. A really nice guy asked me to go to town with him, have dinner, maybe catch a movie. I think I'll say yes. If things go south with the gods … at least I gave it a shot."

My throat was tight as I wrapped an arm around her. "Movie and dinner sounds kind of perfect."

Ilia groaned as she entered the room, shaking her head, springy curls back to their usual perfect disarray. She dressed and straightened, looking more herself in leather pants and a red tank. "I feel so much better," she said with a smile, rubbing her hands across the smooth black pants she wore. "I might even come and watch this little SSW match today. It's been so long since I've seen a decent few rounds."

"I'm heading to the fields, too," I said, "Asher and the others are there. We want to stay together to wait for Louis's call."

Like he'd heard me, his voice was in my mind. *Louis just called, baby. He's ready for us.*

The world seemed to both slow and speed at the same time, and it took a concerted effort not to pant in rapid breaths as panic rocked through me.

I'm on my way, I sent back to Asher, successfully managing to hide my emotions from him and my girls.

A tingle of his energy ran along my spine and I almost closed my eyes so I could enjoy it uninterrupted. This new bond between us, it was like a long-forgotten muscle that we'd just started to use again. At first it felt heavy and sometimes painful to control the energy flow, but the more we used it, flexed that "muscle" the easier it became. I could see one day I wouldn't even have to think about my intentions. The muscle would just know, remember, and it would be like breathing. A reflex.

If we lived that long, of course.

We started walking again, moving faster than before. Just as we were leaving the edge of the paved path, ready to step onto the grassed area toward the students visible around the SSW fields, there was a crack of what sounded like thunder above us.

I reacted immediately—it was a perfect, cloudless day, and I knew this wasn't natural. Last time something "not natural" cracked above my head, it was energy that killed Asher. I would not let that happen to my friends. They didn't have a second life to come back with.

Shoving them aside, I used my power to protectively surround them, before I rose into the air, heading straight for the strong presence I could feel hovering above. Whoever they were, they were powerful, but not familiar. It wasn't any of the gods I'd met, and Louis would have been here sweeping us away if they were legitimately free.

This was something else.

The barrier above the Academy extended high into the sky, but I was fast, hitting it in seconds. I would not let anyone hurt this school. I might not know and love all the students, but they were mine to protect. As I burst through the barrier—no match for my power—it reformed behind me, and I was left to face the last thing I actually expected to be above the Academy.

A fucking dragon.

It was gold, almost blindingly bright as it glittered in the sun. I had to squint to make out the gigantic body with heavy, thick scales. It was also rocking four claw-tipped legs, huge powerful wings, and a jaw as large as my body, with teeth the size of my palm.

Gold. It flashed at me again, and ... I was pretty sure I knew who this was. She wasn't a threat, as far as I'd heard.

Letting my energy fall, I cautiously moved closer.

"Are you okay?" I asked, softening my voice. I'd never dealt with a dragon before and had no idea how temperamental they were. Especially a powerful queen.

As I got even closer, I caught a glimpse of two prone figures over her back, and I was just opening my mouth again when the dragon swung one of those giant wings in my direction, clipping me across the face.

As it hit me, a strong burst of energy followed, and I had one thought before everything went dark.

I thought she was our friend…

CHAPTER 19

It was Asher's voice shouting in my head that woke me.

Maddison! Baby, come on, wake up so I can figure out what's happening! He was angry, a red raging power following his words. I got the quick sense that he was covered in gold right now, and probably rampaging around the school.

Ash? I shot back, wincing as I tried to gather my bearings. *Where are you? What … the golden dragon attacked me.*

His reply was fast and brutal. *Following, but she's using her power to throw us off the trail. It's original energy, and it's tricky. I need you to help me, love. I won't let you go again.*

I blinked again, and as more of my senses fired I realized that we were flying still. I was clutched in the huge taloned feet of the dragon. She had me tightly encased and I could see nothing at all.

Not even slivers of light ... but then again...

I pressed my face closer, and I was almost certain that wherever we were right now, it was not daytime. There was no visible light. I'd learned in class that dragons could move between the realms, so we could technically be anywhere in this world or in Faerie, or even the demon realm.

Fuck.

Are we still on Earth? I asked Asher.

There was no reply, and I shook my head, searching frantically for his energy. It had been there, so strongly, and now ... gone.

Sorry, little one.

The voice in my head was not Asher's. It was strong, powerful, sounding like it was filled with a thousand other voices, ringing like magical instruments.

I need to cut your communication off. I left it long enough so that he would know you were alive, but now it's time for us to move along the only path left to save the worlds. I just hope we're not too late.

Terror welled in me, and with it, confusion.

Why are you doing this? I thought you were on our side?

I used the same method of communication, following her magical energy.

I'm on your side. I had no choice but to take you by surprise. Jessa, Mischa, and you are all the same ... powerful females. You're the ones who need to follow the path.

So why knock us out? Why not just talk to us?

A brief pause, and I didn't bother to move, knowing there was no point fighting her. Even if I were strong enough to take her on, I'd only drop out into some unknown situation that might be worse than where I was now. She said she was on our side, now she had to prove it.

I have seen, she started slowly, *that you would not come without your mates. And this is a journey that no man can take.*

I spluttered, before biting back. *I'm sure if you explained it, we could have figured out a way. None of us need our mates at our sides all the time. We can function without them.*

Fuck. I hadn't lost that much independence, right?

I have seen, she repeated, in her calm bell-like voice. *It's not you that was unreasonable, it was the other three. Braxton, Maximus, and Asher. They would not let you go, and the time wasted arguing was the time needed to save the world.*

My reply died in a loud exhale of annoyance. I wanted to argue further with her, but I really couldn't. She had a point.

I didn't know Braxton that well, or Maximus at all, but I knew enough about both to know they were strong, dominant, and hugely protective of their mates. I mean, Louis was another prime example—his mate was one of the strongest magic users in the world, rivaling him for power at times, and he still couldn't quell his protective instincts.

They protected us because they loved us. I'd never doubted that about Asher, and he was actually really good at walking the line between protecting and smothering. But if this dragon believed they would have hindered us long enough to cost us the battle, then I was sure they would have. We knew the gods were to be free at any moment. Maybe she really had no choice…

How dangerous is this journey?

We dipped down then, like she was banking to come in for a landing.

It's most certainly going to be the most dangerous thing you'll ever do. But it's the only shot we have. I've followed every possible path, looked into all the futures. This is our one chance.

She spiraled further, dropping much faster now, and I fell silent, trying to piece it all together in my head. I had no idea how she'd managed to block Asher from me, since all I'd read about these sorts of bonds had them beyond most magical manipulation. Original magic was clearly the exception, but I wasn't sure she'd done the right thing blocking him out. Asher was powerful in his own right now, and I knew he wouldn't rest until he tracked me down.

Will you allow me to explain this to Asher? It's better for the world if he doesn't lose his shit. I doubt he could get here in time to stop us, so you've got nothing to lose.

I thought she was going to ignore me. There was no reply for so long.

I will give you all a chance to say goodbye as soon as we reach our destination. It will be no more than a minute, because the moment we step into the path, we'll be cut from the mortal world. And we must step onto the path right as the first beam of sunlight strikes the land.

About half of what she said made sense to me. I mean, I understood the words, but I didn't have the context to truly get it. No doubt I'd find out soon enough. It sounded like this path was close, and I was really starting to hate that word. *Path.* It reminded me of my tiny fairy friend. For a second, I wished Mab was here, but she'd told me she couldn't be part of this journey, for whatever reason. So I'd just have to be content with her soul-sister, the other obscure, riddle-talking, original-magic-bearing, dragon.

My stomach twirled as the dragon went into a death spin, plummeting us to the ground. I held on best I could, within the confines of her giant claws that covered most of my body, and then it was over. I could hear the gush of wind as her wings slowed, lowering us the last few feet to what I assumed was the ground.

When I was released, I pulled my power around me, cushioning my fall, but it was only a couple of feet. I landed smoothly, straightening and testing out all my limbs. Everything was in working order.

The golden dragon stood tall, towering what felt like miles above me. It was still dark, very dark and cold, wherever we were, but I could see her just fine. She emitted her own glow that was unlike anything I'd ever seen. The closest was probably Asher and his mother when they were powered up, but it still wasn't quite the same.

Original magic is beyond all other. There are not many of us that can draw from that well, not directly.

She shifted to the side, just a single step, and I could see two prone bodies. *Jessa!*

I rushed over and knelt beside two faces that were almost identical.

Are they okay?

They were breathing and their faces looked relaxed.

The dragon nodded, her huge head slow as it moved up and down. *Yes. They're not as strong as you. They won't wake until I allow them to.*

I blinked at her. *And when will you allow them to?*

She almost looked shamed as she tilted her head. I mean, I wasn't totally sure what shame looked like on a dragon face, so maybe I was more sensing the emotion.

Jessa will be upset with me. She keened in my mind. *The same way you are. It hurts me when she's angry, as she is my twin soul.*

I didn't know the full story of Jessa and her dragon, but I knew it had been something that broke Jessa's heart. Whatever she'd gone through, it seemed her dragon felt the same way. Some of my annoyance at the scaly beast faded and I let out a sigh. The queen's intentions were good ... actions sloppy, but a good heart should always be rewarded.

She was trying to save the world.

I let my anger go.

Standing, I took a step toward her, placing my hand gently onto her leg. *Wake them. Jessa will understand, and I'm sure it's not long until this sunrise that you require to take the path.*

Her huge eyes stared into mine, and I almost flinched away, because they were so all-seeing, powerful and scary in their intensity. Under that though, there was a well of kindness brimming in the depths.

You have a soul built of strength and magic, Maddison James. I'm not surprised you were chosen for this task. You will be our greatest asset in this war.

For some unknown, probably stupid reason, I was fighting tears. To have someone acknowledge that maybe I wasn't a complete screw-up ... shit. I shouldn't need that reassurance, but I loved that she'd freely given it.

Thank you.

She nodded again, before taking a step back, her long neck snaking around toward the twins, briefly touching each of them. I couldn't see exactly where her snout brushed, but within seconds they were both awake, on their feet, eyes wide and confused.

"Josephina!" Jessa bit out, voice husky. "What did you do?"

There was silence while the dragon communicated with them, both girls wearing expressions of confusion and exasperation. A moment of observation was all I needed to see that Mischa was better at containing her emotions. Jessa visibly vibrated with her anger.

Whatever Josephina said it slowly calmed the twins. They turned away from her, both of them walking right up to me.

"Freaky," I murmured, staring between them. Minute differences only, otherwise it was like looking into a perfect reflection.

Jessa's lips quirked as she hurried forward for a hug. "Hey, girl!" she said, holding me tight. "I knew we were going to chat soon, but I definitely didn't expect it would be under these circumstances."

I snorted, hugging her back. "Yeah, Josephina had a pretty good reason, so I'm okay with it, but I'm pretty sure Asher is destroying something on Earth as we speak."

Jessa's jaw tightened, tension spilling into her blue eyes. "Braxton too."

"And Max," Mischa said with a sigh.

She forced a smile, holding her hand out to me. "Hi, you must be Maddison."

I shook her hand and returned her smile. "I am. It's really nice to meet you, Mischa. I've heard a lot about your life, and … well, we have more than a little in common."

Her eyes were more green than blue, a lot like Axl's current eye color, and her face was softer than Jessa's, somehow, despite their identical looks.

"I'd love to talk to you about your time in the human world," she said softly, "and the transitioning phase going from human to supernatural." She looked around at the dark landscape surrounding us. "Guess that might have to wait for another day, though. We're apparently booked up with saving the world today."

My laugh was strangled. "Apparently."

It's time.

We all turned to Josephina, who was facing toward a very small speck of light in the distance.

You have twenty seconds to say goodbye to your mates ... then we must step into the light.

Whatever had been blocking me from Asher vanished, and without pause I reached for his energy.

Ash, love. I only have seconds. We're safe. Going to take a path into the underworld. Don't destroy the world. I love you.

Maddison!

His roar was deafening, but I had no more time for words, so I sent all the loving emotions his way.

Tell me where you ar—

He was cut off, and I hunched forward in pain, my hands on my knees as I fought through the devastation. I was acutely aware of how it felt to lose Asher, to experience his "death," and this blocking of our connection had a similar feel.

Jessa and Mischa were pale beside me, their normally tanned skin blotchy.

"Braxton is fucking furious," Jessa whispered. "I mean ... he's probably going to be in a supernatural prison when we return."

I swallowed hard. "Good luck containing Asher in a jail. He's basically a god now, and I'm scared of what he might do."

"They're all together at least," Mischa added, her voice thick with emotions. "And the kids are safe."

"They're together?" I bit out.

Shit, was that a good or a bad thing? I felt like that many powerful, pissed off males in one place ... kind of a recipe for disaster.

"They're going to come after us," Jessa warned Josephina.

She shook her head.

Where we are going, they cannot follow. Not unless we manage to make it through our task, and then one of us might have the power to open a path for them. It felt like she was looking at me when she said that, but I couldn't be sure.

Her huge wings swept to the side, pumped a few times, stirring up an unnatural gust of wind. It hit us just as a long ray of light spilled down the dark path ahead. The illumination was not that bright at first, simply showing us a bridge surrounded by darkness. The bridge itself was made of no material I'd seen before, metallic and etched through with a plethora of colors, giving it an almost iridescent appearance.

The rainbow bridge is the only remaining path for the living into the underworld.

I figured Josephina was projecting this to all of us.

But it's a path guarded by Heptashia. She was the original mate of Draconis, until he betrayed her for Lotus. Ever since then, she has barricaded almost all entrances into the underworld for the living. All that remains is Atlantis, and this one back entrance. There's a chance she will allow females of worth to cross, and you three are the worthiest of any I know.

Her wings were pumping harder, the breeze lifting our feet from the ground. I didn't fight it, trusting in the dragon queen. The light grew brighter with each thrust of her wings, and I had to force my eyes to adjust so I could continue to see.

"Are you coming with us?" Jessa shouted over the wind.

I am. But not in the form that you know me.

With a flash of brilliant glowing gold, the dragon was gone, and we were all being sucked up in the wind. Jessa, Mischa, me, and a golden-haired woman that I was almost certain had been a dragon not two seconds before. With a final shot of power, we were propelled along the rainbow bridge.

At first it was smooth and fast, but as we got closer to the blinding light at the end of the path, the energy got rougher. It crashed against us, trying to force us back, but whatever magic Josephina used, it was just strong enough to counter it.

ASHER

The storm raged overhead, and I let it grow.

"Ash, dude, you have to calm down."

Jesse was trying his best to get through to me, but Maddison had just been cut off from my mind again, and I was acting on the basest of instincts. My power swelled, the gold of my energy filling the air, and as it rose higher it streamed into the clouds. I was not in control, and normally that fucked me right off—I was too powerful to lose control.

But in this moment, I wanted to destroy it all.

Lightning cracked and my friends ducked for cover, but I wasn't so far gone that I would sacrifice them in my rage. My protection extended to them, and that was it.

The two dragons in the sky. They were on their fucking own.

The beasts roared, and I felt a powerful source of energy coming from somewhere close by. This being was trying to counter my own power.

They were dead if they got any closer.

"Asher Locke, you need to stand down."

The voice rumbled through the air, and it was definitely the source of the power.

I blasted lightning in their direction. A warning.

The only one they would get.

The return shot of energy grazed across my skin and I felt the slightest flare of surprise break through my fury. Their spell had been strong enough to slice my biceps. It healed instantly, but that spoke of how powerful this being was.

He stepped into sight, just as the two dragons from above dropped from the sky.

I knew him. Another dragon.

There was an infestation of scaly lizards here, wherever the fuck we were. I had no concept of time or place, I'd just followed Maddison, but I was reasonably sure we were in Faerie, a land I'd wanted to visit more than once. The land of my ancestors … my family. But now I didn't care to even look around. Now I would raze this fucking world to nothing but cinders and ashes if it meant that Maddison was returned to me.

"Asher, you know me. We might not have always seen eye to eye, but we respected each other. Don't let me have given my respect in vain."

"Fuck off, Rayge."

Who was this asshole, and how was he so damned powerful?

A rumble rocked his chest, the dragon inside of him always one step from losing control. It was the issue I'd had with him long ago. The issue

I had with his friendship with my mate—he was not to be trusted. The dragon who killed his parents.

Sure, I didn't know the entire story, and more than likely there was a good reason, but it made me wary. Family was not immune from punishment, I knew that better than anyone, but he always seemed one step from completely losing control. That was the part I didn't trust.

"You need us, Asher." Another fucker approached me. More dragons. None of them could control me.

"Braxton Compass," I said with a dark laugh. "Didn't figure you for suicidal."

He roared back at me, stuck in some sort of in-between dragon and supernatural form. He was huge, standing a head above me, his arms as thick as my fucking chest. It was impressive, but I didn't fear the dragon. He was strong in this world, but I was not from this world.

"Jessa is gone too!"

I finally deciphered his roaring words, and a stab of something other than fury in my chest. "Maddison is not alone?"

The lightning raged again, slamming into the earth between us, but no one moved. Not me, or Rayge, or Braxton, or the final member of our fucked-up crew. A vampire-dragon hybrid—Maximus, I was guessing, another of the Compass quads.

"My mate as well," Maximus rumbled, his fangs extended, voice filled with violence.

The three of us turned to Rayge. "What are you doing here?" Braxton asked, voice low and deadly. If I wasn't too angry to even see straight, I'd have been cautious if that voice was directed at me, but Rayge was a cocky bastard. He feared no one.

The four of us were probably the worst beings to be in close proximity like this. Especially missing our mates. Someone was going to die.

"Josephina has undertaken a fool's journey," he said softly. "All to try and save a world that doesn't deserve her. I will not let her sacrifice herself. Not even for Jessa, whom she loves more than anything."

Braxton growled and the ground rocked where we stood. "Who the fuck is Josephina?" I bit out, sure that I'd heard the name before, but right now I couldn't think.

"The dragon queen," Rayge said, and sorrow filled his eyes. I wasn't sure I'd ever seen a soft emotion from him. Not a real one. The few times we'd interacted, it had either been uncontrolled anger or a complete blank slate. There might have also been a sliver of humor when he was with Maddison in the bar—my girl had that effect on people.

Like he'd heard me, his eyes met mine. "I won't let Maddison die. She's important and special. The world needs her, and something tells me that if she was to perish, you would kill us all. You clearly have the power to do so."

I didn't deny it. I couldn't deny it. Maddison had been strong and fought for the world when she thought I was dead, but I could not do the same. My rage would know no bounds. No one would be safe from me.

"Maddison is mine," I told him, not sure if it needed to be said, but I was saying it. "Mine to save. Mine to protect. Just fucking mine. And I'm getting her back now, so you all should step aside."

My brothers were still a few yards away—I was using my power to hold them in place. Protect them from whatever went down here. Jesse in particular was cursing me. I could see his angry gestures and raised fists. But he'd forgive me eventually. As long as he was alive, it was all good.

The ground around Braxton shook, the land he stood on charring black as his own fury radiated out in visible waves. "Jessa is all that matters," he said. "She is mine."

"Mischa is mine," Maximus added, his voice low. "We have wasted enough time. Let's move."

Rayge's lips almost twitched then. "Okay, now that we've laid claim to our mates, I think it's time we get them back."

Braxton's head instantly jerked in his direction and he took a step closer. "Who is your mate? Who do you lay claim to?"

If the name that crossed his lips was Maddison, I was ending him. Fried dragon was my new specialty.

Rayge rubbed at his forehead. "No mate. But Josephina, as stubborn as they come, is my kin and I will not let her be harmed."

I was almost certain I wasn't the only one that stared, unblinking, trying to figure out how the fuck a dragon and a supernatural could be kin. I mean, clearly it was through their dragon side...

Rayge did smile this time, the slightest quirk of his lips. "I'll explain on the way," he said. "For now, all I'll say is that the queen of the dragons is not like regular dragons. She has another form. And we are family. She's the best friend I have. One of the only friends I have. I would not survive without her."

I didn't know him well. One of our few interactions was when he killed his parents and was brought before the supernatural courts. He'd been found not guilty, and I should have taken that to mean he was innocent of evil, but there was always something in his eyes that spoke of a soul-deep rage. He lived up to his namesake.

As he talked about Josephina, though, I could see the reason Maddison befriended him. Rayge had hidden depths...

Maybe he was someone worthy of her friendship after all.

There was a click inside my mind and I immediately reached for Maddison, hoping to feel her. She'd been there before, long enough for me to know she was okay, but there was nothing now. In fact, it felt like we had no connection at all. She was no longer in Faerie...

My storm exploded, huge bolts of gold slamming into the ground around us. Everything rocked as my power grew, so much more now that I held Sonaris's energy. Fissures cut through the rock around us, forming small crevices that would soon grow larger if I couldn't stop.

"Asher!" Rayge shouted. "What are you doing?"

I whipped my head in his direction, reaching out and without touching him, cut off his words, lifting him with my energy. He didn't fight me, or he tried at first and realized it was futile, so he chose to remain stoic, watching me with those ancient-as-fuck eyes.

"Maddison is not in my bond. She's gone."

Braxton dropped his head back, his skin covered in scales as flames spread around him. "Jessa too."

The guttural nature of his words made it next to impossible to understand what he was saying.

But I understood. We were speaking the same language.

Fear and fury.

Rayge continued to stare me down and I reluctantly lowered him back to the ground. Maddison was not dead, I had to believe that, and I wouldn't kill someone who might hold more information about whatever this Josephina was up to.

Rayge didn't wince or rub his throat. "We need to move now," he said. "Josephina is still on my radar. My dragon can track her. Follow me."

He shifted so fast it was almost instant. Braxton and Maximus did the same, large beasts filling the space around me. Rayge nudged his head at me, and I knew he wanted me to step onto his back, but I shook him off.

"I don't need help," I said, barely managing to speak around the energy filling my body, my throat, my blood. My insides churned. "I can follow."

Using my powers, I lifted myself into the sky, gold sparkling around me. I was no doubt going to leave a path to follow, but good luck to anyone that did. If a single being tried to stop us from getting our women back, they would regret it.

I'm sending you all back to the Academy, I told my brothers. *I'll let you know when I find Maddison.* I used my powers to open a step-through, hoping they would be smart enough to get out of this unknown area.

Focusing on the dragons, I went after them. Rayge zipped across the sky and I followed at the same speed, wishing they could go a little faster. If I had a clue how to track Maddison, I would not be relying on these dragons.

For now, I needed to keep reminding myself that she wasn't dead. That she was in the company of powerful supes. And that my Maddison was both brilliant and powerful. She wouldn't go down easily. She would be fine.

If she wasn't, it was already too late for the world.

CHAPTER 21

If this was a Grimm brothers' story, that rainbow bridge we crossed would have been full of difficult tasks. Trolls. Labyrinths. Impossible riddles and dangerous creatures. That was kind of what I expected after Josephina's cryptic and downright terrifying "this will be a hard journey" speech.

Instead, we had a clear and smooth path, and in what felt like a single blink of an eye, we were no longer flying. We landed on a round stone platform. Unlike the rainbow bridge, there was nothing glittery about where we stood now. It was hot, filled with an acrid scent: a combination of sulfur and freshly burnt wood. The scent both enticed and warned us we were entering territory that was not our own, and maybe, just maybe, the Grimm's portion of this journey was about to commence.

"Stay close," Josephina said, and I couldn't get over what she looked like now. Her skin was a soft glittering gold. Her eyes were even more unusual, still gold, but with hints of caramel.

"How?" Jessa said. "How are you…" she waved her hand, "like that?"

Josephina smiled sadly, her teeth brilliant white, and maybe more perfect than I'd ever seen on another being. And I'd seen some damn perfect teeth. Still, no one would ever suspect that this golden woman before us was anything other than … well, *other*. She was flawless.

"As the queen of the dragons, host to an ancient magic," she started, "I have some abilities not available to my brethren. My mother had the same, and her mother as well. It's passed down through the maternal line. This is my other form—that of the original dragon gods from whom I descend. There are not many left who draw power from the originals."

We silently stared at her. "You're a god," Jessa breathed, her eyes shiny as she launched herself at the golden figure. "You're beautiful."

They hugged for many seconds, and it was such a heartfelt moment that I found myself with a tight throat and shiny eyes. They had never hugged like this … I already knew that dragon to person wasn't quite the same.

"Why didn't you tell me?" Jessa asked as she pulled away.

Josephina shot a rueful smile at her. "It's not encouraged that we step away from our dragon for this form. My mother always warned me about overusing it, that I would grow addicted to the power in this body. This gold that coats my skin, it's the same gold of the original magic. It's filling my body, my blood, my soul. It's addictive. Inviting it in is never encouraged, even for those naturally acquired of it."

A chill ran through me. Asher. Asher had gold magic too, born from his mother, who was born of the fucking mother of all. Original magic.

That's what happened to him when the gold took over and he lost control.

"I need to talk to Asher," I said in a rush. "He has original magic. And if he doesn't know I'm okay..." I had no idea what he would do, but I knew it wasn't good. If this ancient powerful dragon was worried about losing control, what did that mean for Asher?

Josephina at least had the decency to look sorry. "We no longer have access to them. We have stepped into an in-between world, and now we must journey to the underworld. Through the path of *Heptashia*."

Fuck.

"Fuck," Jessa muttered, and I wondered if she'd read my mind.

I mean, it was the logical response to this situation, so probably not.

"Best thing we can do is finish our task and get back to them," Mischa said, sounding very levelheaded. She was clearly upset too—I could see the tension in the lines on her forehead—but she was holding it together.

"Girl gang," Jessa said softly.

Mischa blinked at her, but I smiled. "Girl gang," I acknowledged. "It was a premonition apparently."

She reached out and we fist bumped, because solidarity, sister.

"Girl gang is highly appropriate," Josephina added. "Since only those accepted will cross. And no man has ever made it through. This goddess is very particular. And men ... she hates them."

Not hugely surprising since she was no doubt super-pissed at being betrayed by Draconis. I wanted to know more of this story. There was no time right now, but hopefully there would be one day. It was kind of my family problem after all.

Dad the fucking douchebag. Shit father. Shit mate.

For a brief moment I wondered if understanding Heptashia's story would help us make it through...

"No," Josephina said. "Understanding will not help with this first part." She could still read minds apparently.

"This is a simple test of worthiness, and no one knows what's used to weigh your worth, but everyone faces the same scale."

"Worthiness means something different to every person," Mischa said, solemnly. "I don't understand how this test could be fair. I've certainly done some things I'm not proud of, and more than likely won't pass."

Jessa growled, a fierce sound. "You have to forgive yourself for what you did. Nothing was malicious. You were hurting, and if I had been in the same position as you, I would have probably done worse. You're so much more levelheaded and kinder than me. I'm violent. Quick tempered. And very unaccepting of other people's flaws when they irritate me. I'm *so* far from perfect."

Josephina smiled at the twins, and it was clear she had a soft spot for the sister of her beloved Jessa. "You're both perfectly flawed and that's okay. You don't have anything to prove to anyone ever. You've both saved the world more than once, and at great personal and emotional sacrifice. As I said initially, you are two of the best supes I know. You are worthy." She turned to me. "And Maddison is worthy, for multiple reasons. I have almost no doubts that you'll all pass, but it's hard to know for sure when this test is designed by Heptashia. It's what she considers worthy, and as I have not traveled this path before…"

"What about you?" Jessa asked, her concern for the dragon queen obvious. "Will you have to go through the same test?"

The golden woman nodded. "Yes. I will be at your side, as always."

"You are more than worthy," Jessa agreed. "You are right not to be worried."

Josephina shook her head. "I'm not worried, but it's not because of what you think. I'm no more worthy than you three. I don't worry because I am with you. There's no others I would be with, even if this is my time to end this life."

I'd never seen anyone lose color as fast as Jessa did; there were already tears tracking down her cheeks. "I will never accept that," she choked out. "I don't fucking care. Let's turn around now, because I won't accept losing any of you. Not Josephina, or Mischa, or Maddison. No one."

I felt the same. Fuck knows why, because these people had been in my life for all of five minutes in the grand scheme, and yet I knew I would mourn them greatly if they were not around. Sometimes it takes one second to click and know that these are your people, deserving of your love and loyalty.

The dragon queen smiled, a beautiful display of womanly strength and grace. There was no way to tell she was a dragon, outside of the ancient eyes, and powerful energy. "We will do this together. We are strong and worthy," she murmured, and the words seemed to resonate across the rocky patch we stood upon.

In a second, the ground cracked open, like Josephine had whispered the magic password to break the rocks. As we all dropped, I heard Jessa mutter, "Fuck. Not again…"

Then darkness closed around us, and I reached for my power to slow the fall, but it was wispy, slipping through my grasp.

Looked like there was no cheating here or circumventing the next step on this "path."

We all just had to hope we were worthy.

CHAPTER 22

We didn't fall for long, and when we landed, it was in a squishy substance. The darkness was the sort where it felt like no light would ever penetrate it, and since my magic was still beyond my reach, I remained in that dark hole, wondering what the fuck was around me.

I ran my hands over the ground, noting it was both soft and firm, with a velvety coating, like you'd find on the outside of a peach. "Jessa?" I called softly, not wanting to alert anyone to our presence, but also not hearing any sound of life around me.

No reply.

"Mischa? Josephina?" I'd reached a whisper yell.

No reply again.

True unease slithered through my body. It was strong and fast, and it almost crippled me with the need to get out of here, to run and run and run until I was no longer in this place that had creepy tendrils chasing down my spine.

I fought against my panic, refusing to let hormones and instincts scare me. I was stronger than this reaction.

Like I'd just issued a challenge to the universe, whatever was affecting my central nervous system kicked up some more fear. With it came the brief thought that I was being controlled.

It was too unnatural to be anything else, but what was I supposed to do to counter it? Should I wait until something happened and react from that? Or was it a better use of my time to move through the darkness and find my way out of here?

With my mind moving in frantic, jagged thoughts, it was so hard to think rationally.

Getting out of here was appealing, but I wouldn't leave without my friends.

Sucking up some bravery, fighting through the falsely induced panic, I shouted: "Jessa Lebron!" I was standing now, ready for the enemy to attack in the dark.

"Jess! Mischa! Josephina!" I called their names loudly, and then, like that's all the darkness had been waiting for, everything lit up.

Bright. Blinding. Scorching my eyes until they adjusted.

Blinking, I found myself standing on a path of pure gold. It glinted without a visible flaw, so shiny that I felt like I'd slide right off it if I took a step. The darkness still lingered on the edges, leaving the path clearly defined, but I'd never been one to just blindly follow the obvious route.

I took a second to really think about what I wanted to do. All of this was a test. Now that I was out of that dark, squishy-floored room, I sensed that part was designed to see how I'd react when my fear and anxiety were ramped up while alone and vulnerable. Apparently screaming loudly for my friends had been step one.

This golden path was another test, and for the life of me I couldn't figure out what I was supposed to do.

I took a step, bracing myself for the slide, but my foot landed firmly on the surface. Glancing down, a distorted view of my face reflected back at me, and even with the abstract nature of my reflection, I could see the tension lining my forehead.

Get it together, Maddison. I had to get it together or it'd be over before it began.

I took another step. And then another. The next step I moved right of the path, pushing the sphere of light across. The darkness receded further as I stepped to the right. Soon the lit path was so wide that it was closer to a field of gold. Joy lit up inside me, and with it came a push to take that beauty for myself. So much gold. I would be rich. Richer than anyone.

The gold is everything. The gold is strength. The gold is power.

It took me a minute to realise that was not my inner voice chanting those words at me. It felt so much like my own thoughts, and even when I shook my head to dislodge the voice, it would not abate.

No! I bit back, the same way I would have talked to Asher. *Gold is not everything. It's not even in the top ten things I love. STOP!*

The chanting continued, and my hands itched to reach down and touch the beautiful path. A path I now realized was no longer smooth but littered with gold bars. Large and small, up and down the surface, piled high in some places and almost flat in others.

No! I repeated, and I jerked my hands higher. *No one controls me. I don't need gold. I need answers. I need a way to save the world.*

The chanting stopped. The gold faded. The path turned to a dark gray rock and the gold bars became nothing more than stone.

All that glitters is not gold.

One final whisper of words and then the voice was gone.

The stone under my feet turned bright red, like it was filled with fire. I couldn't feel the heat but I knew it was hot. I also knew that if I moved from the one spot I stood on, I would burn.

Fucking hell.

Literal Hell, apparently.

I was already over these tests. My patience had faded to a mere sliver inside, and when I reached this point I was pretty much all "screw it." Without another worry about my death, I started to run. My brain winced at the first step, but I didn't let it deter me. It hurt though, and when a sizzling hit my ears, I actually cried out. I was wearing shoes, but it burned from the sole of my feet right up to my knees, like the bottom half of my legs were on fire.

Picking up the pace, I moved faster than ever, my entire focus on finding my friends and getting through this shit. The pain got worse and worse, each step more agonizing than the last, but I didn't stop. I'd been through pain before. And if I was honest, physical pain was much easier to handle than emotional pain. Heptashia would not best me. I would not let anyone best me again.

I had no way to measure the time that I ran for, but after what felt like hours, tears streaming down my face at the agony, I slowed. Was this how it would all end? Was this the test I couldn't pass?

My heart ached as a deep-seated disappointment pressed against my previous hope and determination. The pain was wearing me down.

The moment I stopped moving, the agony burning my body faded. The ground was still red, but there was no pain. And my feet and legs looked whole and healthy.

What in the actual…?

What did this even mean? Was I supposed to keep running? Or was this a test of intelligence and I was failing miserably by aimlessly moving and causing myself unnecessary pain. Standing here for the rest of my life didn't seem any smarter though.

Red land spread out as far as I could see, holding me hostage until I figured out how to pass its test.

My energy swirled inside of me, but it fizzled into nothing when I tried to use it.

I had to move again.

It was harder than I expected to take that first step. Knowing how bad the pain was going to be had my brain rebelling hard. But there was no other choice.

My foot lifted, and I closed my eyes, bracing myself, before I sprinted, hard and fast.

I'd never been burned alive of course, but in my head I imagined this was a similar feeling. My second attempt lasted less time than my first, as cries and sobs spilled from my lips.

Doubts followed soon after...

What if I was running in the wrong direction? Maybe I was supposed to run into the darkness behind us. I couldn't seem to get my head straight and make a decision.

The pain was breaking me down to a point where I wasn't even sure who I was anymore.

I stopped again.

My breaths wheezed in and out, harsh and almost deafening in this silent land. My face was cool as the tears streaked across it. I remained standing, though, with my shoulders back, and a core of steel.

"*You won't break me!*" I screamed. Fuck knows where that came from, because I was almost certain that whoever controlled this had already broken me. The force of those words came from deep inside, where they could not reach, where my bond with Asher lived, where my power and my ability to keep fighting to save the world existed.

Their fires would never touch that.

CHAPTER 23

I had just closed my eyes, searching for the mental fortitude to move again, when a lilting song filled the air. At first it was just the melody, low and powerful, sending a shiver across my skin. Words followed, and I recognized the lyrics … I knew this song. *The Sound of Silence*. What an ironic choice, since there had been nothing but silence until the music started. Not to mention they were singing about darkness and how it was their friend.

As the voice got louder, I realized who it was.

"Jessa!" I yelled.

I took off, following the sound of her voice. Before I could think twice about it, I was singing too, the familiar lyrics giving me a sense of home. A sense of purpose. Something to focus on through the pain…

Wait.

The pain was gone.

A quick glance down had me blinking at brilliantly green grass, in shades of khaki and gold.

Whoever the goddess controlling this path was, she was clearly a little insane.

But hey, weren't we all.

The singing grew louder, and it was definitely Jessa's voice. She had this beautiful rasp at the end of her words that was sexy and sassy at the same time. I'd recognize it anywhere.

I couldn't see her, but as the singing grew louder, I figured I was heading in the right direction. When the singer hit a particularly high note, a smile split across my face as I sang along. When the song ended, it didn't start again. The silence bothered me, and since Jessa might be looking for me too, I continued to sing.

I grew weak and tired as time went on—it had been hours—*days?*—since I'd rested or eaten. My mouth dry and parched, I'd have killed for some water, but I didn't stop running and singing. I couldn't stop until I got to the end of the path, until I made it into the underworld.

I had to be strong enough.

Out of nowhere, Jessa appeared in the distance, her face filled with terror as she sprinted toward me. My boots skidded to a halt, heart thundering in my chest. Where had she come from? And what was chasing her?

Jessa didn't strike me as the kind to fear anything, so this was most unnerving.

Not Jessa.

I blinked, mulling that idea over in my mind.

Maybe this wasn't her...?

The Jessa running toward me was close now, arms out like she was gonna throw them around me. I prepared myself to fight.

"Maddison!" fake Jessa trilled, voice trembling and ... empty. "I finally found you."

Yes, you did, pod person.

"Where have you been?" she asked, launching herself at me.

I didn't let my guard down for a second, even when she hugged me tightly and smelled exactly like Jessa. *Not her.*

"What were you running from?" I asked.

"Follow me," she said quickly, not answering my question.

I shook my head. "No, I think we should continue moving forward on this path."

Jessa tilted her head, examining me with those blue eyes that matched the real Jessa but were vacant in a way hers weren't. I sensed I wasn't supposed to know this about her—that her imitation usually fooled everyone.

I knew my friends better than that.

"Don't you trust me," Jessa said suddenly, her moods as variable as the landscape here.

As I opened my mouth to answer, a shimmer of light flashed across "Jessa's" body, and for a split-second I saw another being superimposed over her.

It was gone in the same heartbeat, but I'd definitely seen another female, unnatural in both her beauty and appearance. She'd had hair down past her feet, whiter than the purest snow I'd ever seen, spread out on the ground behind her. Her eyes had been huge and white too, cold and empty.

Was that … Heptashia?

"What are you?" I snarled, reaching out and wrapping my hands around her wrists. I was at a disadvantage here, not having any powers to access, but I was pissed off enough not to care. "And where is Jessa? If you've hurt her…"

There was a moment where our eyes remained locked—she was examining me on a deeper level. I knew it. I could feel her probing beneath the surface, searching…

I couldn't return the favor, but as uncomfortable as it made me, I didn't let go.

The Jessa facade flashed again, one more time, and then it melted away.

A luminescent woman, silvery white, stood before me. She smiled, teeth strangely more ivory than the rest of her body. "Follow me," she said, and she turned and walked away.

Another hard choice.

Was it a trap?

At this stage, it almost didn't matter. I was just ready for something else to happen, even if it meant I would end up fighting for my life.

So I followed.

Her hair trailed out in a long river of white, cutting through the green, like a train following behind her. It seemed to grow further as she walked and, eventually, I had to move to the side or I would have stepped on it.

She never looked back once.

I was tempted to reach out and yank on all of that glorious hair, mostly because she was irritating me. Bitch better start talking or we were gonna be straight-up playground style brawling.

"Hey!" I finally said when the walking had gone on longer than I could handle. "Where are you taking me?"

She didn't turn back, but she spoke: "You lasted far longer when you were burning."

My fingers itched, and I was reaching for her hair when she chuckled. I stumbled to a halt, blinking at the crazy chick.

"I can read your mind," she mused. "It's intriguing. You're full of thoughts and strengths."

At this point, I was almost certain she was the crazy goddess running this shit show. "You're Heptashia, aren't you?"

"I am," she said simply.

"Did I pass your tests?"

She stopped, finally turning back to face me. I hadn't moved since her laugh, and I wouldn't until she explained herself. I felt no power from her, just a cold emptiness.

The coldness scared me more than anything else I'd experienced so far.

"You have proven many things to me. That you care more for others than your own safety. You have a strong sense of right and wrong. You are determined. You are strong. You persisted through the pain." The slightest of pauses again. "Did you know that when you've experienced a debilitating pain, and then you have to experience it again, it's worse the second time. See, your brain already understands what will happen if you choose that pain again, and it's trying to save you from the agony. To do this, it will make you feel the pain even stronger, as a deterrent."

Her lips twitched. "Your brain did that, and still, you chose to step forward. You chose that pain again, no matter how strong it was. Very few make it past that part of the test. Even more important, you saw through the mask to the truth beneath. You knew your true friend and was never fooled by my ghosting her essence. Only those strong of mind can do this. In all ways, you passed my test..."

But...

I knew there was a but coming.

"But there is one final step on this path, and none can circumvent it. You must move through to be part of the whole."

What? No, seriously. What?

She started walking, and the green grass morphed to snow, her white hair no longer contrasting but blending in perfectly.

"Where are my friends?" I asked with a sigh, moving again, my boots crunching against the snow. "Are they okay?"

No reply.

"Does this world change at your whim, or at its own?"

This gave her a moment's pause.

Her eyes flickered to mine, the light depths almost translucent. There was actually a violet hue to them. "What an interesting question."

I could feel my face scrunching up. She was that irritating. "What an interesting answer," I replied.

Her tinkling laughter filled the air, and I felt a stupidly uncontrollable urge to join her in laughing. Maybe this bitch was part centaur.

Her laughter cut off, and for the first time she was looking at me like she really saw me. No vapid, cold, empty shell, instead a fire burned deep in her soul, and the color of her eyes morphed to a bright, almost blinding, purple.

"We could be friends," she stated. "I didn't think it was possible. But maybe many of the impossible things have just yet to meet you."

"We're forming a girl gang," I told her dryly, half kidding. "If you want more than one friend."

I mean, why the fuck not? The rest of us were our own brand of weird. This chick would probably fit right in.

She smiled. "I'll keep that in mind."

She started to walk again, and this time I followed silently.

Chapter 24

The snowy landscape started to scale up, like we were walking to the top of a cliff. It got steeper and steeper, but I never lost my balance, or had to reach forward and use my hands to steady myself. Just call me a mountain goat, or whatever those little furry things on the side of the cliff were.

As we elevated, I hoped to gain some perspective over this land … to truly see what was out there. But that persistent veil of darkness never lifted, not from above or below.

Whatever this place was, it hid its secrets well. Or it hid hers.

Heptashia didn't falter in her trek up the mountain either, and again she never looked back for me. Just when I thought there was no way we could continue to climb, considering we were almost vertical now, it leveled out, and we ended up on a plateau above the clouds.

Yeah, there were clouds now, because this land was fucking insane.

"Here is your final judgement," she said, no smile, no inflection, just a wave of her hand as the clouds drifted away to reveal a giant scale.

"Now this is more what I expected," I said, stepping forward to examine it closely. The scale was golden, shiny like the path I'd walked along earlier, and shot through with white writing. The script wasn't in English, and my brain didn't automatically translate it for me, so I had no idea what it said.

It fit my knowledge of scales, with two sides balanced over a middle stand. One side was empty, nothing more than a flat space. The other side was filled with a swirling … magic, maybe. It was hard to know exactly what it was, with no corporeal part to the mass.

"This judges your future," the woman said.

I hadn't forgotten she was there, but I also hadn't heard her move so close to me. Schooling my face to hide my surprise, I turned minutely. "My future? How can I be judged for things I haven't done yet?"

Her eyes widened like she was shocked. "Easily, of course. Your path is pre-ordained. Your future actions are already in motion, even if they haven't yet come to pass. And right now, if this scale determines that you are beyond saving, you will forfeit your life and walk forever in this land of nothing."

Well, with that recommendation…

"And if I refuse to step on the scale?"

The model-perfect bone structure of her face started to change, morphing into something that no longer resembled the silvery woman. There was a new snake-like quality to her now, dark lines marking her cheeks, eyes larger, and pupils diamond shaped.

"Best not to find out," she hissed, and I swallowed roughly, because … dude. What the hell was that?

"Fuck it," I muttered. The fact that I was more than over this bullshit propelled me forward.

I stepped on the scale.

The moment my feet were flat on the gold surface, energy locked my body in place. Old fears resurfaced, and I forced myself to bring up an image of Asher. The best calming tonic I had. Asher was my peace … my sanctuary.

The magic on the other side of the scale started to swirl harder and brighter; white light bisected through the midnight energy. The woman watched it all without any inflection on her face, so I had no idea if it was going well or not. None of it actually affected her, and she didn't care either way, but it would have been nice to know if I was failing miserably.

Red lights split the white, and then they turned black. My pulse started to pound until I could feel it in my throat. Was I evil as hell in the future, because that was a ton of black…

The woman walked forward. "I'm sorry," she said, her gaze locked on my face. "I would have enjoyed being part of your girl gang."

"What?" I snapped, not sure what was happening. My arms and legs moved again—I was completely free from the energy holding me on the scale.

That was the only good news.

The scale started to shake under me, my body rattling along. Trying to get free, I flailed and lurched forward, but the gap that was my exit continued to shrink smaller and smaller until I was surrounded by gold. "Let me out!" I screamed, but there was no reply, and from the tiny gap still available to me, there was no visible sign of the goddess.

I'd definitely failed this part of the test. A scary thought when it was something to do with my future, but I'd have to worry about that later. Right now there were much more pressing concerns. Like the fact I was trapped on the side of a godsdamned scale. Or that I was going to walk this crazy fucking world forever if I didn't get myself out of here.

My energy swirled, as it had been since I arrived here, stuck, not able to be accessed. That wasn't going to work for me any longer though, and I reached for it, yanking as hard as I could. Like when I'd gone up against Sonaris, I needed to free myself from any worries or blocks that held my power back.

This was my one and only chance; the last sliver of space between the bars on my cage was almost gone. I sensed that when it disappeared, I would be trapped as she'd predicted.

The world would fall to the gods. Millions would die.

Everyone was relying on me, and even though I wanted to curl up in a tiny pathetic ball and cry, I found some fucking strength, deep inside, and slammed my hands against the bars.

"I'm a god!" I screamed. "You will never contain me."

The energy swelled. It pulsed and fought its containment.

"You have no control over me." The guttural words didn't even sound like me. "You. Do. Not. Control. Me!"

A physical fissuring started inside of me, and Heptashia's block on my power detonated in a blast of white dust blowing out the side of the golden cage, splintering it like it was nothing more than a dandelion misting into the breeze.

As I rose up into the air, water swirled around me, refilling my strength and sanity. Being without my power was like being without the sun. At first you thought it was okay, not noticing as you grew weaker and depressed. Eventually I would have died, cut off from my energy in that way. I needed it to not just survive but to blossom.

Asher's presence slammed into my mind and I soaked up his energy, my soul literally screaming as it was reunited with its other half.

Maddison?

His voice sounded like thunder in my head.

Asher, I choked out through our mental link. *Asher. Fuck. I missed you so much.*

There was nothing but silence, deadly, echoing silence. I knew he was still there, but it was beyond his ability to speak.

Are you okay? I pushed.

Another second of heavy silence.

No. Where are you?

He was barely holding it together. The words were strangled, like they were being forced out, and since this was mental speak, that told me about the state of his mind.

I took a back entrance to the underworld. An entrance, I think, that will bring us to the Hellbringers and give us a chance to take the gods out.

Thunder echoed around me, and when lightning struck the ground, I looked around, wondering if Asher was close by. Josephina had said that there was a chance of opening a path for them ... had I managed to do that?

Maddison.

He drew my attention back to him.

I'm coming for you.

The feelings inside of me...

I'd never felt anything with this much intensity. It was almost too much for me to deal with. I lowered myself to the ground, trying to find an equilibrium.

Tell me what happened.

He sounded closer; my heart was hammering hard enough that it hurt my chest.

I quickly told him the condensed version of everything since I was stolen away by Josephina.

How I'd failed the final test.

I broke free from her cage. No one can hold a god. I just had to finally admit that's who I am. This is who I am now. I shuddered, arms wrapping around myself. *I have no idea what they saw in my future, Ash, but it must have been bad.*

My power wrapped around me like a protective blanket, and I closed my eyes at how soothing it felt. Asher didn't say anything, but he was moving closer.

His energy raged. A stormy sea filled with whirlpools, riptides, and debris.

I'm on my way.

This path is only for females, I reminded him.

His chuckle was low, dark, and rumbly, sending chills down my spine. *Not any longer.*

Before I could ask him to explain that, I felt a tugging on my power, and then in a flash there were three very large men standing around me. Two I knew well: Asher and Braxton.

The third was a vampire ... uh, vampire with dragon energy? I had no idea what that was all about, but I could see a definite family resemblance to Braxton, so I was going with another quad.

Mischa's mate no doubt, judging by the fury on his face. I mean, all three wore faces of men who'd had their mates abruptly stolen from them.

Scary, scary men.

Before another thought could cross my mind, strong, hard arms were hauling me into his body. Our bond sent a pulse through us both, and some of the chaos inside settled. The gold of Asher's magic burst around us, and more storms rocked across the land. Before I could figure out what that meant, or how it was possible, all of my attention was on my golden god.

Asher held me with a desperation I'd never felt from him. "Fuck," he growled, voice hoarse. "Don't ever do that to me again. Ever. I almost destroyed the Academy."

"He almost destroyed the world," Braxton bit out, sounding far less relaxed than normal. His eyes were also very yellow, and since it was bad news when Asher's changed color, I figured it was the same for this dude.

"Where are Jessa and Mischa?" Braxton asked. "And where the fuck are we?"

Beside him, the vampire's chest rumbled, his eyes as black as the world around us. These two, both powerful, tall, beautiful ... they reminded me of Asher. Those blessed in life with more than just stunning looks, but immense power. They were not used to being scared, to being out of control—this situation had them on the edge of completely losing it.

My heart ached at the pain we had caused our mates … unintentionally, of course, but it had happened.

"They were totally fine the last time I saw them," I said softly, still cradled in Asher's arms. I made no move to separate us, needing this closeness as much as he did. Our bond was practically purring. "When the trials started, all of us were separated. I have no idea where they are. I'm guessing somewhere in this darkness. The goddess called it the land of nothing, but it's a weird adaptable landscape, and … maybe there's a chance we can bend it to our will…"

It was a random thought, but I'd never seen anything like this world. It was almost fluid in its structure.

"This land responds to Heptashia's magic," I mused. "Maybe we can tap into it and get it to guide us to the others."

Another figure appeared then, stepping through the shadows, and I tensed, expecting the goddess.

It wasn't her. It was another dragon.

"Rayge!" I shouted, surprised by how happy I was to see him.

I wiggled to get down, but Asher growled and pulled me close. Titling my head back, I was about to remind him that I was not a possession. When our eyes clashed, though, I swallowed down my argument. "You're keeping my power in check," he murmured, his voice a blast across my senses. "I can't let you go."

I wrapped myself tightly around him. "You never have to," I whispered. "I love you more than anything, and I don't care what that stupid scale says. If you're in my future, it's bright. I might not be perfect, but together we will keep each other in check. I have to believe that."

He was already tense, his muscles hard and unyielding, but somehow his body went even tenser. There was no time to explain though, because Rayge had reached our circle.

"Where the fuck did you go?" Braxton snapped.

Rayge just shook his head, addressing me instead. "Maddison, I'm glad you're okay." I got an actual smile, which I returned. Asher's eyes were drilling into the dragon shifter, but he didn't say a thing. We didn't have time for any of their alpha bullshit, so I was grateful.

"I scouted around," Rayge continued. "There's a veil just to the south. It's a magical barrier, but I'm pretty sure that between the five of us we can break through no problem."

A veil. I hadn't seen anything like that, but she'd kept this land deliberately mysterious for those in the trials. Even now, as we stood atop "judgement-mountain," I could only see darkness.

"She hid the land," I told him, exhaustion hitting me. I rested my head against Asher's cheek, enjoying the feeling of his skin on mine.

"It's a large piece of land built by magic," Rayge said. "I'd describe it as an oval shape, with some pointed offshoots at the southern end. It's strongly coated in magic."

"It protects the entrance to the underworld," Maximus finally spoke up. "Our mates are either still in the trials of this land, or they've crossed through the veil."

"One way to find out," Braxton roared, and seconds later he was no longer in human skin. A very large, very intimidating dragon stood before us. Braxton was massive, his scales dark and shiny. I couldn't tear my eyes away, trying to figure out how it was possible that a human could turn into a creature as gigantic as this. I mean, sure, Braxton was a big guy, but nothing on his dragon.

My brain attempted to explode at the insanity—the fact that I was a god and this still freaked me out was bizarre—but before I could have my mental breakdown, two more dragons stood in front of us. I barely got a glimpse of them before they took off into the air. I did have time to note that Rayge, a bronze beast, might have been even larger than Braxton.

Asher gently set me on my feet, a deep breath lifting his chest under my hands. "Fuck, Maddi," he said, closing his eyes briefly, like he was still fighting for control.

"You're covered in gold," I murmured, leaning up to kiss him. "It's kind of hot, but it's also scary. Josephina said that the original magic is addictive, and you shouldn't use it too much."

He shook his head. "This is who I am now, love. I have no other magic to access. And I feel no addiction to it."

He meant what he said, I could feel it through our bond. Since there were three bazillion more pressing concerns on my radar, I let it go for now.

Asher lifted me higher, capturing my mouth in a brutal, possessive, scorchingly hot kiss. "Wait until this is all over and I finally get you alone," he warned against my mouth, and it probably spoke of how fucked up I was that I couldn't wait to find out what that meant.

Reluctantly, Asher used his magic to pull us into the air, his hand firmly wrapped around mine. We followed the dragons into the darkness. Like before, wherever we moved, the mist of this land faded and we could see more, but then it closed in behind us again.

I hoped Rayge knew what he was talking about, because I had no idea how he'd managed to see anything.

"You have to look with your power, not just your eyes," Asher said, picking up on my thoughts. "Look beyond the obvious."

I wrinkled my nose at him. "Now you just sound like Heptashia, and since she's legit one hundred percent crazy, that's not a compliment."

His lips twitched, and for the first time since he'd stormed up to me, there was a sliver of green back in his eyes.

The gold was growing on me, but green would always be my favorite.

Chapter 25

Despite the speed of the dragons, we caught up to them quickly. I wasn't sure when it happened—probably after Sonaris—but Asher was stronger than ever. He carried both of us with ease; no strain showed on his face or in our bond.

"I can see the veil," he said, looking ahead.

I'd been too busy watching Asher to try that "looking with my power" thing, and to be honest, I really didn't need to. I trusted Asher. I would let myself lean on him this one time.

He shifted to look my way, eyes lit up with emotions that were both dark and light. A contradiction. A perfect mystery, as always.

We're a team, Maddison James. His voice was strong. I will always be whatever you need. If you need strength in your arms, I will lift for you. If your legs can't walk any further, I will carry you. If your heart grows weary, I will find hope in mine. And if your mind is tired, I will take some of your burden. That's how partners and teams work. We all carry life's heaviness at times, you more than any other, but when you have a team, you know you'll never have to carry it alone.

Fuck.

Fucking fuck.

He destroyed me.

Fire burned through my chest and into my soul. The pain and worry and anxiety from being in this land faded, almost like Asher had taken some of it, just as he said he would. The surging in my chest was strong and brutal, like a wave crashing against unforgiving rocks, the strength of my emotions destructive, but also a perfect display of nature.

I spoke from my heart, as he had done: *I love you more than I thought it was possible to ever love. You are the team I dreamed and hoped for. The family I prayed to the gods for. I will never take you for granted, and I will always ease your burdens as well. I will be enough for you.*

He wrapped his arms so tightly around me that I couldn't breathe, and it was perfect.

You are beyond enough, Maddison. You're a fucking gift, and I will never let you go.

A small part of me feared this type of fatalistic conversation. Usually they preceded us both dying in a fiery catastrophe, and considering where we were going, and the unknown we were facing, my fears were not unfounded.

I didn't regret it though. Asher had my chest burning in the best way, and this moment was worth any temptation for the Fates to destroy us.

When we finally reached the veil, even with my shitty non-power eyes, I could see it clearly. An unbroken curtain of darkness that couldn't be moved or penetrated—demonstrated by Rayge as he pushed against it.

"How do we get through?" I asked.

Asher and Braxton had some sort of silent conversation, before the huge dragon flapped a few times and turned back to the sheet of nightmares.

"He's going to see if it's immune to dragonfire," Asher said quickly, "since it's able to cut through most magic."

He moved us further away, and we both watched as a blast of flame scorched the air across the dark sheet. The other two dragons joined him, and I shook my head at the intense blue-black flame.

"Remind me not to piss off a dragon," I murmured, and Asher shot me a slow smile.

"You could take on a dragon any day, and if you want my opinion, you should start with Rayge."

I narrowed my eyes at him. "What's your issue with Rayge? Seriously. It's time to finally tell me."

Asher sucked in a deep breath, his gaze conflicted. Through our bond I could tell he was sorting out his thoughts, so I didn't pry further. "Our parents were friends," he started in a low voice. "Rayge and I didn't know each other that well, he was already much older when our families would catch up, and was never really around." He sucked in another lungful of air, anger spilling into his next words. "The first time I really saw him, he was on trial for killing his parents. I went because mine weren't alive to be there, and I felt like they would have wanted to go. Rayge sat in that room, and his expression never changed once, and whenever I went near him, my fucking hair stood on end. There was something in his gaze, Maddison … he's dangerous." His eyes left mine to rest on the bronze dragon.

"He killed his parents," I breathed, turning my head to see Rayge as well. "Did he go to prison?"

Asher shook his head. "No. He was found guilty of killing them but wasn't punished. To this day, I have no idea what happened between him and his family, and the fact that he wasn't sent to a supernatural prison should be enough to ease my worries … but my initial assessment hasn't changed. He is dangerous. Just … maybe not to you."

Rayge shifted his head, dragon fire cutting off as he met my gaze. No doubt with his supernatural senses, he'd heard everything.

"He's not dangerous to me," I said to Asher. "I'm pretty good at judging someone's nature, and that's not a supe you have to worry about turning on you. If you deserve his trust and loyalty, you have it for life."

Rayge's eyes were shadowed as he nodded. Before I could say anything else, he'd turned back to the veil, dragon fire once again spewing from his jaws.

Asher watched us both. "I will trust you on this. No doubt my past clouded my judgement of him."

Asher lost his family. He believed they'd been murdered, and no information ever came out about it. Someone choosing to kill their parents was probably a decent trigger for him.

"The dragon-fire isn't working," Asher snarled, startling me from my thoughts.

He moved us closer, a blast of heat blowing my hair back and giving my cheeks a stretched, stiff feeling. "We need to help them," I decided. "My energy is back in my control again ... I'm willing to throw it at the veil."

Asher moved us further along, so we weren't at risk of being burned, and I reached out to touch the sheet of darkness. "The fire was breaking the bonds, just not fast enough," I noted. "At least we know it can be parted, all we need is to find the right power to do it."

Asher reached out as well, and when my hand finally landed on the dark sheet, I expected it to feel how it looked, like a thick, heavy, curtain. Instead my hand went right through to the other side, and I lurched forward with it.

"Maddison!" Asher cursed, reaching out to grab me, both of us tumbling through.

The other side was nothing like the side of darkness and mystery.

Crystal clear blue skies, clean air that smelled like sunshine and flora, and a creek casually cutting through the green grass below. An animal chirped near my ear, and I thought it was a little bird until I turned my no doubt astonished eyes on a tiny fluttering ... fairy. I mean, that's what it resembled. Like Mab crossed with a lightbulb, shining brightly.

The chirping formed into words. "Welcome to Heptashia's underworld. Please, do not panic. You may have left your previous life behind, but here you will be safe and content and happy for the rest of your eternity. You will find your family and loved ones here, including all of your pets. You will find your greatest heart's desires. Please follow me."

Turning to Asher, my words died on my tongue. *What...?*

The look on his face ... dread and pain.

"Ash?" I said softly.

He snapped out of it, shaking his head before turning to me. "Nice place they've got here," he said, trying—and failing—to sound casual. "Welcome committee isn't bad either."

Reaching out, I rested my hand on his arm. "Are you wondering if your family is here?"

I could think of no other explanation for that expression he'd worn.

"Yes," he said without hesitation. "I should not see them though. There's a reason that we don't cross here until we die. A very important reason. We must wait until our time is done, but it's just so…"

"Tempting."

And it really was. A land where you would be safe and protected. None of the fear and pain and loss we'd had on Earth. Fuck…

"Why doesn't everyone want to die?" It was a horrible, morbid thought, especially considering a lot of people did want to die, and actively chose it to end their pain and suffering.

Asher took his time in answering. Not a surprise considering the context of my question. I mean, it was one of those very deep, possibly painful introspective questions. Getting to the true nature of life and death.

"I think … that our time on Earth is filled with so much more than this land holds. New experiences; true, strong love; emotions that take your breath away; and yes, fear and worry and sorrow. But if we didn't have the lows, would we truly feel the highs?"

Unease slithered through my chest, replacing an iota of the peace I was feeling. I mulled his words over. "Yes, you might be right. Everything here is peaceful, but it's also the same, forever. It's a nice retirement, but we're too young for that now."

Asher pressed his lips to mine. A brief, perfect kiss. "Exactly. Here there are no babies. No new life. No change. As you said, this is the perfect retirement for souls to be at peace. We're not ready for that yet, but it helps to know it's there."

It did help. My heart was just a tiny bit lighter than it had been before I stepped into this world. A sliver of hope and light was sometimes all anyone needed. Unfortunately, the real world still awaited us … and it still needed saving.

Turning back to the veil, I reached forward, parting it with my hands, like a waterfall broken by a rocky ledge. On the other side, a dragon head appeared. Braxton was waiting right where we'd disappeared.

He pushed through my gap, having no issue making it to the sunny side. They'd just needed someone to make the first part.

"I can't break through it," Asher said, trying again. "It's not an Atlantean power that allowed you entry."

"Draconis," I said drily. "My parents might be crazy, power hungry bastards, but at least they left me with some wickedly useful skills."

Asher's chest rumbled. "Heptashia shouldn't have had power over you in those fucking trials."

I shrugged. "When I first arrived here, my power was locked down by that land of nothing. I'm assuming that's standard practice. If I'd tried even a small amount, I would have broken the lock long ago. I played the game like a sucker."

He nodded. "Your father's energy is probably the reason you could open a path for us as well. This land should respond to you, if you can just figure out how to tap into it."

Braxton, back in human form, dressed head to toe in black, heard the end of our conversation. "How is Draconis locked away in the underworld, if technically he's the god of it?"

"Sonaris trapped them," I said with a shrug. "To be honest, I never asked him how he managed that, but whatever he did, it kept them there for a few months."

Asher shook his head. "If they didn't have Draconis with them, they would have been locked in there for an eternity. None, except maybe the Mother of All and the god of the underworld, can manipulate the power of the underworld. It stands alone. Draconis is how they got out so quickly."

The other two dragons approached us, both back in their human form. Rayge was pulling a shirt over his head and I wondered if he was the one to magic them their clothing. Seriously, dragons were as ripped as Atlanteans. But I wasn't tempted—I barely gave them more than a glance—Asher fucking eclipsed all other dudes.

But ... I still had to glance, right?

I'd go with Axl and call that one research.

Strong hands wrapped around me, throwing me up and over a broad shoulder. "I should smack your damn ass, Maddison James," Asher grumbled, and I snorted, threading my fingers through his hair, mostly because I liked doing it.

"Have some respect. We're in the ... afterlife."

Asher shook me gently, before he walked us over to the other guys. None of them blinked an eye to see me up on his shoulder, but I felt uncomfortable. Wanting to stand on my own feet, I wiggled to get down.

Braxton's face was grim, his eyes sad pools of blue. "Jessa got used to being carried around," he murmured. "It still pissed her off at times." The pain on his features was the sort that crumbled lesser people. "We're men who love our women, and we have dumb fucking ways of showing it."

"We'll find them," I said, solemnly. "Nothing is going to take your mates down. They're strong."

"You're strong and you still failed the test," Maximus said, the rumble in his voice matching the black pitch of his eyes.

I shook my head. "The last part of the test judges your future actions. Apparently future-Maddi is planning on doing something really bad. Pretty sure it's to do with my fight against the gods, and whatever happens, I'm a risk to the world." I wasn't a moron, I knew that controlling the Hellbringers might destroy me or the world, but it was literally our only option.

"Can any of you feel a stronger connection to your mates?" Asher asked, abruptly changing the subject. In his thoughts, he was pissed that anyone might consider me a threat. He really didn't have to worry. None of them seemed to care. This wasn't their first rodeo.

"I can feel her," Braxton said quickly, "but our communication channels are still closed. She's alive, at least, and that's just enough for my beast to remain calm."

"Mischa is alive," Maximus confirmed.

Rayge lifted his head, eyes flashing to a dark gold. "I can sense Josephina. We're not mates or bonded in that way, but we have a different connection ... a magically created life-debt that allows me to feel her. She's also alive."

As confident as I had been that they were okay, it made me feel a lot better to have it confirmed.

"Would you please follow me…" The light fairy was back, trying to usher us along. She never flinched or questioned our presence here, remaining calm and glowing. "You need to go through processing. Then your eternity awaits you."

Lucky it was the fairy and not Heptashia who was the welcoming committee. That goddess would definitely give the underworld a bit of a reputation.

Gates of Hell, anyone?

CHAPTER 26

"Let's follow her," I suggested, not sure what else to do. "Maybe Jessa and the others had to go through processing and we'll find them there."

No one argued, and since the light fairy was still waving us on, like a tiny automated robot attendant, we walked in the direction she was frantically indicating. Nothing changed as we moved; the light breeze stayed the same, the sweet smell in the air was consistent, and the sprinkle of warmth bathing our faces never faded. It was nice, but unnatural. Especially compared to the Academy, where the weather was changeable within seconds. Maybe I liked that more than I thought, the unpredictability. The longer I stayed here, the more I wanted to leave and return to my real life.

The light fairy disappeared as soon as we followed her instructions.

We continued along the stream until we reached a large open lagoon, surrounded by wildflowers. There didn't appear to be trees or shrubbery here, just grass and bunches of flowers, ranging from the starkest white I'd ever seen, to pinks and purples and yellows. The colors were vibrant and eye catching, and the sweet scent had to be coming from them because it was slightly more potent here.

We stopped at the edge of the water, because there was no more path to walk. "What now, little light fairy?" I asked, looking around for her.

She didn't reappear.

"Light fairy, that's highly appropriate," Rayge said. "They're called the *linuettes*, which means lighted guide. They exist only in the underworld. They guide the dead to their final resting place."

Creepy. Very creepy.

"Do you think it's because we're not dead that we're just standing here staring at the water? Because this doesn't seem like much of a processing … uh, process."

Yeah, okay, I was a tad impatient at times.

Rayge took a step toward me, hand lifting like he was going to touch me, but a rumble from Asher's chest stayed his hand. My possessive Atlantean was in fine form today, but I felt the same way about him. The world kept tearing us apart, and we were frankly done with it.

"We're still standing here because our transport hasn't arrived yet," Rayge said. The tension between Asher and him faded as fast as it had appeared.

We were all adults here, and Rayge respected Asher's claim as my mate. He was also too old to give a single fuck about dick measuring. Not that Asher was doing that, but Rayge could have chosen to respond like he had.

He was apparently secure in his supernatural skills. It was one of the things I liked most about him. The other was his ability to drink me under the table.

This was all forgotten as the water started to ripple before us. I wasn't sure what I was expecting for transport. Since we were standing on the edge of a waterway, probably a boat of some sort, captained by the ferryman. Okay, I might have been delving a little deep into another mythology. I knew very little about the supernatural and Atlantean "death" process.

No boat arrived. The water rippled, waves increasing in an outward flow, until there was a single path through the lagoon. Grass lined this path, despite it having just been under water.

Okay, then. I'd just keep reminding myself that normal rules didn't apply here. Saved my brain from fracturing under all the weird.

Braxton stepped out first; his mate was missing, and he was done waiting. I really couldn't blame him. I was next, then Asher, Maximus, and Rayge last. The path was wide enough for one person only.

"We should have flown over," Rayge said, looking around. There was nothing to see as the path took a downward trajectory. Not a single living creature was visible in the clear blue water around us.

"I don't think over would have worked," I breathed, noticing how dark and high above our heads the water was getting, like we were literally walking to the bottom of this waterway. "Looks like we're going into the depths."

Silence remained our constant companion. It was only that I was so accustomed to the sounds of the ocean and the birds and the air that I truly noticed the lack of it here. When we'd been walking for some time, the water surrounding us—which was now too high for me to even see the top of—started to ripple. It was the first change since we started, and I braced myself for what might happen next. If this amount of water crashed onto us, we would be crushed.

All of us stopped. Asher's face beside mine was tense. My power churned, teasing across my fingertips as I readied myself to use it. The ripples in the lagoon grew stronger, and I blinked as water spiraled out of the wall beside us, swinging arcs of color and pattern. It was not clear, as one would expect water to be when separated like that. The strings were teal and purple and red, and as each wound around and through us, I felt them sliding across my skin and down my arms. The water left just as fast, and I looked down to find a teal mark—a perfect match to my hair color—twined across my arm.

Like a water tattoo.

It was not the same as an Atlantean tattoo, this one slightly elevated above the skin. Rubbing a hand across it didn't move it though.

Asher got the same aqua mark, but the dragon shifter brothers had red swirls across their thick forearms. Rayge's was a dark navy color, the most intricate mark of all, spanning almost his entire right arm.

"What does this mean?" I whispered, as the remaining water fell away and we were back to standing in the middle of the never-ending lagoon.

"We were processed as we walked," Asher guessed, "and now we have been placed into … categories of some sort."

Asher and me. Braxton and Maximus. And Rayge was on his own.

"Don't let them separate us," Rayge said, pushing in closer.

We didn't have much of a choice in the matter though. No one can truly fight nature.

Not when she's ready to take you.

CHAPTER 27

Darkness crashed into us at the same time as the water. It didn't squish me flat like I expected. A ball of aqua wrapped around me and Asher and we were jetted off through the side of the path, out into whatever lay beyond.

I heard the angry roars of the dragons, before each of them disappeared in their own ball of water, colored to match their marks.

"The colors have to refer to sections of this land," I said to Asher, holding on to him as the world flashed past. Everything was dark outside our bubble as we zipped through the underworld. We could have broken free if we wanted, no doubt, but I decided to play this out. See where we ended up.

"I'm guessing it separated us by race and power," Asher said, eyes tight. "They kept us together because of our energy. Brax and Maximus for the same reason. And Rayge, he's not one easily classified, and I'm guessing that wherever he's going, it's probably a place that very few venture."

This was all great, except we were losing track of the reason for being down here.

"I need to get to the Hellbringers," I reminded Asher. "Those guys will find their mates, I'm sure. Their determination was spectacularly obvious. So, for now, let's not worry about them. We have a job to do, Asher Locke. We cannot let the gods destroy the world."

The golden glow of his magic hit me in the face. "Why does it always have to be you?" he growled. "Every single fucking time we deal with this shit, you're the one who has to step up and take the hit."

I laced my fingers with his, and we moved toward each other, as much as we could in this bullet of a bubble. "It's not *always* me. It was you once, and then it was Axl. I have been hovering in the background *not* doing all the things I should be. We've run out of time. I can't procrastinate any longer. I have to step up and do what I was born to do."

"All of us, Maddison. All of us can control the Hellbringers."

I wanted so badly to keep Asher and Connor out of it. Asher because I loved him, and would not risk him, and Connor because I didn't trust him. There was no lie in what Asher said though.

"Yeah, and there's a lingering worry inside of me, because everyone kept harping on about how we have to work together. I wonder if we will fail once more because we didn't force a true and strong bond with Connor."

I admitted it out loud, because he was already hearing it in my thoughts. I breathed out my frustration. "Connor should be here."

Our bubble was starting to slow, more light filtering through the water around us.

Asher spoke quickly, since we appeared to have reached our destination. "Let's just take it all one step at a time. Firstly, we'll find out where we are. Secondly, find out how to reach the Hellbringers. And thirdly, figure out if it will require all three of us to control them. Connor lost our trust. This is on him, not you, and I find it hard to believe that we need him to take out the gods. We've done everything without him so far, and we're all much stronger since Sonaris. We can do this."

I nodded, desperately hoping he was right.

The bubble was all but stopped, and for the first time the water filled with an abundance of light and sea creatures. Creatures I could see through as they moved…

"Souls," Asher said. "These are the souls of animals."

I swallowed hard. "How … how many animals have died through the years? It must be billions and billions. Surely they couldn't all be here?"

Asher looked around, taking in as much as he could. "It won't work the same way as when they're alive. They're not fighting for space or food or territory here, they're just existing. Here, everything fits and works. This is not the physical plane you're used to, this is the spiritual plane."

"Would all the dogs, cats, birds … all the pets be here somewhere?" The light fairy had said they were, but I hadn't really paid attention to her then. Seeing the animals was … a lot.

Asher nodded. "Could there be a peaceful afterlife without our most loyal companions?"

"Absolutely not," I said with resolve, thinking about the few animals I'd loved in my life. A small mangy dog I'd fed from my own meagre portions.

Tom. He'd been brown and white, his fur matted, and one leg damaged so he always limped. He'd been my only friend for three years, but then, one day ... he just stopped coming around.

I'd cried for weeks, because I'd never known such unconditional love. I'd never known any love. But Tom, he got me through more than one tough day.

Then there was a tortoiseshell cat that arrived in my life a few years later. Mystique. She was not as friendly as Tom, or as cuddly, but she was loyal. She always came back to me. Until she didn't.

It was a harsh world, and I figured that both died on the very streets they lived. They'd been gifts wrapped in matted fur, giving me so much love and joy.

Knowing they might be here somewhere had my heart hurting and soaring in unison. A small glimpse of what Asher might have been feeling before.

Our bubble rose to the surface, blue water around us and aquamarine skies above. More lands came into view as we were released onto a small island. There were lots of islands scattered about, and *so much water*. It spanned as far as the eye could see; everything looked like a beach paradise.

"How is it that they haven't noticed we're alive?" I asked, looking around. There wasn't another "soul" in sight.

"*Because this land sees only your energy ... your soul.*"

The disembodied voice came from somewhere above us, like a narrator to our story.

"*The vessel is not important. It is all that dies. The soul ... lives forever.*"

The voice faded and I blinked at Asher.

"Ask it another question," he suggested, looking around. He was tense, but no one would know that unless they were in our mate bond. His face was calm and confident.

"Where are all the other souls that are part of this land?"

The energy returned. *"They are here. This specific island is yours for the rest of your peaceful afterlife, but if you seek the energy of others, please, step off your land and you will be rewarded."*

This was just getting weird, and we didn't have time to indulge no "voice in the sky," but I also couldn't stop from wondering who else would be here in this land.

"We should step off," I decided.

Asher looked at me a like I might have fallen and hit my head too hard, but he didn't argue. He was learning to trust my instincts, just as I was, and right now my power was urging me to find the others. He stayed close, watching my back, as we walked to the edge of the island. The water looked so damn inviting, but I ignored the call.

"Our afterlife narrator said to step off," I said with a shrug, and I did just that.

My foot remained steady on top of the water, like it was solid ground. "Can I not enter the water?"

A small surge of energy and the voice was back. *"You can if you want to. We know your wants. We respond to them."*

"This narrator is pretty useful," Asher remarked in a dry tone. "I mean, who wouldn't want an all-knowing Google in the sky."

I thought up the millions of questions I'd want answered, wishing there was time to voice them all. Stepping again, we all but glided across the surface of the water, moving to the next island. The second I tried to enter it, though, a gentle force repelled me back.

Underworld Google was back. "*You cannot enter private property without permission. Please have the inhabitants add you to their accepted list. Otherwise, please make your way to the central meeting place for interaction.*"

The central meeting place.

"That's what we need," I murmured. "A meeting place."

The water lit up beneath my feet, a glowing path that dotted its way in the opposite direction of this island. "Looks like it wants us to follow," Asher noted, both of us staring at the golden glow.

Original magic was everywhere, even here apparently.

We wasted no time, hurrying across the path. The faster we moved, the faster the scenery blurred around us, like we were traveling at warp speed. There were countless islands, and way more off in the distance. "True mates must share an island," I noted, and Asher went predatorially still at my side. I slowed a little, turning to see his face better. "What's wrong?" I looked around, because generally that reaction meant danger was close.

"The thought of our deaths…" His hands clenched. "I'm not dealing so well after losing you in our bond."

I understood more than I wished I did. "Yeah, I feel the same. But at least we know that when we both die, we'll be together."

His chest rumbled, jaw working as he fought for words. "I have no real response to that, other than … let's not test the theory anytime soon."

Reaching up, I cupped his face in my hand, holding the dearest thing in my life. "That's fine by me, Ash. I have too much living to do with you."

He kissed me, fast and hard, because that's all we had time for, but my body responded anyway. One day we wouldn't be rushing sex and quality time together in lieu of saving the fucking world. One day. I had to believe we'd earned that much at least.

Since it wasn't today, though, we set off again at that running pace, following the path that never wavered. The central island came into view about twenty minutes later and I blinked at how fucking huge it was. The largest island I'd ever seen, on television or in real life.

The moment we stepped onto the sand, the yellow path faded, and with a pop, like a bubble bursting, sound slammed into us hard and fast. It was overwhelming after so much silence.

"Guess we should explore this meeting place," Asher suggested, taking my hand. Urgency hit me deep inside, spurring my steps on. Asher was feeling it too, the sensation intensifying in our bond.

Whatever we were about to find ... there was a chance it could change our lives.

CHAPTER 28

The noise level didn't grow louder as we moved closer. This land didn't work on the same principles as the living realm. The noise remained consistent, but we still knew where to go.

Asher shook his head. "My energy is uneasy with how unnatural it feels here. Normally, if things were this easy, we'd be two fucking steps from an ambush. The underworld is messing with my senses."

"Right?" I shook my head. "It's freaking me out. I'm hoping in death this seems much more normal."

He didn't have time to chastise me over my morbid obsession with our deaths—come on, when does anyone ever have the chance to experience the afterlife before they die? To know that there was this kind of paradise waiting on the other side for us? It was a lot for anyone to process.

Asher grumbled but kept his thoughts to himself, and I didn't pry into his mind.

Especially since we had arrived at the source of the noise.

"Holy afterlife party," I snorted.

There were people everywhere. I couldn't count them all, but I would guess ... tens of thousands. And like the fish and creatures in the water, there was a transparent vibe to those closest to us. They all touched each other and interacted without issue, so it must be the nature of souls in this world.

"Some are transparent, and others aren't," Asher said suddenly.

Wait ... he was right. As we pushed further into the party, I saw more of the "solid" souls.

"What does that mean?" I whispered.

Asher, knowing as much as me, didn't have any answers either.

No one paid us any attention as we passed groups sprawled on the beach, playing in the sand, swimming in a small lagoon. They chatted like old friends, happy and bright. There was no sense of darkness or danger here. No sense of time or schedules. It was just ... peace.

Asher released a long drawn out sigh and I chuckled. "Keep your shorts on, dude, I'm just observing. If you don't like the thoughts, stay out of the head."

He shook his head, but his lips twitched at the corners. He wasn't as mad as he wanted me to think he was.

Turning from him, I started to walk again, not realizing a soul had been moving closer. I bumped into it, one of the translucent ones.

The soul jumped back. He was a male, taller than me, with young features—he looked all of fifteen. "Gah, I hate when you live-souls do that," he said, and I blinked because he wasn't speaking English but I understood him perfectly like he was. "Touching one of you is like walking through a freezing rainstorm."

Asher leaned in close. "He's speaking ancient Atlantean," he whispered.

I blinked again, forcing my own smile toward the soul. "We're kind of new here. Can you tell me why some of you … us … are transparent, and others are solid?"

I spoke English, and he answered in his native tongue. But all of us could understand.

Wicked cool.

"You're new," a soul said, tilting his head as he observed us. There was an echoing quality to his words. "You're one of the ones who didn't die but were banished to these lands. There have been no new Atlanteans for longer than most of us remember…"

It hit me the same moment Asher muttered *fuck*.

Atlanteans. Our Atlanteans! This was where they were, stuck here in the underworld for thousands of years. The solid souls were our trapped people.

My throat grew tight. More souls and Atlanteans drifted closer to us, all of them observing us with no malice. "How did you get here?" The soul was not suspicious. This world did not have any need for suspicion, but he was curious.

I decided honesty was our ticket. "We need to find the Hellbringers, destroy the gods who are trying to destroy us, and release the Atlanteans from their prison."

Whatever noise had remained after my first revelation completely died away. Somehow they'd all heard me.

Those who were solid pushed forward, and I ran my eyes over as many as I could, noting that they were dressed in what I could only guess was traditional Atlantean garb. Their clothes were natural colors, ivory and brown and white, with some splashes of cerulean and aquamarine to break it up. The women wore silk saris tied at their waists, and another strip across their breasts, the men just around their waists, and all of them were covered in the sort of ink that Asher had marked me with. So many tattoos covered their skin.

"Who are you?" one of the women asked, her long white-blond hair falling almost to her ankles.

Most of them had white blond hair, with just a few other shades of blond sprinkled about. How had I not noticed all of this when we first walked through?

They were hiding their true selves. Asher said in my mind. *Blending in with the dead among them.*

"My name is Maddison," I said to the waiting Atlanteans. "I am one of the children that your last kings and queens had, one from the gods."

Some chatter burst through at this revelation.

"We did not see the birth of those children," someone said, from further back in the crowd. "Atlantis was sunk before it was possible. We were thrown into the underworld and had to fight our way to this land."

Looking around, I took a deep breath. "We don't have much time, so I'm going to give you the condensed version of everything that has happened since you disappeared."

Asher remained silent at my side, but his support was consistent as

I explained as much as I could. "It has been ten thousand years since you left—" none of them had aged a damn day in that time—"and the gods are back again, wanting to destroy the world. For good this time. They believe they can remake it, with themselves as the supreme leaders. We must stop them."

"How are you … so young? Where have you been for the last ten thousand years?" These questions came from another woman.

"Atlantis sank," I told her, "but the three god children were kept in stasis, only freed in the past twenty years. The gods were freed as well, and now they want to finish what they started."

I went on to explain about my parents, Asher's parents, and how we were determined not to let them win.

"We're on your side. We want to free you and return you to Atlantis, your home."

"What if we don't want to return to that land of the living," a small girl asked.

I looked down and my smile fractured … as did my heart.

Dropping to one knee, I got down on her level, my eyes clashing with huge dark gray ones, the color reminding me of an early morning storm. She was innocent, but there was a sense of ancient energy about her as well. "Hi," I said softly. "My name is Maddison. What's yours?"

Her perfect pink lips, with a cupid bow, stretched as the smallest of smiles tilted the corners. "My name is Nameen. I'm six."

She was six, and she'd been six for ten thousand years. My gods.

"It's so nice to meet you, Nameen."

Before I could stop her, she moved forward, and in the innocent way only a child had, wrapped her arms around me in a gentle hug. "You look like a princess," she whispered against me, and my heart ached so hard I wondered if it was still functioning in my chest. "I love your hair."

Unlike the translucent soul, she felt solid, and I sucked down tears as I held on to her for a few seconds longer. Eventually, though, I had to let go.

"I'm scared," she said as she pulled away. "It's safe here. Mumma talks about home, and it doesn't sound safe there."

Placing a hand on her cheek, I brushed her super soft skin. "I understand, sweetheart. You have no idea how much I understand. But … wouldn't you like a chance to grow up and experience everything life has to offer? You are not meant to be here … this paradise is for those who have passed on."

She regarded me silently, and I wasn't sure she truly comprehended what I was saying. Eventually she smiled and nodded, and I released her back to her mother, who was hovering close by.

The silence was heavy after this, the pain palpable. Asher wrapped his hands around me, bringing me back to stand, supporting me as everything hurt in my body. This was the point the transparent souls started to drift away—this was not their business, and they had paradise to get back to.

"We're ready to return," a male said, stepping forward. He was one of those who had marks across every inch of his skin. "Back to Atlantis. We will trust in your plans. The previous royals stayed behind and went down with the island. That's why you were stuck in stasis for all those years."

We were finally with the very people who could tell us everything about being an Atlantean, and their final days on the island.

They went into the underworld before we were even born, Asher said in my mind.

Yes. And apparently our mothers didn't flee. They stayed and had us, and then everything went to shit.

His arm anchored me close.

That little girl broke me, I told him, my energy drenched in sorrow. *She fucking broke me, Ash.*

He soothed me the best he could, with love and support and the reminder that we were going to change their circumstances. All of them.

They were going to freak when they saw the world today.

But first we had to figure out how to save them all.

"I need to find the Hellbringers," I said. "Without them, I can't defeat the gods. They're too strong, and their power is too great for me to control alone."

They'd been here for ten thousand years, and they weren't like the dead, content in their afterlife. Surely one of them knew something.

"The land they exist in is not one we can venture to," the heavily tatted man said. "But you are born from the gods." He turned and pointed across the island. "They're in that direction. You'll know when you reach the dark veil."

Great. Another fucking curtain of nightmares. Hopefully I could part this one just as easily.

"I will be back for you," I promised them. "I'll figure out a way for you to all return to the land of the living. Atlantis has risen again, and it needs its people back."

The man reached out to touch me, just on the forearm, and there was clearly no malice in his move. When our skin connected, I felt a flash of everything they'd been through to this point. How one of the gods—Sonaris by the looks of it—had saved them by sending them here. He'd cared about his people, in his own weird way.

"We will make this right," I whispered. "Just hold on a little longer."

I felt their collective hush, and then as one they slammed their fists against their chest, the thump echoing like a crack of thunder, and then they returned to the party.

The tatted man was the last to turn away. "We can't interact with those who are dead, even though they can touch each other no problem. It's been hard, but at least we weren't alone. Everyone that comes to this island has Atlantean blood. We have seen our descendants, those who escaped and have died over the years. We have each other. But it would be nice to return home. This is not a land for those still with their vessels. It feels … unnatural."

"That's one way to put it," Asher grumbled. He'd been letting me take the lead and I was overflowing with his support. "We will not let this injustice stand. We are Atlanteans of our word, and we will return y—"

His words were cut off as two translucent beings drifted past, their eyes alight as they chatted to each other.

Asher blinked, staring at them. "Mom … Dad," he murmured.

The tatted man stepped in front of him. Asher's eyes blazed as he nailed the man with a dark glare. The Atlantean was smart enough to take a step back, hands held high.

"They won't remember you," he got out quickly, before Asher made another move.

My mate paused, giving him a second to explain.

"Those who have died come here for peace, and in that peace they do not remember their loved ones. They don't mourn for those they have lost. It's part of life here. When their loved ones die, though, and their souls arrive here, that's when all the memories return. The dead don't remember the living, but they know each other in death."

"But you all remember?" I said softly, and he nodded.

"Yes. My mate, she escaped with our children before the fall. They are here … their souls are now … but they don't know me. So I watch from afar and feel joy that they are at peace."

Holy fucking hell. Literal hell. I couldn't even imagine his daily torture.

"You want to return to the land of the living and leave them?" Asher asked.

The man's chuckle was brittle. "I must live first so that one day I can die and return to them. One day we will exist together in this perfect paradise. Until that moment, I will have to live for them. I'm ready for both."

I willed my tears down, because while this was one of the most heartbreaking stories I'd heard in a long time, this man did not want my tears.

"You deserve your happiness," I said, voice a touch husky. "We will make it happen."

The man inclined his head, eyes never leaving mine, even as he backed away.

It was time for us to get out of here too, but before we could leave, I had to check one thing.

"You okay?" I asked Asher, giving him my full attention. "If you need a second to deal with your parents, follow them to see how they're doing, you know I'm right with you."

He shook his head, barely any hesitation. "Nah. They looked happy, and it would only be painful and confusing for them not to remember me. I'll let them have their peace, until it's time for us to meet again."

I pushed lightly on our bond, because if Asher was hurting I wanted to feel it too. There was mostly peace in his emotions, a little pain, but it was barely perceptible. He had me and his brothers, and the few others he considered family. The loss of his parents was always going to be a sore spot for him, but it had actually helped to see them briefly. To see their peace.

"Let's go save our families," I murmured, hugging him tightly. "We're almost at the end. We can do this."

"I got you, baby," he said, as he crushed me to his chest. "You and me forever. We will not fail. I refuse to let that happen."

Forever. We were coming for you.

CHAPTER 29

By the time we reached the edge of the island, the noise had faded, leaving us with that echoing, unnatural silence. There were other changes too. It felt colder here, and the water on this side was slightly darker. Murky almost. Like a warning not to cross.

"The souls would feel it stronger than us too," Asher said, eyes alert as he searched out dangers.

"It's a good system to keep them in their areas, but why are they segregated anyway? I mean, that's a very 'living person' thing to do."

We stepped out onto the turbulent water and it held our weight.

"This world is controlled by living gods," Asher replied. "No doubt they have categorized souls into what they think is the most peaceful afterlife for them. Shifters wouldn't want to live with all of this water, but Atlanteans do. Most of the time they probably get it right."

Except for those like Rayge, who was no doubt difficult to classify.

"I hope the others are okay," I said, concern for them creeping into my thoughts. "I mean, I'm sure they are. All three are capable as hell from what I can tell. It's just hard not to worry."

Asher ran a hand through his hair, sending the black and gold strands into sexy disarray. "This world doesn't play by the fucking rules. No amount of capability can overcome that, and those three are not born of gods. I'm worried too."

I liked that his circle of friends was extending. I mean, I was in a girl gang with their mates now, and it would be nice for all of us to hang out in a different capacity one day. One with a little less mortal danger and end-of-the-world worries.

"You ready?" Asher asked, his eyes locked on the dark veil. It was without a single flaw or crack, just like the last one.

"Let's do it."

I stepped forward, the water swirling in murky disarray beneath my feet. Just before I was about to reach out and touch the veil, I heard a shout from behind. Spinning around, Asher shifted in front of me, chest swelling as he extended his arms protectively.

Peering around him, I caught a glimpse of the tatted man sprinting like his life depended on it.

"Wait!" he shouted again, and Asher straightened, allowing me to see the ancient Atlantean clearly.

The man wasn't just sprinting, he was sprinting while holding two gigantic tridents. How he hadn't tripped over them was beyond me, but I found myself fascinated by the glint of their jewels in the dusky light here.

Storms suddenly raged overhead and he picked up speed.

"Should we go to him?" I shouted to be heard over the torrent of winds trying to push the man back. They had legitimately sprung up out of nowhere.

Asher linked our hands together and then we were racing. Despite this world's attempt at keeping us apart, we made it to the Atlantean, steadying him as he sucked in air. It was clearly a reflex leftover from his life above, because there was no shortness of breath here. I didn't even feel the slightest strain.

"Is everything okay?" I asked him, tightening my hold so he was upright.

"These are the weapons of the royals," he said, between breaths. "We managed to find them and I figured you might need the extra help."

Extra help would never go astray on this mission.

I reached for the closest one but he waved my hand away. "No, this is for him," he said, handing it to Asher. It was pure gold, from the tip of the very shiny prongs all the way down the carved handle. On the end was a large, smoothly-polished jewel. A ruby, I would guess from the color and texture.

"This was your mother's," he told Asher.

Asher's eyes flared the same shade as the weapon, and his skin turned a darker shade of bronze as he flexed his fingers around the trident. "It … feels right," he said, running his gaze down the handle. "My power responds to it, much more than any of the others I've held."

I was paying some attention to Asher, but most of it was on the other weapon. *Was this finally it?* Was I finally going to find the weapon that called to me? I'd been trying for nearly three years at the Academy, and outside of a mild affinity for some, nothing had stirred my power.

The man lifted it toward me. I held my breath as my fingers wrapped around the middle. Like a hallelujah moment, everything went still and silent, before the surge of power shocked me deep in my chest. *Fuck yes.* My fingers tingled, head tilting back as that surge rocked all the way to my toes.

Storms raged above us, the once aquamarine sky now dark as ash. "This has never happened before," the tatted man said, looking above. "You're upsetting the balance. You should hurry before the souls are affected."

The power was still riding me, but I wasn't so far gone that I would risk their afterlife. I nodded, sucking the energy back into my center. The trident pulsed, working with me, like we'd been besties forever.

"They're gorgeous," I noted, and I might be biased, but I was pretty sure mine was even better than Asher's. His was pure gold, sure, and that was pretty cool. But mine was a deep rich copper, with a large aquamarine stone. It felt like a sign. So much of my year had been connected to this color, and now I knew I'd chosen it for a reason.

"Copperite is a mineral found only in the oceans of Atlantis," the man told me. "It's one of a kind, almost indestructible. Please use it to save our people."

That was all he said before he took off, racing back across the stormy seas.

"Holy shit," I said to Asher, both of us staring at our pretties. "I almost want to stroke this thing and call it my precious."

His eyes flashed as a rumble of laughter left him. "Trust me, baby, the only shaft you'll ever need to call your precious is not a fucking trident."

My eyes wandered down his chest, before I shook my head. "No, Ash.

No! Not the time. We have to get our asses through that veil."

At this point, I wasn't sure if I was convincing him or myself.

He muttered some choice words but didn't argue. Making our way to the veil, the winds buffeted against us but my trident stayed steady.

"We need something to anchor it to," I thought out loud. "Leave our hands free until we need to use it. Like a scabbard, but the trident version."

Asher's smile stretched across his face and my damn heart skipped a few beats. "Don't do that," I scolded him. "You're too distracting. We've already wasted too much time. We need to focus."

More fucking gorgeous smirking. My thighs clenched automatically against the sensations rocking through my traitorous vagina. Bitch was greedy and she clearly didn't realize that this was an end-of-the-world situation and no fucking was allowed.

Asher laughed, and I was gone. So freaking gone.

"Come on, baby. Let's do this thing so I can spend some quality time loving on you."

Our trident situation forgotten, we ran, and as I moved, the weapon seemed to grow lighter and lighter until I could barely feel it.

"It's adjusting to our power," Asher said, twirling his as he sprinted. "Now that's the sort of weapon everyone should have."

I didn't disagree, and I was doubly glad our ancestral weapons had found their way back to us. They'd clearly been sent into the underworld to keep them from falling into the wrong hands. Someone had been looking ahead, and my heart really hoped it wasn't Sonaris. I couldn't correlate the god I knew with the one who remained strong in the memories of his people.

They were like day and night.

We reached the veil in moments and I didn't stop, stretching out with my free hand, smashing through the darkness. Asher slipped in after me, and on the other side was a completely different land.

Only there was no actual land at all. We were suspended in the air, and in a single heartbeat, both of us started to plummet.

Chapter 30

Before we'd fallen more than a few feet, my powers kicked in and I slowed my descent. Asher did the same next to me.

"We keep moving?" I asked him, hovering, my trident barely even a blip in my hand. It was so light, and I was almost certain it was shrinking. Soon I'd literally be able to shove it in my pocket.

"Yep, let's move. This world is built on lands connected and separated via the veils. The souls go where they'll have the most peaceful afterlife. We have to keep moving until we find where the Hellbringers rest."

As we zipped across the air, I had a thought. Maybe we were going about this all wrong…

"Where are the Hellbringers?" I shouted, demanding an answer.

A path lit up in front of us, visible across the pale-yellow sky. The lighting here was akin to a sunrise, warm and soothing, and I could see lots of bird souls, a pterodactyl or fifty—holy fuck, dinosaurs—and other flying beings I didn't have names for. I did recognize fairies, and … a few that looked like angels.

This was their land.

They paid us no mind as we dashed through them, intent on their soaring journeys. When we reached the next veil, Asher was a little ahead of me, knocking me back when he was rejected.

I laughed. "Just had to give it one more shot, didn't you?"

His lips twitched. "No idea what you're talking about."

With a chuckle, I tapped his forehead. "I'm in here, buddy. You can't hide anything from me. Don't worry, your strengths lie in other areas."

"Damn right they do," he said, moving back so I could do my thing.

The next land was filled with cities, lots of shopping and restaurants and a very human-like existence. The souls here, they looked like supernaturals or … humans.

"Do humans come to this afterlife?" I asked Asher.

He was watching them scurry about below us—we were still high in the air, our powers shooting us along.

"I have no idea. I guess there's no reason they wouldn't. We all exist on the same Earth together."

This was true.

Something about the sight of a familiar cityscape was soothing. I'd been homesick without even realizing it, and seeing streets so similar to where I grew up was the shot I needed to bring me back to reality.

"This world messes with your head," I said to Asher, zooming toward the next veil. "I keep forgetting the urgency of our task."

"Yes," he agreed. "It's a constant battle to remind my power that we must move forward. No time to hang out and play with our new weapons."

Speaking of, the trident was no more than a few inches long now. I shoved it into the back pocket of my jeans.

"Remind me not to sit on that and stab myself in the ass," I told Asher, and he chuckled.

"You got it, Maddi." His features tightened. "I really don't like being here. It's not right for the living to walk this existence. I have no idea how the Atlanteans haven't lost their minds."

Another question without an answer. Another thing to worry about. We hadn't spent a lot of time with the Atlanteans, so who was to say they weren't suffering a lot more than we had seen. Maybe we were too late. We wouldn't know the answer to that until they were back in our world … back with the living.

The next veil approached, and we pushed through it, and then the next, and another. We crossed lands and territories until I despaired of ever finding the Hellbringers.

Maybe they didn't even exist here.

When we entered the next section, the heat hit me hard, and for the first time since this whole weird trip began, the path we were following dipped down, cruising close to the red ground.

Was this finally the right area?

I snorted. "I mean, the lava is a nice touch, but also, what a way to be a cliché, *Hell*hound."

Asher didn't answer, he was on alert, scanning the lava fields below. "The path remains," he finally said, when he was satisfied that there were no immediate dangers. "Stay close to me."

Now wasn't the time to argue, so I didn't point out what a bossy asshole he was.

I might have thought it though.

We sailed across the land, heat turning me into a sweaty mess. It was the first time since entering the underworld that I'd felt anything remotely normal like sweat. The dead didn't have skin to sweat, but I did, and it was as hot as balls in this section.

"Where do you think they are?" I murmured, feeling an urge to stay quiet.

Maddison...

I was growing used to voices in my head now. Not just Asher, but the multiple energies existing within my own. I could feel the Atlantean five and my brother. I knew they were alive and not in pain. It was something I was growing to love and appreciate.

But this ... the being calling my name was not family.

It wasn't completely unfamiliar either. I'd heard it the last time we took a back entrance into the underworld, its enticing tones urging me to step out into the darkness.

"It's calling me," I told Asher.

His head jerked toward me, gold threading his eyes. "I don't hear anything. Not in your thoughts, or in my own head."

Yeah, and he was not happy about it.

"It called me last time as well, only I didn't realize at the time that's what it was."

We've been waiting for you...

I shook my head, and Asher's eyes were even brighter. "What did it say this time?"

Turning to him, I moved closer. "You heard it?"

"No," he said, shaking his head, "but I saw the change in your eyes. They shimmered. Briefly, but it was enough for me to guess it was in your head again."

I swallowed roughly. "It said that it's been waiting for me."

If thunderclouds had a face, it would have been Asher's in that moment. "Why are they so fixated on you? Why is everyone so fixated on you? I don't like it, Maddi. I fear what this will mean if you allow these creatures too close."

I wasn't without my own fears, but really… "What other option do we have?"

It was a genuine question. If Asher could think of one other option to try to defeat the gods, I'd be all over it. I'd been trying for months to find a solution to our problem. We kept coming back to this.

If Asher's jaw clenched any harder, he was going to break some teeth. "Fuck. I'm not sure this is the right thing to do."

I captured his hand. "I need you to promise that if I lose control of them, you will stop me before I hurt anyone. You have the power of destruction and creation in your energy. What you did with Sonaris and Axl … I need you to do the same for me. Don't let me turn evil."

There was no chance for him to answer because a burst of light and power slammed into us. I was shot back toward the veil we'd just used to enter this world. Usually I would have been able to slow myself in seconds, but the invisible force didn't fade, pushing us further.

My natural protections kicked in, and I managed to counter some of their energy, shooting my own back. Not that I could see who we were fighting.

Was it the Hellbringers?

"Maddison!" Asher's shout sent another jolt through me, a literal jolt that strengthened me, allowing me to break through the force holding me. Finding Asher through the energy, we linked hands together, taking off along the path still trying to lead us to the Hellbringers.

"What attacked us?" I asked breathlessly, trying to get myself under control.

Asher was grim faced. "The gods. They're not out yet, and that means they're still in…"

"Here with us…" I finished softly.

Shit. I hadn't expected that. Louis seemed so sure they'd break free in hours, and it felt like we'd been in the underworld for so long.

Maybe time didn't move the same in this world.

Also… "The gods have been in the same section as the Hellbringers all along?"

Asher nodded. "Looks like it. They can't control them, though, so their focus would have been on escaping only. They need to control us to control the Hellbringers."

Their plan was complicated and full of holes. Not huge holes, but decent sized ones. I guess they hadn't expected to lose touch with us for so many years, hadn't expected we would be strong and independent and think on our own. They'd lost the advantage of not raising us to be evil and power hungry like they were.

No doubt they'd had Plan B's on how to ensure our cooperation, which probably involved killing our loved ones if we didn't, but nothing had worked out for them. Something I was going to be super grateful for. Maybe the Fates didn't completely hate us.

Maddison. Come to us...

The voice again, at the end of the golden path, which was leading straight into the lava that ran like a river across half of the land here. In the distance I could see cliffs, and something told me that was the edge I'd stood on very long ago. The world had been dark to me then, my powers locked away, so I hadn't seen what lay beyond. But now I could. I could see it all.

I wasn't going to reach the lava in time though, because a bunch of fucking gods had just exited from those cliffs, and they were rocketing toward us. There were more than I expected. Ten at least. Were they multiplying down here like fucking rabbits?

"We need a plan," I said quickly. "Some way to contain them so one of us can get to the Hellbringers."

Deep in my heart, I knew I had to be the one to deal with the Hellbringers. How I knew that was anyone's fucking guess, but it had to be me. I was the one they called. I was the one to take the risk. That meant I had to convince Asher to try to buy me some time.

He heard my thoughts, and his were dark and angry, but he didn't spill any of that out into the world.

"I love you, Maddison," he said so fast it was almost a blur of words. "This is ... wrong. I don't want you to be the one to control those beasts, but ... it's the path." He pulled me closer, expression fierce. "I will kill every god here and destroy the worlds above and below if you're hurt. Don't die, okay?"

My heart. My fucking heart.

Asher's lips crashed into mine, one last kiss. "Find the Hellbringers. I will keep the gods away from you."

Storms raged around him as everything lit up gold, his skin, eyes, hair. He was my golden god, and despite the urgency, I needed one more second to stare at him, to drink in everything that was Asher, just in case this was the end for all of us.

"I love you," I whispered, and his face tightened. He brushed a gentle caress across my cheek, turned, and took off, heading for the gods. One versus ten. It was not great odds, so I needed to move my ass. He could maybe buy me a few minutes.

I wouldn't waste them.

Chapter 31

"**M**addison! You belong to me. I'm your mother, and you will stop what you're doing *right now*."

Lotus's voice blasted across the world but I paid her no mind. She was my mother, but she had not raised, loved, or wanted me. I was a means to an end, and even if I had thought of her as a true member of my family, there was no way I'd be on board with her plan.

I wouldn't bend to the will of others.

I heard the gods clashing. Storms raged around, fueled by Lotus, Asher, and me. My power was stronger than ever, lightning bursting from my fingertips when I swirled my hands too fast.

There was no time for me to play with electricity though. Asher wouldn't be able to hold them off for long. I needed to kick my ass into high gear and find those Hellbringers.

Keeping my mind locked with Asher's, I saw that he was hitting them with everything he had. I gave him as much help as I could, our energy drifting almost seamlessly between us.

Just as the Atlantean text said. True mates that were also gods could share power.

Enough, Asher said, cutting off the flow. *You need all your energy.*

He was probably right, but the urge to send more his way was strong.

Focusing on the path again, I followed it straight to the river of lava, hoping that when I got closer I'd know how to find the creatures. Surely, they didn't expect me to plunge into that river of red, oozing, spitting lava, clearly hotter than the fucking sun itself.

Sweat was running in my eyes now, but it was easy to ignore when one was busy trying not to die. I mean, this was our first decent shot at stopping the gods. And to find out they were all still in the prison, no havoc or loss of life above…

A fucking gift.

You're so close. Don't stop. Find us…

How do I find you? I shot back.

I was mere feet from the surface of the lava. If I wasn't supernatural, I would be dead from the hot air simmering around me.

How?

My descent slowed until I was hovering inches above the bright red field.

You know how…

They legitimately couldn't be serious.

It will kill me.

No reply. No flicker of that voice in my mind. It had withdrawn and was now waiting for me to make my decision.

With nothing more than a thought, I lowered my body to the point where if I breathed too deeply my chest would touch the fire. Since I didn't actually need oxygen to survive, I just stopped. Safer that way.

My fingers brushed across the surface, grazing the red lines, and I flinched at the immediate and deep burn. I wasn't immune to this lava, and it didn't appear to be like the fire fields in that test by Heptashia. This was actually going to burn me. My fingers were already covered in angry red welts.

Maddison ... baby. No!

That was Asher. He sounded labored, but he was paying enough attention that he knew what I was thinking.

It's the only way.

No! he said again, more command in his voice. *Don't blindly trust the Hellbringers. We have no idea what their agenda—*

He was cut off by their power as they spoke to me again.

We are without agenda. We are not beings with sentient thoughts. These words you hear are a reflection of your power and the bond you hold to us. We are nothing more than a wisp, but nothing comes without sacrifice.

Fucking fuck.

I floated for seconds, trying to figure out if I had the strength to do this. Not physical strength—it was of no use here. But the mental strength.

A long time ago, when I was still in the human world, I'd read a news article about a man who cut his own arm off to save his life. At the time, I couldn't imagine how he must have felt, knowing those were the only two choices he had, and that both of them might mean his death anyway.

But at least one of those choices held a sliver of hope. Sometimes a sliver was all a person could rely on. It was all they had.

Agony burst through my mind and it wasn't my own. I screamed for Asher, rising up, my energy ready to shoot me straight toward him.

Don't come to me, he choked out through our bond. *Get out of here. Get the others to help you.*

He was hurt. Badly. The gods had him pinned, and even though he'd taken out a lot of them, and hurt Draconis, Lotus had managed to slip through his guard. Like the slimy bitch she was. Swear she had a guardian angel and nine fucking lives like a cat.

Asher's power burst free in a shimmer of gold, raining across the land, and I knew this was his last-ditch attempt to power me with his own energy. I couldn't leave him like that though. I couldn't leave him to be tortured by them and possibly killed. Maybe they thought the ten of them could handle his energy. I wasn't close enough to know if they'd bonded themselves in the same way I had to the Atlanteans.

More gold filled the air, and this time it wasn't from Asher. It was from his mother.

Galindra, bound with magical ropes, was dragged forward by Draconis. "If you don't want to die, G," Draconis choked out—Asher had hurt him good. "You will kill the child. He's an abomination."

Asher remained tall and strong, not a sign of pain or fatigue on his face. I could still feel him through our bond, but he was blocking me as best he could, hiding the worst from me.

My eyes darted between the god standoff and the lava below, and I found my fortitude. I found the strength to remove my arm. Because I didn't need two arms if I had no Asher. I didn't need them if there was no world.

Gritting my teeth, I dived back down toward the lava, and when I neared the surface, threw my left hand out and plunged it straight into the boiling river of fire. My intention had been to keep my pain to myself, grit my teeth and get through it, but it was so much more than I'd imagined.

My skin melted away, reduced to nothing more than bone in seconds. My skin was diamond, but even diamond had a melting point. My bones, though, must have been something stronger than diamond because they did not succumb to the heat. Once I'd screamed through the pain of losing my skin and muscles and organs, there was nothing but a cold chill against the parts of my body still in the flames.

Where are you? I called to the Hellbringers. But there was no reply. Swirling my mutilated arm in the fire, I started to wonder if this had been enough. Did they require me to go fully into the flames? Did I have to sacrifice everything except my bones to control them?

Before any of those questions could be answered, something heavy and solid grabbed my bone-arm and yanked me under.

CHAPTER 32

Asher's voice was the last thing in my mind before everything went black and pain like no other destroyed me.

I burned.

Every part of me burned. There was no escape. My screams allowed the lava to seep through my throat, melting me from the inside, and within a minute of the worst kind of torture I'd ever felt in my life, there was nothing left of me, nothing but a fractured mind and a skeleton built of fragmented memories and original power.

As I floated in the lava, it felt cool against my bones, and I wondered what it really was. What was this substance, filled with an energy I had not felt before?

Come to me.

This time I was in control, fears stripped away. I could never experience the sort of pain like that again. Softness had been burned from my body, and I was now the perfect machine to house the Hellbringers.

I was the perfect god killing machine.

Our special one.

The energy surrounded me, a swirl of darkness and ultimate power.

The three of you would have controlled us. It's better this way.

I had a flickering thought of two others, their faces shrouded. Better this way for sure. This was what I was made to do. What I was made to be.

Why am I special? It was time to know, even if knowing changed nothing.

You and the other two contain a tiny essence of the Mother of All. Her energy lived within you when she died to save the worlds. She spilled her blood and power. We are the original energy she used to build it all, and now you will have it. No other could harness the energy of the universe in the same way you do.

This information was new to me. I'd never expected that the Mother of All's energy would reside inside of me, but it explained why I was here now, controlling this power.

I was the Mother of All ... the second.

Bony fingers appeared in front of my face, held together with my power alone, since any connective tissue was long gone. The dark power wrapped around my hand and my energy welcomed them. They sank into me like the missing pieces of my essence. Light pierced through the darkness of this world below and I wanted to smile, only there were no lips left for me to do so. I settled for embracing the contented feeling of completeness.

Complete power.

Time to do what we were born to do.

The Hellbringers had not been born, but they were one with me now, and had embraced my thoughts and memories. They'd lain here in this elemental ooze since the fall of the last Mother. They had been waiting.

With ease I lifted myself in the air, moving through the fire like it was water. Something caught my eye when I was about to break through, and I wondered for a moment why there was a bronze trident in the lava with us.

Why had it not burned?

You don't need it.

The voice pushed away my curiosity and I dismissed the trident then as nothing more than a trivial Atlantean thing. Akin to caring about an ant. Or the slimy trail of a slug.

All were insignificant to me. I would waste no time on them.

When I sailed out of the lava, it was to find a world built on chaos and tragedy. Screams and fire licked across the world; gold covered every surface, and two gods fought with blows that would have killed any other being.

Flicking my hands to either side, I pinned them against the wall. The cracking of their bones was somewhat satisfying. These were supposed to be the most supreme beings in this system of energy, and it was like swatting a fly.

Gliding across the air, I approached the closest one. A woman. Her power buzzed against my bones like electricity. A goddess of storms.

"What the fuck are you?" she stuttered out, fear creasing her almost perfect face. In the reflection of her eyes, I could see the glowing skeletal vision of myself, see the flames in my eyes, the darkness shrouding the rest of me.

"The Mother of All," I whispered back. Or tried to. My voice boomed much louder than I intended, and she whimpered as blood trailed from her ears.

I didn't attempt to keep my voice down again. I was not made to consider others. I was made to right the wrongs of this world.

Use us.

My perfect Hellbringers.

They were the omniscience to my power, the ones to allow me to reach out and drain the goddess until she was nothing more than a husk. When her body puffed into a dusty residue, I directed it toward the lava.

The power I'd drained from her swirled inside of me and I briefly contemplated keeping it.

No. You are not made to bow or worship the storms. That must belong to another. Find the one who will remake it in your image.

The entire world of beings flashed before my eyes, and for some reason I paused on one with perfect dark skin and hair the color of the flames from which I was born.

Her.

I didn't know her. She was nothing to me. But I sensed that she would embrace the storms and bring back their glory. If I couldn't take on the power, I had to keep the balance.

The balance was everything.

The original magic that had borne gods seeped from my bones, Hellbringers at my center helping me control it all. The storm power disappeared into the universe.

A new god was born.

While I had been focused on my internal view of the world, more gods appeared. They were attacking me with power and energy and their own specific brand of godhood.

Sweeping out with my power, I trapped all of them one by one, holding them in stasis. Each came before me, and each of their powers became mine.

As I stripped a godhood, I then returned it to a new being, one that my power deemed worthy.

When I was done, only two remained, two who glowed with the same molten gold that filled the bones that was all that remained of the being I used to be. Two beings born from the original Mother of All.

Their names were already forgotten. Purpose insignificant.

My power wrapped around them and I dragged them forward. The first was a woman.

"You cannot do this," she spluttered and I cut her off before she could speak another word. They were all corrupt. They all had to be remade.

This one didn't really have any significant role in the balance. As long as the Mother of All existed—and she certainly existed inside of me—there was no need for an understudy.

Crushing her in my grip, I destroyed her in the next beat of time. Her power settled inside of me and I decided to hold on to it. For now. There was no need to rush and fill her position, and I had more than enough strength to control her meagre energy.

The Hellbringers didn't respond.

We moved on to the next being, and a flicker of recognition touched deep within my energy.

"Maddison," he said, face streaked with blood, eyes wide and gold as they pleaded with me. "Maddison. Baby. Please come back to me."

Pulling the male closer to me, I examined his energy. Similar to my own, and to the energy residing inside me now, he was another born of the original Mother, the being that controlled the Hellbringers before me.

We are not called that. That's the name given to us from the mortals. We are Setra, the source of life. We make the Mother of All.

I understood it all now. Every aspect from before and still to come. The Mother of All was not a god in the way supernatural beings knew them. She was a vessel for the Setra. That was the true power behind her creation.

Do we need this creature? I asked, for some reason hesitating to destroy him as I had all the others.

The original energy was quiet. Together, we searched through the past and the future to find the importance of this one.

Keep him. He has merit.

I released my hold on the golden god. He caught himself before he plunged into the lava below. In a flash, I disappeared from the world below, emerging on the land above.

There was a lot of work to be done here. I needed to start now.

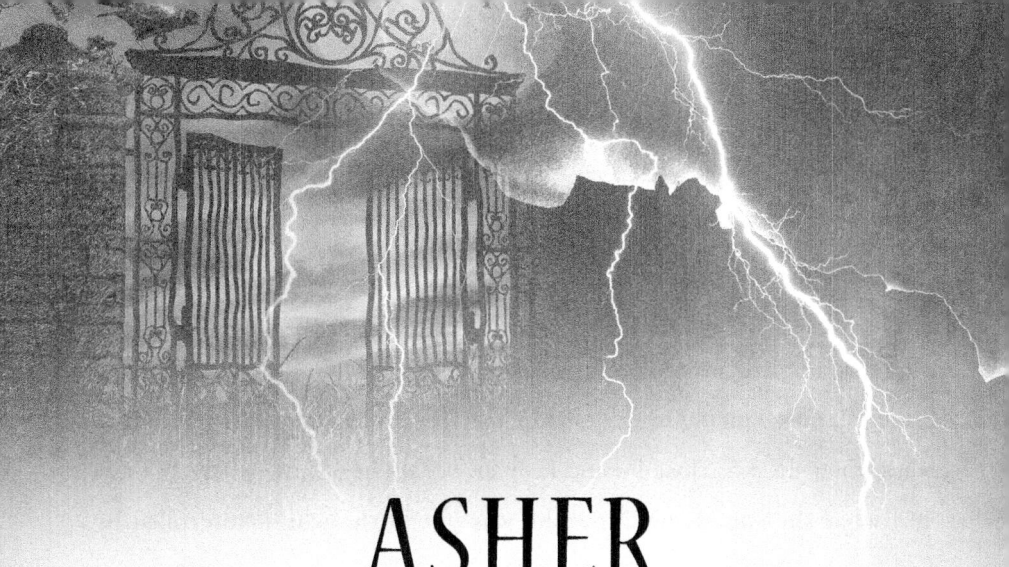

ASHER

Despite the futility of my actions, I couldn't stop reaching for Maddison through our bond. I knew she was gone. Nothing left of her but a glowing, murderous skeletal figure, filled with darkness and fueled by the Hellbringers.

She was scary as fuck. Yet somehow still beautiful. Her power wrapped around her, gold as my own, but it was not the same. Only a fool would think we were even in the same league…

Was I fool to keep hoping that my Maddison existed within her still?

Her soul was blocked from me, but I had to believe it was still there. That belief was the one fucking thing keeping me functioning.

She spared me.

I was the only god she spared. That had to mean there was still some of my Maddison left, trapped by the power of those dark souls pushing against her. Turning away from the lava, I was maneuvering myself up behind her when she snapped out of existence, disappearing in the blink of an eye.

"Fuck!" I shouted, frustration slapping against my face. Maddison might be nothing more than a set of murderous gold and black-speckled bones, flames dancing in the orbs of the eyes and a tongue of fire, but at least when she was close I could keep an eye on her, know where she was and what she was doing. Now she was out in the world, controlled by fucking darkness, and lacking her kindness and compassion.

The Hellbringers … I'd had a terrible feeling about them. How the fuck were we going to fix this?

Gliding across the now-empty cavern, I entered the stone tunnel that led to the exit, to Atlantis. Scorch marks and gouges littered the walls, evidence of where the gods had been smashing against their prison. All of those gods were gone now. Maddison's parents. Mine. The others who had teamed up with them.

The entire supernatural pantheon had just been remade, and there was nothing anyone could do to change what Maddison had created. She was the only being with the power to remake the world. And right now she wasn't exactly taking suggestions.

We'd all better fucking hope she didn't decide the entire world was a complete lost cause and raze it back to two single cells bumping together.

Asher!

Voices slammed into my head when I powered out of the prison, all of them loud and demanding, except the one I needed to hear more than anything.

My brothers raced toward me.

"What happened?" Axl demanded, his voice a snap of elemental power that not very long ago wouldn't have been possible for him.

"Where is Maddison?" Jesse demanded.

I paused, my gaze taking in the glowing quality to his skin now, the surge of energy crashing inside his chest. "What the fuck happened to you?" I asked him.

His expression was shuttered. "I'm a god now. What sort of god, I have no fucking idea, but all of us were hit with a burst of power. None of us are Atlanteans now."

Maddison.

"She killed the gods," I breathed. "She sent their fucking power out into the universe and she somehow selected you all to be worthy of it."

I touched my brother's arm, our powers crashing together.

"You're a god of shifters," I told him, immediately recognizing the earthy and elemental power that all shifters were blessed with.

Jesse's eyes, more forest green than ever, widened. "The fuck you say?"

He didn't know how to react, and I couldn't blame him. "You're the god of the shifters. I don't know what else to tell you."

"Where is Maddison?" Rone interrupted, his eyes burning red hot for a beat.

"God of the Underworld," I muttered. Fucking hell, Maddison. Way to keep it in the family.

My brother's eyes were filled with a shade of red that was similar to the lava fields below. He opened his mouth, probably to rage at me, but I got in first.

"Maddison found the Hellbringers," I said, shortly. I'd done my share of losing my shit when she'd first plunged into the lava, thinking that I'd lost her to the burning depths. Now I was in survival mode. Getting Maddison back was the only way I could continue in this life. She was still there, buried deep inside.

Calen slammed his fist into a nearby tree, but instead of it smashing to pieces, new plants blossomed out of the side, hard and thorny, like a weapon made by nature.

"God of fucking nature," he cursed. "I hate fucking plants."

It would be humorous if we weren't in the worst situation that I'd ever known.

Louis pushed forward, face lined with fatigue and desperation. His eyes implored me to have some good news, but I was afraid he was going to be greatly disappointed.

"How do we bring her back?" Axl asked, his hands itching like he wanted his magical pen and paper to take notes. "Maddison … if she has remade all of the gods like that, she must have the Hellbringers. What did they do to her?"

"Is there a way to neutralize her?" a dickhead from the crowd shouted. "Before she destroys us all."

My power slammed into him, knocking him halfway across the island.

Louis let out a harsh breath before his power burst free and he silenced all of the supernaturals. "It would be a good idea to remember that Asher has the power to destroy you all with little more than a thought. Now is not the time to try him—he's barely holding on. Let's not antagonize the angry god further."

Barely holding on…? I was running on autopilot, my sole objective to save my mate. The rest was white fucking noise.

"Asher, talk to us," Jesse said. His anger had died down, even though his new powers were still burning through him.

"What happened down there, Ash?" Rone rasped, his eyes red-rimmed.

"What happened?" I said with a dry, fucked-off laugh. "What happened is we fucked up and now Maddison is controlled by the Hellbringers. Or whatever the hell they are. They stripped away her humanity, her softness, and now she's just power and vengeance. She remade all the gods in a blink of a fucking eye." I threw my hands up. "I've never seen anything like it."

I ran a hand through my hair, the urge to smash Atlantis to the ground slapping against me. "This was not the fucking way I thought this would play out. I'd thought we would fight, that we might get hurt, that we might lose people we cared about. Don't get me wrong, I didn't want it to end like that—I hated that might be the worst case—but I was trying to prepare for it. This, though? No one could have prepared for this possibility, because no one knew it *was* a fucking possibility."

My roar of words slammed into the wall of silence that filled the land.

Louis, the only one brave—or stupid—enough, stepped forward. "There must be a way to save Maddison. Do you have any thoughts about how to pull her back to us? She's stuck in a powerful void right now, but she still exists. The essence of who she was born to be is there. Someone … or something, needs to remind her."

"Don't you think I tried?" A growl ripped from my chest, and those in close vicinity were wearing a nice coat of golden energy. I was fucking shedding magic like a fairy. "She didn't even know who I was."

Louis shook his head, and I was wondering why I hadn't ripped it off yet. "She didn't kill you. She killed everyone else, right? That's all you need to know."

Reaching through the bond, I got nothing but white noise and static, like Maddison was no longer operating on the same plane of existence as the rest of us.

What do you need from me, Maddison James? How do I bring you back to me?

There was no existing in this world without my mate. The only positive was that she was pretty much indestructible at the moment. Nothing could hurt her.

More than she'd already been hurt anyway.

When I closed my eyes, all I could see was her skeletal figure, all I could hear were her screams as she plunged into the lava.

"The scales," I muttered. "The fucking scales saw this coming."

They'd tried to trap her, but there was no circumventing her future. Maddison was the one controlling the Hellbringers. The one remaking the world.

There had to be something that meant more to her. What did she need…?

"The Atlanteans…"

"The Atlanteans?" Axl asked, his eyes greener than ever as power rode him.

"They're in the underworld," I said, starting to pace. "Trapped there. We need to free them. Returning that much power to the surface might be enough to draw her attention."

A sense of grim purpose and determination gave me something to focus on. I was already striding toward the Amphitheatre, ready to return to the underworld. This was the right step. I needed to bring them back to the surface.

"I need to free them now!" I snapped, my brothers rushing to keep up with me.

Louis tried to follow as well, but I shook my head. This was a family matter, and as much as I liked the sorcerer, he was not family. Not yet.

Maybe if we got Maddison back, it'd be a different story.

"Keep everyone safe here," I told him. "Prepare for anything. Maddison is not herself, and everyone in the world is at risk."

Louis looked like he wanted to argue but refrained. He stared me down for a few minutes, before he nodded and returned to the group of powerful supes that had been preparing to defend the world from the gods. "Find Jessa, Braxton, Mischa, and Max," he called after us as we entered the path to the underworld. "Find them and bring them back too."

"I'll do what I can," I told him.

My priority was Maddison. The rest would have to wait.

Chapter 34

The world was a mess. I hadn't noticed until this moment, but now, with my ability to search through and beyond the current timescape, I saw it all. Using my abilities, I followed the path of destruction, through wars and murder. Mistake after mistake. I had a vague recollection of learning about war in class. The teacher had asked us what we learned from war. What it showed us.

It showed me that maybe my work here was greater than just remaking the gods. My work would require me to remake the very fabric of this world, because the inhabitants were beyond corrupt. They never learned. They sacrificed … everything … for their own gain.

This is your role. We were there at the beginning. We will be there at the end.

The longer I spent time with the spirits of the Mother of All, the more I learned about them. They had been in control of the original creation, and they were in control now. They had been lost for many years, sleeping in the original lava of power.

Yes. The lava that had stripped my humanity, was the very material that scorched the earth and formed the mountains and oceans, the trees and plants. From that original energy, everything grew.

You can reform your skin. You can reform yourself.

I knew I could, but I didn't want to. For me to do the job I needed to do, there could be no softness about me, no humanity. Already some of my life before was coming back. Memories. And with those memories were feelings. They were diluted, faded so I barely even recalled the life I lived before.

But they were there.

I almost remembered their names.

"Enough!" I said out loud.

We were above the water, in the middle of the Indian Ocean. Close to Australia. There was a fishing vessel out there; it had drawn my attention because it was linked to a sister line that was razing our oceans to the floor. They overfished, taking everything: whales and dolphins, sharks and dozens of others that were mine to protect.

One thing that hadn't been stripped was my love for the water. The lava formed the landscape, but it was from the water that we all came. The water and the lava were the original magics, and when someone hurt my oceans, they would pay.

Hovering above them, I sent a wave across the ship, knocking most of the crew into the water, fishing nets tangled around them, trapping them, as they had done to so many creatures. I let the ocean do the rest, ready to welcome them into the watery depths. A part of me wanted to draw out their suffering, make them really pay for what they'd done, but there was too much work to do. The last action was to splinter their ships—not just this one, but every single ship they had or was connected to them, most of which were out in the water.

More of them would face the wrath of the oceans … and the animals within it.

"Why am I bothering with this?" I wondered out loud. The spirits twirled against my energy, sinking deeper. "Should I just clear the lot and start anew? Maybe the next world will be one with less greed and corruption?"

Less evil.

"Are there any worth saving?"

The spirits were fairly neutral in regard to making these decisions. They provided the power and I was the hand that wielded it. I would strike the final match and blow this place up.

So they gave me no answer.

Using their omniscience, I followed my path to the next disaster … and the next. I cleared up diamond smuggling. Rainforest razing. Overmining conglomerates who were more interested in a piece of paper than in the actual damage done to the Earth.

My head spun. It was too much. It was way too much. I felt like I was cutting off one evil head only to have five more spring up. When I discovered a pedophilia ring in the process of selling tiny innocent children … that was when I lost my mind and released all of my power.

The world froze. Every part of it. It remained in stasis as I tried to make up my mind.

You cannot hold this for long, the spirit warned me. *Everything works together for a reason. If you throw the balance off, it's very hard to get it back.*

Apparently not even I had the power to do that.

"I don't know what to do."

It was a chink in my armor, and I wish it wasn't there.

"There are people I cared about in this world. Every now and then their faces flashed across my mind, taking me by surprise. But I also don't think there is a reason to save this world. I've had the smallest glimpse and it's horrific."

Maddison James!

The blast of my name did not come from the original energy. It came from another source, one that sent a blossom of heat to my chest. Glancing down, I blinked at the skeletal frame that was all that remained of me. There was no heart or visible organs. I didn't need them to survive, so how was there heat?

Baby, I need you to listen to me. This is not you ... these are not your decisions to make. You don't have to be alone.

How was he communicating with me? I did not allow anyone to enter my energy...

Not to mention, everyone was frozen, every single living being, including the beautiful world they were destroying.

For the first time since setting out on my task, I was curious about something other than the state of the universe. This male, he was somehow immune to my power, because while the entire world was frozen, held in the grasp of my limitless power, he was not.

Maddison James, I know you better than any fucking person, living or dead. You're the other half of my soul and I need you to know ... I will love you no matter what. I support whatever decision you make. If you remake our world, I will find you in the next one.

A brief pause.

You and me, water baby, we're end fucking game. End game, baby! Repeat it after me.

No! No, I couldn't let this voice ... let this energy entice me from my task.

Do you want to see him?

This time it was the spirits, and I couldn't tell if they wanted me to look or not. They didn't hold opinions about things. Not really. They just existed and had their part to play in it all. They just needed a vessel to play that part. That was where I came into it.

Maddison James.

The voice again. He wouldn't leave me alone.

Impossible, my love. There's no alone when you have a true mate. I will give you space when you need it, but you're never truly alone.

Get out of my head! I screamed, sending power with the command.

I felt his flinch. I'd hurt him ... badly. But he didn't leave me.

Maddison James.

That fucking name again.

There's my girl. Not hearing you curse six ways to Sunday is probably the weirdest part of it all.

In my new fury, I released my hold on the world, everything lurching back to life in a plethora of sights and sounds. Energy crashed into me, into the void I'd been deliberately holding over all life.

When I find you, I warned the man, *you're going to wish you never meddled in my energy.*

His laughter was short, deep and rich, and if I had skin to still get goosebumps on, I would be covered. *Find me...*

Those last two words sounded labored, and I wondered if I'd hurt him even worse than I thought with my last blast. For some inexplicable reason, that bothered me, and I found myself wanting to discover who he was. Before it was too late.

ASHER

My body dropped to the ground. I groaned as Jesse caught me before I could sprawl like some uncoordinated newbie fuck. My girl packed a mean punch when she wanted to. Not to mention I'd had to literally bleed to get the connection through.

Louis's mate, Elizabeth, was a powerful sorceress. She'd done some quick research while we were in the underworld rescuing the Atlanteans, and had discovered a way to break through the protection of the spirits.

"We had it all wrong," she told me. "The Hellbringers are not actually creatures that can kill the gods, they're literally spirits of the original Mother of All. They are the creators. They just need a vessel to wield their power." She was protectively cradling her tiny baby bump, and I found it hard to believe she was due to give birth any day. What the hell did I know about babies or gestation?

"You should leave now, Tee," Louis argued with her, off to the side, but she stubbornly crossed her arms.

"The literal goddess of creation is crossing the world as we speak," she shot back. "She might decide that no one here deserves to survive, and in that case I'd like to end this all at your side."

There was agony in the sorcerer's eyes, one of his hands pressed to her stomach while the other pulled her closer. "You're going to be the fucking death of me, Elizabeth Teresa Montgomery."

He kissed her, softly, and I closed my eyes because I couldn't watch.

I focused on Maddison—she was coming back to me. Whether to kill me, we'd soon find out. Either way, I was ready to fight for her. For us.

If I could just find the energy to stand on my fucking own. I didn't want to be leaning on Jesse when she arrived. That was not how this would go down.

Atlanteans surrounded us on all sides, and I felt some satisfaction that at least I'd done that for her. It had been important to Maddison that we save them, and despite it taking me a while to figure out that the trident could part the veils, it hadn't been too hard. My brothers, stumbling over their new powers, had helped too.

We'd found Jessa and the others, pissed off and cursing in the shifter section of this world. For the first time in ten thousand years, no living being remained in the world meant only for the dead.

"At least Josephina and Rayge took the children to Faerie," Jessa said, crossing her arms. "If Maddison remakes this world, they might just survive it all."

"I think we should have gone too," Mischa said, her voice wavering even if her eyes were dry. "It would have been better that way."

Jessa's face crumpled and I waited for her to fall into her mate, take his support. But she didn't. She stood tall and pulled herself together. She was strong. Just like Mischa. Just like my Maddison.

We were the fucking lucky ones to have them.

Braxton went to her, holding her the same way I would have killed to hold Maddison. Sometimes I wondered if we were the ones who needed them just that little bit more. Women were so strong and resilient. Without their strength, we'd just be over here smashing fucking walls and fighting each other. Maddison tempered my base instincts, while also bringing them strongly to the forefront when needed.

It was a contradiction. But it worked.

"You okay, bro?" Jesse asked, concern lining his face. He still had one hand under my arm, half keeping me up. The newly-formed god of the shifters was falling into his power with ease, and I was glad to finally have my best friend back, the tension between us gone.

"Been better," I grunted, managing to get my feet back under me. Jesse let me go when my legs were steady.

Closing my eyes, I felt for Maddison's energy, but the spell was gone; she was blocked from me again. The puddle of my blood under my boots had already cooled. I didn't have the strength to access that sort of magic again. The original magic within her was too strong, and it was actively working to block Maddison from remembering her other life.

"I still don't understand how blood got you through to her," Calen said, looking a little green around the edges, starting to take on the hue of the plants he hated so much.

Axl made a frustrated sound. "It makes sense and doesn't at the same time. Maddison is, for all intent and purposes, the new Mother of All. The original creator. She holds energy that was here when the worlds were first formed, and it takes a sacrifice to communicate with her. But it shouldn't be like this. The original mother was not a swirl of darkness and insanity. Why is it affecting Maddison so badly?"

"Because it should have been all three of us," I said, admitting out loud what I'd known for a while. "Everyone warned us that we needed to form a solid bond and we ignored them all."

My eyes drifted to Connor, who was sprawled out on the ground, seemingly passed out. Useless fuck. So much of the blame lay with him, but I wasn't blameless, so I wouldn't kill him today.

"Maddison is not strong enough to fight their power on her own," Axl said, sounding like he was cataloguing that information in his super brain. "Yes. That makes sense. It needed to be the three of yo—"

Power slammed into Atlantis, sending shockwaves through it. Louis turned, eyes drifting up to the sky. The tension in his body told me everything, but I already knew she was close. Her power was literally simmering in the air, visible to all.

"She's almost here," the sorcerer said, reaching for his mate, holding her close. Neither of them looked afraid though, facing this challenge with a stoic strength that was mirrored on most of the faces around me.

Come on, baby girl. Don't waste all of this life.

Maddison loved a lot of the people here deep in her soul, where those spirits couldn't touch.

I just had to hope she found her way to that place in time.

Chapter 36

I could have appeared on the island in an instant. I knew where the voice was, I knew where everything was.

He was waiting for me on Atlantis, along with thousands of supernaturals, and a few gods.

For the first time since becoming the Mother of All, I felt an urge to gather my thoughts … to pull myself together.

There was also a brief urge to return my skin, cover the bones of my power with the vessel they all wore.

I didn't, because it felt like a weakness, and someone with the task I had been assigned, could not be weak.

Sending power ahead of me, I had them focused on that approach while I snuck in from behind, wanting to observe them secretly, as I had done with the fishing boats, with the smugglers and mining moguls.

Giving them a chance to prove me wrong.

So far none had, but everyone deserved a chance.

One single shot at proving they shouldn't be wiped from existence.

"...children to Faerie."

They were discussing their children. One wanted to stay with them if this was the end, and another was grateful they might survive it all.

More heat stirred. That was surprisingly altruistic, and brave. Both of them could have been in Faerie too—if they'd had time to send their children there. It wouldn't have saved them, but they didn't know that. Instead they were here, with friends and family, ready to stand against the threat.

I was the threat, of course, and none could stand against me.

That in itself made them even braver.

Girl gang.

That asinine name ran through my mind and I wondered at the familiarity of their faces. There were so many scattered around, original Atlanteans, their energy ancient and slightly different to the current breed of supernaturals that populated the world today.

I recognized the new gods as possessing the energy I'd shared out into the world, and as I examined each of their faces, I felt more stirrings of heat in the place where a heart should sit, phantom emotions from an organ long gone.

I drifted closer as my false trail of energy got stronger, sending them all on alert. They faced the way they expected me to arrive, allowing me to approach from the side.

A puddle of fluid caught my attention, the blood darker than normal, tinged with blue and black ... and gold. Standing in the middle of it, staring straight at me, was a man.

A familiar man.

The man I'd spared in the underworld.

Somehow he knew my other trail of power was a distraction. He knew I was here, the one strong enough to break through my protections and speak to me.

His skin was bronze, his hair dark with steaks of light, his eyes were green and gold. Original magic infused his essence, born from the daughter of the original Mother of All. There was something about him that stayed my hand, even though I wanted to strike him from the Earth at the same time.

He crooked a finger at me, calling me closer, and I almost lost control and went to him.

Memories flashed at me, faded broken memories.

Swimming, family dinners, movie nights.

This man, he'd been part of my life … before. He'd been important and special.

You're no longer that being.

The spirits had been quiet, but they started to stir now.

Any that distract should be eliminated.

It caught my attention, because they had been without much opinion until now. No real direction from them, just their powers guiding my vision. But maybe I'd been relying too heavily on their guidance, not realizing that was the same thing as an opinion.

Did they show me truth, or just their warped version of it?

Always truth. Truth is truth. No matter what.

Right. That was right. But … if black was black and white was white … what was gray?

Because there were shades of all three in truth. I'd learned that through so many of my life's battles and journeys.

Moments I was just starting to remember.

Removing the cloak from around me, I appeared in the air, visible.

The male had never taken his eyes from me, and wasn't remotely surprised. But the others, they jumped swinging in my direction, their various powers ready and waiting should I attack.

They didn't strike first though, and I found that … interesting.

"You all know who I am?" I said, my voice thundering because that's what it did now. Too much power to be quiet.

The man … the man I could not tear my eyes from … stepped forward, almost protectively standing before the mass. "You're Maddison James. You're my mate."

"Our family," another, dark-skinned man said. He had green eyes, piercing in their intensity, and he carried a cloak of shifter energy around him. Another of my newly reformed gods.

"My friend," a third man said, with arresting violet eyes and an ancient, restless energy. He was unique, and … kind. He had helped me. I remembered him. I remembered them all.

"Hey, girl!" A fourth. This time a woman with jet black hair, stunning, aristocratic features, and sky-blue eyes. "You wouldn't kill your girl gang, right?"

Girl-gang. Again. That was why it had crossed my mind, because these people were my friends.

The spirits stirred again. *Not your friends. Maddison's friends. You are no longer her. You are the Mother of All.*

Energy swirled and crashed around me, my own turning the seas that surrounded this land into a mass of tropical storms. "The world is corrupt," I told them. Why I was explaining myself, I would never know, but I ... I wanted them to understand. "I've tried to remake small parts of it, but ... it never ends. I can't find a reason to save it."

They pushed closer to me, none of them concerned by the force of the power surrounding me. They were brave. Or stupid.

Or both.

"There is so much good here," someone said, and I didn't know this person, but they faced me with kindness in their eyes. "Your vision is shrouded ... maybe you need to step into the light."

The spirits stirred harder, fighting to cloud my judgement again, but here, surrounded by all of this power, they couldn't quite achieve what they wanted.

"Show me," I said suddenly, deciding this was it. The last chance.

The final song.

CHAPTER 37

One by one, the supernatural beings on this island stepped forward and allowed me to touch their skin. This gave me the most direct access to their energy, and through that energy I could see their past and future. I could see lifetimes lived through multiple worlds.

Some of them had been through so much. Fought to save the world. Fought to save each other. Loyal and just and kind.

I hadn't seen this side of humanity since absorbing the spirits. But there it was.

A reason.

I released Jessa and she winked at me. "Like your new look. Very … skeleton chic."

None of them had flinched away from me, and I'd seen no disgust in their faces. The ones who considered me family … my appearance did not change anything for them.

Maybe it was time to bring my skin back. To close the gap between the two states of mind I inhabited now.

NO!

It was a single command, and my power surged as the spirits locked around me, tightly.

Release me! I told them. *You need me. You have no control here otherwise.*

"Fight them, Maddi," Asher said, eyes flaring gold as he stepped closer. "They're controlling you. Manipulating you."

"Shut up!" I shouted, cutting him off before he could say anything else. That didn't stop him though. He wrapped his arms around me, hauling me into his body. I'd stopped him from speaking but I hadn't stopped his movements. I'd never have guessed he'd be comfortable with hugging a skeletal mass of darkness and spirits.

He hadn't even hesitated.

Needing to hear his words, my power released its hold on his tongue.

He wasted no time.

"You are mine, Maddison James. I'm going to say your name until you remember. I'm going to love you forever, no matter what you look like. If this is the only way I can have you, then I will embrace it. Just ... don't let them take everything. I want the funny smartass of a girl who fears nothing and cares too much. I want her back. I need her back." His voice got low. "You're my light, Maddison James. My. fucking. Light."

It hurt. His words physically hurt me, reminding me of the lava burning through my skin to what lay below. I didn't have skin to burn any longer. I thought the softer side was gone, but he managed to dig into my bones. Into my essence.

"NOOOO!" I screamed, throwing my head back, blasting them all away from me.

Bodies went flying, but the gods amongst them managed to reach and save most of them.

I was too far gone to care though.

You have a job. Remake the world.

The spirits pulsed, restless, inside of me. Pushing and pushing. Forcing their will back into me.

We slept for too long. The world is corrupt.

My power flickered weakly against theirs, my perceived strength mostly from their abilities.

No, there is good too. Look at these people. Look at them! You saw what I did, and there is good. I can't remake beings like this. They deserve better for everything they did and sacrificed.

I saw it coming and I was already running. I just didn't know if I'd get there in time.

My body zapped out of existence, back into the underworld. It didn't come from my own knowledge, but I understood there was only one way to save the rest of the world. I had to get the spirits back into the lava from which they came. I had to return them to their resting place, because there they were mostly harmless. Barely a blip. Waiting for one who would be strong enough to wield them.

There would be no more though. Asher, me, Connor. We were the only ones. So if I could return them, the world would be safe. But I had seconds, because they were grasping for my power, my control, my soul.

Slowly. Piece by piece.

They were going to take away my free will.

The lava was right before me, and I was almost part of it, when my body was jerked away, inches from the molten red. I'd taken too long—the spirits had enough control now.

Let it end… I was all but begging, the faces of everyone I cared about flashing across my mind. They allowed my memories back, and my soul screamed at everything I'd done. Everything I'd almost lost.

If we go back in the original source, you will have to stay too.

Deal.

Deal.

I didn't even have to think twice.

A shadow flashed over the top of me just as I was dropping into the red heat. A familiar face.

Connor.

"I got you, sis," he said. "You don't have to do this alone."

He landed on top of me, power and body weight sending the pair of us—spirits included—tumbling into the fire below.

For as long as I existed, I would hear Connor's screams. They reverberated through me. When he was nothing more than bones, he came at me, dragging the spirits from my body and letting them absorb into his.

I couldn't figure out how that was better, because he definitely wouldn't be able to resist their call. And sure enough, in seconds he stopped fighting. Flames danced in the sockets where his eyes used to be and the darkness was now part of his soul.

"Connor!" I screamed, effortless to talk in this primordial fire.

He drifted toward me and I looked around, trying to figure out if there was anything close by that might help me.

Anything at all.

A glint of copper caught my eye, and I was reaching for the trident before I could even think about it.

Connor charged at me.

"Release them!" I shouted. "It's not too late."

He never faltered, looking like someone's worst nightmare come to life.

You can't control them. Trust me. This time I used our mental link, and it got through.

He was silent for many moments, then light infused his bones. *I'm the supreme being ... born to destroy the worlds. The Father of All.*

Don't make me do this, Connor.

I couldn't let him escape. There was no zapping from the lava, he'd have to rise through it like I did. And I would fight him all the way.

It will be better. This is the right path.

I recognized the words. They were the spirits, controlling him. He was so pliable, but I couldn't be mad. I had been too, because one of us was never supposed to control them. The three of us was the only way, and we'd missed our shot.

You were trying to save me, I reminded him. *Remember that. You didn't want the world to end. You're a hero, brother.*

I felt him, for a split second, through our bond. *Maddi...* A whisper of his voice.

Before I could do a single thing to stop him, Connor zoomed at me, and by instinct I lowered my trident, plowing it straight into his chest.

No. Gods. No, no, no, no!

I was screaming and sobbing as the tip pierced his body, sinking deep. The original lava did not break our bones, but this ancient weapon, forged by our people ... it was our weakness. Everything had one.

I love you, Maddi.

That was his last whisper before the world exploded around us, and my world went black.

Chapter 38

It was the sun that woke me, as warmth seeped into my skin, sinking through to my organs.

Skin … organs…

Connor.

The memories were there, partly shielded by my brain as it gave me time to try and deal with everything. I remembered though. I remembered it all.

My body had returned to me.

And my brother was lost.

Prying my lids open, I lifted a hand, examining the tanned skin and perfect nails before me. There were no flaws, no obvious signs of the trauma I'd both caused and suffered.

My scars lay beneath the skin.

It should worry me that I had no idea where I was, how I got here, or what had happened after Connor plowed into my trident.

I remember that part so clearly. I'd lowered the weapon but tried to move it last minute so it didn't hit him directly. He'd shifted with it though, making sure it cracked right through his chest, into the center of his power.

Numbness in my body and mind was the only thing keeping me from experiencing the sheer overload of agonizing and painful memories. Best to just lie here. Wherever here was.

Maybe I was in the underworld.

I didn't look transparent, but from what I understood of that place when you were dead, the souls just looked normal to each other. There was no peace in my body, though. I was filled with restless energy that slapped against me, urging me to release the numbing void. Release it and feel.

"Maddison fucking James!"

The voice was loud, pissed off, and it came from one of my favorite people in the world. Ilia stomped over to stand above me, staring down with a furious look on her face.

"Girl. You better get your sandy ass up. Right. Now."

She was angry, clearly, but there were tears in her eyes too. I blinked, feeling some of that numbness slipping away, the pain clawing at my insides. Tears trailed down my cheeks, and while I didn't make a sound, my body was screaming.

Ilia didn't say anything else. She just sat beside me, close enough that her hip touched my shoulder.

The pair of us remained like that for hours, silent but together.

"How did you find me?" I finally asked. With those words, I found the strength to sit.

She snorted, her eyes distant. "I tracked you for years, girl. I could find you any fucking where, especially with my newly gifted powers." She grimaced briefly, before a smile ripped across her face. "Thank you for that. I mean, I kinda love that we're almost related now, since I have your mother's old powers." Her brow wrinkled. "Yeah, that's weird. Anyways, let's just say it has taken some getting used to, but I've managed not to send storms raging across the world in the last few weeks."

"Weeks..." I whispered.

As naked as the day I was born, white-blond hair—my natural color that I hadn't seen for years—cascading down my back, I turned to face my best friend. "It's been weeks?"

She nodded. "Yeah. You've been missing for weeks. None of us had a goddamned clue what happened to you. Asher near lost his mind. This morning, when I picked up a signal from you, I rushed off before I could tell anyone. Scared you might disappear again."

She looked around.

"Nice island. You know it wasn't here yesterday, right?"

I took a moment to look around it too. Perfect sandy white beach, aquamarine water surrounding the tiny section of land, and about fifteen trees scattered about, offering a tiny slice of shade.

"I think I was existing between worlds," I said softly. "I had all this energy from Galindra—it allowed me to remake my reality for some time." Imagery flashed at me ... darkness where I'd hidden and mourned. "At some point I released her energy, after having used most of it, and ...

it was time for me to return." Guilt and pain had trapped me in a void of my own making.

Ilia shocked me when she wrapped her arms around me, pulling me against her, holding on like she was anchoring me to this world. "I thought I lost you. When the guys told me everything that happened, I fucking cried for a week. And then I started hunting you." She pulled back and her eyes were as stormy as her new power. "I refused to believe you were gone. No one could find you in the underworld. Or in Faerie. Or in the demon realm. You had literally ceased to exist."

"Asher..." I murmured out loud, devastated at the pain I must have caused him.

Ilia paled. The fact that someone with skin as dark as hers could "pale" told me that it had not been a good time for him these past few weeks.

"Asher found Connor's bones. They were washed up on the edge of the lava in the underworld, your trident still sticking out of them. He said the spirits tried to entice him into the lava, so he knew they were back where they belonged, but ... you were gone. He almost went into the lava just to see if you were there, but he figured if the spirits were calling, you were not available to them."

I swallowed hard, my throat suddenly dry. "So ... Connor is actually dead? He hasn't reappeared like me?"

She squeezed my hand, her face sad. "We found him in the underworld. His spirit is at peace. He didn't even remember us, but he was happy, Mads. He was happy."

Sobs burst from me and I buried my head in my hands, bringing Ilia's with me because she wouldn't let me go. "I don't know if I can face them all. The things I did. The things I said…"

I killed people. So many of them. Most of them had been legitimately evil, but it wasn't my place to decide if they should live or die…

Ilia snorted again, and using our still-connected hands, jumped to her feet, yanking me with her. "Babe, you know I love you more than anything, but I won't sit here at your pity party for one. A lot of fucked-up shit happened, and we'll be rebuilding the world for years to come, but in the end, you're the fucking hero that saved us all. You killed the gods." She jabbed at my chest, not hard enough to hurt but I felt it. "You fought the most powerful spirits in existence, pretty much from the first moment they took you over."

I shook my head. "No, I didn't. I let them do whatever they wanted."

The look on her face was one of disbelief. "Dude, you know that's not true. They wanted to completely remake the world. We all know that was their ultimate end game. That's the reason for them to exist. They're basically a failsafe when the world is no longer redeemable. You fought them."

Logically, what she said made sense, but the embarrassment I felt at letting them take me over wouldn't abate.

"Did you know that Louis's mate had their baby?"

My head jerked up and I blinked at her. "She did?"

She nodded. "Oh yeah, nine-pound chunker of a boy. Strong and powerful, just like his parents, and already with those fucking violet eyes that can see into your soul."

Happiness exploded in my chest, cutting through the dark depression that had been holding me hostage for weeks.

"Wanna know what they named him?"

I nodded. Already that shining brightness of a new child had me feeling lighter.

"James."

The tears were back, but this time they were not filled with a soul crushing grief. Or shame at my actions. This time ... it was joy.

"James..." I breathed.

Ilia nudged me. "Yes, girl. James. Because you are so fucking awesome, and they could think of no better role model for their child. I mean, his name is James and some other middle name for those twins he's so fond of, but his first name ... it's for you."

I shook my head. "It's more than I deserve. I do need to stop hiding and face them all. I need ... Asher. I fucking need him. He deserves an explanation."

Movement to our right caught my eye and Ilia let out a blast of storm magic before she could stop herself. Asher brushed it away like it was a piece of paper floating on a light breeze.

"Shit, dude! I could have killed you," she burst out, her hands shaking. "You know better than to startle a newly-powered god. I'm a fucking explosion waiting to happen."

She kept raging on but Asher had no attention for anything but me. His eyes, the color a simmering pot of gold, were locked on my face. He stalked toward me, not pausing, not even looking Ilia's way. After some time she just threw her hands up and muttered something about giving us privacy and letting everyone else know I was alive and well.

When she disappeared in a swirl of storm power, I found myself standing before my mate.

"Maddison James," he rumbled, and I crumpled like a deflated tire, falling forward, slamming against him.

His arms were there, strong and sure, keeping me up as I sobbed against his chest. "I'm so sorry," I choked out. "Fuck. I made so many mistakes. You should hate me."

Those strong arms holding me tightened, pulling me closer, cradling me against him. "Stop," he rumbled against my cheek. "Stop apologizing. You have nothing to be sorry for. There's literally not a thing on any world that could make me hate you. Smack that perfect ass? Totally. But never hate." He breathed deeply, eyes closed as he buried his head in my neck. "Just ... let me fucking hold you."

Moisture landed on my skin, and I couldn't be sure, but maybe Asher shed a tear in that moment too. Not that I could tell when he finally pulled back, his face picture perfect.

Lurching forward, I slammed my lips against his, needing this more than anything in the world. I groaned as that fresh air, salty scent of him invaded my senses, filling me with a completeness I hadn't felt in a very long time. Maybe now wasn't the best time, but I'd missed my mate, everything about him. And I was done mourning. It was time to start living again.

Asher's chest rumbled against me, a growl leaving his lips as he yanked me hard into his chest. My body pressed against his was the best feeling ever, and when he picked me up, I twined my legs around his waist.

His clothes vanished in the next heartbeat and we were naked, the long hard length of him pressed to my stomach, and I rocked forward, needing to feel more. We reached the water and Asher plunged us into the depths, allowing more of my tattered soul to repair.

Piece by piece, he was bringing me back to myself.

"Now, Ash," I said breathlessly, water all around us. "I need you to love me now."

He slid inside in one hard thrust, jerking my body back with the force. My nails dug into his shoulders as I held on, keeping myself anchored as best I could as he slammed into me over and over and over again. The first orgasm hit hard and fast, my body desperate for the release; the second started to build immediately.

Asher lifted me so he could take a nipple into his mouth, all the while continuing to possess my body in a way that was designed to kill a person with pleasure. It was a little rough and desperate, out of control ... and totally perfect.

I screamed as the second spiral of pleasure sent stars across my vision, turning the water into a jacuzzi. My power poured heat, as did Asher's, and we would have to finish this soon or we'd start killing our beloved sea creatures, most of whom were thankfully making themselves scarce right now.

I could feel when Asher was close, his dick swelling until it was almost painful. He was big at the best of times, but just before he came it was scary big. "Let me finish you off," I said, scraping my nails down his chest, before cupping his balls in my hands. I could only just reach them in his position, and I honestly needed more.

His eyes darkened, teeth bared as he nodded.

My body protested when I slid off, but she soon shut up as I lowered myself in the water, wrapping a hand around him. His shaft was too wide for me to close my fingers, but that was okay, my mouth was the most important part today.

With one hand cupping his balls, the other wrapped around the base, my tongue and lips worked his knob. His taste was intoxicating, and since I didn't have to breathe, I got to enjoy the full experience, taking him as deep as I could, licking across him over and over. He groaned, palming the back of my head as I worked his cock.

"I'm gonna come, baby," he groaned again.

He was warning me, but he didn't have to. I liked the taste of him, and I wanted it all. My pace increased and he threw his head back, jerking in my mouth once, twice, and again. I swallowed, loving the taste and the knowledge I'd pleasured him like this. It was a pretty big turn on.

When he was finished, and I'd licked him clean, he yanked me up into his chest, lips crashing into mine. "I fucking love you," he murmured against my mouth.

"I love you too," I whispered back, my head spinning at how strong my emotions were.

We kissed for a long time, before Asher carried me back to the sand and this time loved me slowly, bringing my body to the edge of orgasm with his tongue until I lost control and used my power to slam him back into the sand so I could climb on top and ride him.

Turned out my newly created island was the perfect place for us to spend multiple days and nights loving each other. It was only the thought that I had other people to see, to explain myself to, that stopped me from hiding there with Asher forever.

"We don't have to go back," he said, when I was lying in his arms a few days later. There was a peace in my heart now. I'd come to terms with everything that had happened during the battle against the gods, and I had forgiven myself.

Somewhat.

Asher's unconditional love and support made it difficult to continue to place all the blame on myself. And Connor was happy. So that was something.

"You don't owe anyone anything," he said. "You risked everything to save the world. You were going to sacrifice yourself and stay in the lava."

I about pulled a muscle turning my head to see him. "How did you know that?" I asked, wide-eyed.

"Connor."

He'd talked about my brother a lot, but it still hurt to hear his name. "He remembered that?"

Asher nodded. "Yeah, when I got to him, he'd only just arrived from the processing in the underworld. He still had his memories. They were fading fast though, so I got as much of the story as I could, and then let him have his peace."

Playing with the sand, letting it fall between my fingers, I turned back to stare at the moon. "Does he have a family there? He is truly at peace…"

Asher drew me close. "He's at peace, baby. And he does have a family. He's found a soul that he spends a lot of time with. Rone checks in on him."

Rone, the new god of the underworld. Another face crossed my mind, one with an ever changing face.

"Has he run across Heptashia there?"

Asher snorted. "Yeah, apparently he's seen her a few times. She celebrated pretty hard when Draconis died. It's just a shame he didn't procure some photographic evidence."

I choked on some laughter, trying to imagine her acting *more* crazy. Gods, maybe she would end up in our girl-gang one day. As my laughter died off, I found myself swallowing hard. I'd been wanting to ask Asher something, and I feared the answer, but it was time…

"Are the guys angry with me?" I choked out. "I mean, I just forced the powers on them. Forced godhood on them."

He laughed, the rich sound cutting out the natural ambient background noise of the island. "Angry? Fuck no. They're loving being gods, the cocky bastards. They're doing a pretty good job at it though. Larissa is the only one a little pissed. She kinda wanted to be a god too."

I shook my head, laughter bubbling out of my throat.

"I told her the next time a god fucked up, I would destroy them and she'd be first in line for the power."

Turning, I pressed a kiss to his chest. "You're a good person, Asher Locke. I'm so lucky that you're my mate."

His humor faded. "I'm the lucky one, love. And now I think there's time for one last swim before we head back."

There was no avoiding it any longer. My escape here in paradise was coming to an end.

But before it did, one more swim was exactly what I needed.

I mean, we'd eventually get around to swimming.

Chapter 39

Stratford, Connecticut, was a gorgeous town. Bordered by forest, it was filled with supernaturals, who for some reason were crowding around us. We were in what felt like the center of their town, near a hall and huge fountains.

When Asher and I got back from the island, I'd gone straight to the Academy, finding myself part of multiple tearful reunions. Jesse in particular had been a fucking mess, holding me tightly, making me promise I'd never leave again.

He was on my left side today, Asher on my right, Calen, Axl, Rone, Larissa, and Ilia behind me. The eight of us had been inseparable since I returned, and at no point did I ever feel anything but love from them. No judgment. No anger. No accusations.

They just loved me. More than I deserved.

Now it was time to see Louis … and my girl gang. I needed to make amends.

"Maddison!" Jessa screamed, sprinting in the graceful way of supernaturals as she ran for me. "You're finally here!"

Slamming against me, she hugged me hard and I tried not to bawl again at how fucking good it felt to see her. Pulling back, she cupped my face, before shaking her head. "Bitch, you took too long to get here. I was fucking worried something happened to you again."

I choked out some laughter. "No, sorry. I just … I'm sorry for almost killing you all."

Jessa scoffed, waving her hand at me. "Dude, that's fucking nothing. Don't think you're the only one that almost killed everybody. Mischa and I are the OG's of that."

Her twin snorted from the crowd, stepping through to our side. "I really wish she was kidding."

She hugged me tightly and I returned it. I felt like I'd been through so much with these supes. The sound of little footsteps had us pulling apart, and I blinked as three of the most perfect toddlers I'd ever seen raced to their mothers, the twins to Jessa and a doll of a girl to Mischa. Neither had to touch their parents before they were flying through the air and into their mother's arms.

I blinked. Asher stepped forward, his face soft as he stared at the little girl in Jessa's right arm. "They already have access to their powers?" he asked.

Axl looked even more fascinated as he moved closer too. Brother might be the god of the seas now, but no one could take the genius out of him.

Jessa let out a derisive laugh. "Oh yeah. They basically have no limits. One day they'll either save or destroy the world."

I rubbed at my face. "Feeling an urge to fist bump them in solidarity right now," I muttered.

Those closest to us laughed, and Asher even chuckled as he stepped back and wrapped an arm around me.

Out of nowhere, Jessa's daughter shot into the air and straight into his free arm. He caught her on instinct, blinking down as she smiled up into his face. He released his hold on me to adjust her more securely against him.

"Hello, little one," he said, blinking down at her.

"That's Evie," Jessa said. "She doesn't really speak, but she understands everything."

Evie looked three or four, with a heart-shaped face like her mother. Her white-blond hair was long and wavy down her back, and I wondered at how she was so fair when both of her parents had near black hair.

"She'll talk when she's ready," I said, brushing a hand over her hair. "Won't you, sweet baby."

Her eyes locked on mine and an understanding traveled between us. Her eye color was unusual and hard to classify, a mix of blue and green and gray, and when it hazed over I knew she was using her powers. I just didn't know what for.

She beckoned me closer, and when I was in touching distance again, her little hand landed on my shoulder.

Your future is bright.

At the childlike voice in my mind, I somehow managed not to jerk away, even though I kind of wanted to.

"You can see the future?" I asked her, sounding a little breathless.

Her mother's brows furrowed as she took a step closer, her son still held tightly in her arms.

Evie nodded, lips turning up in a beautiful smile. She patted me on the shoulder one more time, before turning and floating back to her mother.

Jessa coughed. "Well … fuck. Should be easy to keep her out of trouble, what with her seeing the future and knowing everything before it happens." She looked a little shell shocked, then her natural resilience kicked in and she returned Evie's smile. With a rueful chuckle, she leaned over and planted a few kisses on her daughter's cheeks. "When you're a teenager, mommy is going to need a lot of girl-gang vacations. Daddy can deal with his superpowered children." Her voice lowered. "Overachiever."

"I heard that, Jessa babe," Braxton said, pushing through the crowd with Maximus at his side. I wasn't surprised; mates were never far apart. They'd probably been following their babies as they ran for their moms.

Maximus waved to all the supes lingering around. "Go on, you've met the gods. Now you can scurry back and return to keeping this town functioning." The vamp hybrid had a twinkle in his eye, but also power in his voice.

Ah, now I understood why we'd had this level of welcoming committee. Everyone wanted to meet a god. Our reputations were already proceeding us. Personally, I was eternally grateful that everyone was treating me just like a normal supe still. No one showed any fear. No one seemed angry at me for what I'd done.

It was a lot more than I expected … or deserved.

"Come on," Jessa said, "we've prepared a meal for you all. Hope you can stay."

I nodded and found myself being pulled along by Ilia.

"I swear," she said in a rush, "ever since becoming a god I've been starving. Which is insane. I don't even need to eat."

Asher called after us. "It's your new powers. You're adjusting, and that's taking a lot of control. You're refueling in the only way you know how."

"I'm glad you can still enjoy food," Jessa said, keeping up with ease. Her children were zooming through the air in their way of travelling. "No amount of power would be worth giving up cake."

Braxton laughed, perfect white teeth flashing. "Jessa's worst nightmare."

She nodded, clearly not at all joking.

They led us across their picturesque town, supes peeking out of the windows as we moved past, but for the most part leaving us alone. When we reached a gorgeous log cabin, built on the edge of the forest, everyone slowed.

Mischa's daughter, her mop of dark curls bouncing across her shoulders, led the way in under the thick canopy. The natural light was cut off, the scent of earth, nature, moss, and flowers surrounding us as we pushed through. It was peaceful here, the contrast almost immediate from the noisy, bustling town. Calen sighed, and despite his recent protests about nature pissing him off, he looked happier now that we were surrounded by greenery.

He might be coming around to his new godhood.

The table came into sight first, as did a sorcerer, child held in his arms, standing at the side of the long bench.

"Louis!" I cried, lowering my voice when I saw his son was sleeping.

Moving toward him, I let him wrap his spare arm around me, and when I sank against him the final part of my fractured guilt surged up.

Louis ... I respected him more than almost anybody else, and I'd let him down. This apology was a long time coming. "I'm so, so, sorry—"

His hand wrapped around my mouth, stopping me before I could get another word out. The child in his arms stirred, and both of us were distracted as James opened his eyes. His very purple, ancient beyond his years, eyes.

"Oh wow," I choked out, muffled behind the hand still holding my mouth hostage. "He's so perfect."

Louis released me, and before I could say another word, slid James right into my hands. "Only family touches my child," he murmured, face close to mine. "You are my family. You do not need to apologize for anything. And..." He cleared his throat. "Thank you ... for saving the worlds ... for allowing me the gift of holding my child. I will owe you for the rest of my long life. And beyond that."

Tears ran down my face, the sort of tears that turned me into a snotty mess, but I didn't care. Forgiving myself was apparently the hardest thing I'd have to do, because these people who meant so much to me ... they were never mad.

"You spent weeks creating a dark void to hide in," Louis said, voice low, "fearing what we might say and do when you returned. Your guilt over Connor ... over it all ... that wasn't yours to hold on to. I'm glad you finally returned to us, because our lives are better with you in them."

I swallowed more tears, squeezing my eyes shut tightly.

"I like your hair."

His words surprised me, and my eyes flew open again as I shifted some of the hair back behind me. "This is my natural color," I said with a shrug. "It's been so long, I almost forgot how white blond it was."

Louis reached out and brushed some of it back, in such a caring gesture that it had me blubbering again. "I think this is the best color yet," he said softly. "You don't need to change your fate any longer. You are finally where you were always meant to be."

Well, fuck. Dude was legit trying to kill me. "I'm so glad you came into my life," I choked out. "You saved me in more ways than one, Louis. I'm grateful for you."

Thankfully, before we could spill out our emotions further, Elizabeth, his mate, walked up to the table, her arms full of trays, with more magically following. The delicious smell of food had everyone moving.

When the platters landed on the table, we all sat.

"Let's eat!" Jessa and Ilia said at the same time, and the morose mood faded as laughter rang out.

Neither Louis nor Elizabeth made a move to take their child back, and I found myself somewhat content to sit, cradling him against me. The little one was still awake, staring up at me, and I smiled down at him, unable to look away.

"You're sort of perfect, you know," I whispered, brushing a hand over his cheek. He wasn't swaddled. It wasn't cold, and he wore a onesie in blue, so his arms were free to reach out, tiny fingers wrapping around mine.

I didn't question if that was normal for a child of his age. This was Louis and Tee's child. He was going to be extraordinary.

Asher shifted his chair closer to mine, his arm behind me so I could rest my body against his, the baby content on my chest. It was the perfect balance, and there was this odd ache in my heart.

"I'm not ready right now," I said to Asher, tilting my head so I could see his face, "but one day I could see this as part of our life."

He leaned over and kissed me, briefly, pulling back with blazing golden eyes. "One day, baby."

The rest of the afternoon was spent eating, drinking, and playing with the Compass babies. James spent most of the time sleeping, content in his parents' arms. And occasionally in mine.

Little guy already owned my heart. All of them did.

"Bye, Aunty Maddi," Jackson called, his baby voice ripping through my body and puncturing my heart.

"Awww…" Ilia pressed a hand to her chest. "He called you Aunty Maddi. That's so freaking cute."

Jessa laughed. "You are all family. You're welcome here anytime."

Thank the gods … well, thank someone anyway, that I hadn't achieved the end goal of those spirits. If I'd remade the world, I would have missed all of this.

Today was going down as one of the best days of my life, and I was eternally grateful to be here.

Chapter 40

"You have one month, Maddison," Princeps Jones said, stern but with a sparkle in his eyes that sort of indicated he might be laughing at me. "Think you're up to the challenge?"

My lips twitched. "I guess we're about to find out."

His laughter rang out and I let my own go free as well. "I mean, I might be a fully-fledged god now, able to access all of my powers, but … I still gotta study."

He shook his head. "I know. And with that in mind, you'll have a modified syllabus. But it won't be easy. One month until final exams, and if you can pass the third and fourth years, you're free to graduate."

Graduation. It was important to me, and maybe a lot of supes wouldn't understand, what with who I was and my power now, but coming to the Academy had changed my entire life. This was the full circle of this journey. If I wanted to move on to whatever was next, this was the path I had to take.

Another fucking path. This time, though, I had a good feeling about it.

Leaving Princeps Jones' office, I made my way directly to the library. I was going to be there for the next month straight, trying to catch up.

I was ready.

I could do this.

And I would not be alone.

Mab was the first one to greet me, the tiny fairy flying over to embrace me in magic and a finger hug, wrapping around my hand. "I am so proud of you," she said, pulling away, chiming bells in my ear. "I've known the destructive energy of original magic, and I don't have to imagine the strength you showed. You've always been the hero on this journey. Always."

"That was why you couldn't be there to help me?" I asked her.

She nodded. "Yes. The risk was too great, but I always knew you wouldn't need me. It ended as I expected it would."

She was a mystery wrapped in a quandary, filled with super special magic. There was so much we didn't know about her, the eternity of years she had walked this world ... and that was okay. I didn't have to know everything to know when someone was a good friend.

"Maddi!" Axl exclaimed, jumping to his feet when I made it into the main part of the library. "What did the princeps say?"

I smiled, taking a deep, fortifying breath. "I have one month. One month to finish the modified coursework he assigned and take the final exams."

His jaw twitched, but not a single negative word left his mouth. "We've got this, sister. Don't even stress on it."

I hugged him hard. "Oh, I know. If there's one thing I trust, it's that with your help I can do anything."

"You helped me stop the erratic weather," he returned.

That was true. Ilia and me to be exact. The goddess of storms was handy to have around when you were trying to incinerate a weather spell gone awry. She didn't have full control still, but with my help we'd gotten the energy exactly where Axl needed it, and then he'd set his spell in motion.

It had been blue skies since that day.

Grabbing my hand, he dragged me across to an empty table. It hadn't been there the last time I entered the Atlantean library, and something told me this was specifically here for me to study on for the next month.

"I'll bring you the books and coursework," Axl said, pushing me into the soft chair. "You start now, because you don't have a second to waste."

He wasn't kidding, and before he'd even walked away, I reached for the book on top. History.

Oh yeah. Let's do this.

ONE MONTH LATER

As the last firebolt burst to life, incinerating the multiple targets, the teacher dropped his hand and I all but collapsed on the floor. For the past month—thirty-two days—seven hundred and fifty hours—forty-four thousand minutes—I'd slaved over the Academy textbooks.

My final exam had just ended, and despite the range and strength of my powers now, I wasn't sure I could get to my feet.

"You did very well, Ms. James," my professor said, standing over my head. "Your official grades will be posted on the wall in the next thirty minutes. Good luck."

Thirty minutes. That was all the time left to find out if all my hard work had been in vain, if I was going to graduate this year. No matter what happened, I wouldn't be back to the Academy next year. None of us would be.

We had jobs to do ... roles that we had to play to keep the supernatural world functioning. Turned out, being a god was more than just zipping around on a cloud of golden energy.

Even Asher and me, with our new roles in Atlantis, had a lot more going on than most.

Despite my hectic study load, I'd managed to get back a few times to find a group of thriving and bustling people, all of whom were adjusting better than I could have dreamed of.

It helped that we'd banned all supernaturals, outside of the Atlanteans, from disturbing them while they adjusted. Right now, the supe world wanted to study our ancient and powerful race, but the last thing they needed was to be a sideshow attraction.

Everyone would just have to wait, just like they did when they wanted some attention from the gods.

Us. We were gods. It was fucking weird.

A heavy body landed next to mine on the floor of the classroom and I laughed as Asher traced his fingers across my side, right in the most ticklish spot.

"I will smite you, asshole," I gasped.

My threat did not deter him at all, so I used my power to send him shooting across the room, taking out a bunch of tables and chairs as he went.

He was back at my side in seconds, hand held out to help me up. "Come on, Maddison James. It's time for you to check the list."

"It's up?" I asked him when I was on my feet. My energy wrapped around his like it had been days since we'd seen each other rather than hours. Our powers were almost fluid now, shifting between each of us.

He nodded. "Yep, but I didn't look yet. I wanted to wait for you."

"Aw, that's sweet. What if I failed though?"

Lacing our fingers together, he led me out. "I doubt you did, but I'm proud of you either way."

The wall was near the Princeps's office. I'd never worried about this wall before—it was strictly for those graduating.

I was finally understanding the stress of it all.

The list was long, the writing small, so everyone crowded close to see better. Up top was the list of academic excellence, and I wasn't at all surprised to see Axl was top of the graduating class. He'd worked hard for that honor, and no one could take it away from him.

He'd been there long before he was a god.

There were so many students around us, and for once none of them were paying us any attention. Today they only cared about graduating and moving forward to the next part of their lives.

Scanning along the list, I saw Asher's name. He was in the top ten of all graduates and had the highest marks in water magic and combat. Continuing on, the rest of my family were all there too. Every single one of them graduated, and they had fantastic grades despite everything we'd been through over the past year.

That left just me.

"You did it!" Axl shouted, wrapping his arms around me and hauling me up.

I saw my name at the same time he reached me. Maddison James. Passed.

Relief crushed me. There had been a few tricky final exams, and I'd messed up more than once. None of my classes had spectacular grades, but that didn't matter. I'd passed. I'd achieved what I needed to, and now we could move forward.

"Woohoo!!" Larissa screamed, barreling into me. "Party time…"

Before she could say another word, Rone wrapped his huge hands around her biceps. I saw a moment of shock on her face before he pulled her toward him and lifted her high enough that he could crush his lips to hers.

All of us blinked at them, and when my brain caught up to my eyes, I couldn't stop my heartfelt smile. Yes. Finally. Finally they were going to give it a shot.

Before a single suggestive remark could even leave Calen's mouth, Rone was gone, chest rumbling, fangs out as he kissed the hell out of Larissa.

"I'm guessing we won't see those two for a while," Ilia said with a snort, striding over. She fist-bumped me. "Great work, dude. You're officially an Academy graduate."

It was surreal.

Calen scooped her into his arms, disappointment over his lost opportunity to heckle Rone gone. "What about me, sexy? I graduated too.

Where's my present?"

Her voice was husky. "Hmmm, let me think. It might be back in my room. Should we go and see?"

He was running. Literally running away from us, Ilia in his arms.

"Don't forget about the party later," she screamed over his shoulder, her laughter ringing down the hallway.

A huge graduation party was going down, location to be revealed soon. We still had a few hours before the big event though, and I really wanted to swim.

The last month had been a touch stressful, and ... everything before that too.

Let's do it, water baby.

Asher in my head. Hot. Damn.

"See you all tonight," Jesse said with a knowing grin. Things were so much better between all of us—he was even seeing a shifter from Stratford. In truth, I think the skeleton thing kind of freaked him out. He hadn't looked at me the same way since.

Asher snorted. "Your bones are fucking sexy. What are you talking about?"

With a burst of laughter, I smacked him. "You're an idiot. Now take me swimming."

CHAPTER 41

The ocean room was my sanctuary here. I'd had plenty of late night "swimming" sessions to wind down from all the studying. My poor animals were probably scarred, but Asher and I just couldn't help ourselves.

Our desires only increased with our bond. Now that we were metaphysically tied in every way possible … I wanted him more than ever. Standing on the beach, staring out across the water, he sent his power out, dimming the sky above, turning it from daylight into a starlit night.

"So fucking proud of you, Mads," he murmured, stripping my clothes off. Sometimes he liked to do it the old-fashioned way, hands scraping across my nipples, fingers sending bumps over my skin.

Sexy bones or not, there were definitely benefits to having skin.

When I was naked, he dropped to his knees, face buried in my pussy, tongue stoking across the sensitive flesh there. It took him about fifteen seconds to have me moaning and rocking against him, and ten more seconds before my knees went weak as the first orgasm slammed into me.

How they hit with so much force was beyond me, but I was straight up addicted.

Asher continued to suck and lick across my clit, sending me into a second ... or continuous orgasm. "Fuck," I groaned, my fingers threading through his thick hair. He didn't stop until I was a weak-legged, completely satisfied mess. Needing to return the favor, I ran my hand across the thick shaft jutting out from his body.

Asher dropped his head back. "Love that fucking firm grip," he grunted, and I tightened even further, dragging a groan from him.

When he couldn't take it any longer, he pressed me back into the sand, huge body covering mine completely. As he slid inside of me, I groaned, wrapping my legs around him.

He moved slow at first, loving me, pressing kisses along my chest and up my neck. Soon our rhythm changed as we both chased the edge of an orgasm, while still wanting to drag it out.

"Come for me, Maddison James."

The command teamed with my full name was too much. A scream ripped from me as that slow build turned into a fucking tropical storm of pleasure. His dick swelled and my body reacted. Asher was coming; we were coming. That was just how it worked. Always together.

When he groaned, he slowed, drawing it out for both of us, the world around us made of twilight and smelling of sex and ocean. I'd never been more content in my life.

Asher dropped kisses on my lips as my body pulsed around his. He was still hard inside of me—once wasn't going to be enough tonight. But he would take me swimming first. Our souls were craving it. We could feel it simmering in the bond between us.

"Plenty of time for me to love you later," Asher said, lips brushing across the sensitive flesh on my neck. "Let's do your second favorite thing now."

With a snort, I smacked him on the chest. "How do you know you're my favorite?"

His smile faded, a serious expression crossing his face. "Because I'm in here," he said, brushing across my temple with a gentle stroke. His thumb moved down my face and to my chest. "And in here."

Another toe-curling kiss later, I sighed. "You're right, my love. You are my favorite thing."

"And you're mine, Maddison James. Now and always."

Now and always.

Always was a long time for us, and I couldn't wait.

ACKNOWLEDGMENTS

This series. Guys. It has completely captured my heart. I find myself lingering extra long in this supernatural world—I love the characters so much.

Jacob's story will be the conclusion of this particular set (Dragon Marked series) and then I have to make the decision if I'll ever be back here again.

Something tells me I will. There is still too much to explore.

For now, though, this is goodbye, and I'm writing this with a heavy (but happy) heart.

Thank you for the love and enthusiasm you've shown for Maddison and her Atlanteans. Thank you for following her journey, for laughing and crying with her, and for never giving up.

I seriously have the best readers ever. I could not be more grateful that you found my books in the millions on Amazon.

Thank you. Seriously, I mean it. You rock.

LOVE, JAYMIN XXX

ALSO BY JAYMIN EVE

Also by Jaymin Eve

The Titan's Saga (UF/PNR Humor and action)
Book One: Releasing the Gods
Book Two: Wrath of the Gods (April 2020)

Royals of Arbon Academy (Dark College Romance)
Book One: Princess Ballot
Book Two: Playboy Princes (May 2020)

Supernatural Academy (Complete Urban Fantasy/PNR)
Year One
Year Two
Year Three

Dark Legacy (Complete Dark contemporary high school romance)
Book One: Broken Wings
Book Two: Broken Trust
Book Three: Broken Legacy

Secret Keepers Series (Complete PNR/Urban Fantasy)
Book One: House of Darken
Book Two: House of Imperial
Book Three: House of Leights
Book Four: House of Royale

Storm Princess Saga (Complete High Fantasy)
Book One: The Princess Must Die
Book Two: The Princess Must Strike
Book Three: The Princess Must Reign

Curse of the Gods Series (Complete Reverse Harem Fantasy)
Book One: Trickery
Book Two: Persuasion
Book Three: Seduction
Book Four: Strength
Novella: Neutral
Book Five: Pain

NYC Mecca Series (Complete - UF series)
Book One: Queen Heir
Book Two: Queen Alpha
Book Three: Queen Fae
Book Four: Queen Mecca

A Walker Saga (Complete - YA Fantasy)
Book One: First World
Book Two: Spurn
Book Three: Crais
Book Four: Regali
Book Five: Nephilius
Book Six: Dronish
Book Seven: Earth

Supernatural Prison Trilogy (UF series)
Book One: Dragon Marked
Book Two: Dragon Mystics
Book Three: Dragon Mated
Book Four: Broken Compass
Book Five: Magical Compass
Book Six: Louis
Book Seven: Jacob's story (tbd)

Hive Trilogy (Complete UF/PNR series)
Book One: Ash
Book Two: Anarchy
Book Three: Annihilate

Sinclair Stories (Standalone Contemporary Romance)
Songbird

Printed in Great Britain
by Amazon